DEAN KOONTZ'S FRANKENSTEIN
CITY OF NIGHT

Dean Koontz was born and raised in Pennsylvania. He is the author of many number one bestsellers. He lives with his wife, Gerda, and their dog Anna, and the enduring spirit of their dog Trixie in southern California.

D0556647

Also by Dean Koontz

DEAN KOONTZ'S FRANKENSTEIN

BOOK TWO

city of night

DEAN KOONTZ

HARPER

Harper
An imprint of HarperCollins*Publishers*
1 London Bridge Street,
London SE1 9GF

www.harpercollins.co.uk

This paperback edition 2012

First published in Great Britain by
HarperCollins*Publishers* 2005

A catalogue record for this book is
available from the British Library

ISBN: 978-0-00-745300-9

Set in Albertina MT by Palimpsest Book Production Limited,
Falkirk, Stirlingshire

Printed and bound by CPI Group (UK) Ltd, Croydon, CR0 4YY

In a sort of ghastly simplicity, we remove the organ and demand the function. We make men without chests and expect of them virtue and enterprise. We laugh at honour and are shocked to find traitors in our midst. We castrate and bid the geldings be fruitful.

— C. S. LEWIS, *The Abolition of Man*

FRANKENSTEIN

city of night

chapter 1

Having come to life in a thunderstorm, touched by some strange lightning that animated rather than incinerated, Deucalion had been born on a night of violence.

A Bedlam symphony of his anguished cries, his maker's shrieks of triumph, the burr and buzz and crackle of arcane machinery echoed off the cold stone walls of the laboratory in the old windmill.

When he woke to the world, Deucalion had been shackled to a table. This was the first indication that he had been created as a slave.

Unlike God, Victor Frankenstein saw no value in giving his creations free will. Like all utopians, he preferred obedience to independent thought.

That night, over two hundred years in the past, had set a theme of madness and violence that characterized Deucalion's life for years thereafter. Despair had fostered rage. In his rages, he had killed, and savagely.

These many decades later, he had learned self-control. His pain and loneliness had taught him pity, whereafter he learned compassion. He had found his way to hope.

Yet still, on certain nights, without immediate cause, anger overcomes him. For no rational reason, the anger swells into a tidal rage that threatens to sweep him beyond prudence, beyond discretion.

This night in New Orleans, Deucalion walked an alleyway on the perimeter of the French Quarter, in a mood to murder. Shades of gray, of blue, of black were enlivened only by the crimson of his thoughts.

The air was warm, humid, and alive with muffled jazz that the walls of the famous clubs could not entirely contain.

In public, he stayed in shadows and used back streets, because his formidable size made him an object of interest. As did his face.

From the darkness beside a Dumpster, a wrinkled rum-soaked raisin of a man stepped forth. "Peace in Jesus, brother."

Although that greeting didn't suggest a mugger on the prowl, Deucalion turned toward the voice with the hope that the stranger would have a knife, a gun. Even in his rage, he needed justification for violence.

The panhandler brandished nothing more dangerous than a dirty upturned palm and searing halitosis. "One dollar's all I need."

"You can't get anything for a dollar," Deucalion said.

"Bless you if you're generous, but a dollar's all I ask."

Deucalion resisted the urge to seize the extended hand and snap it off at the wrist as though it were a dry stick.

Instead, he turned away, and did not look back even when the panhandler cursed him.

As he was passing the kitchen entrance to a restaurant, that door opened. Two Hispanic men in white pants and T-shirts stepped outside, one offering an open pack of cigarettes to the other.

Deucalion was revealed by the security lamp above the door and by another directly across the alley from the first.

Both men froze at the sight of him. One half of his face appeared normal, even handsome, but an intricate tattoo decorated the other half.

The pattern had been designed and applied by a Tibetan monk skillful with needles. Yet it gave Deucalion a fierce and almost demonic aspect.

This tattoo was in effect a mask meant to distract the eye from consideration of the broken structures under it, damage done by his creator in the distant past.

Caught in the crosslight, Deucalion was sufficiently revealed for the two men to detect, if not understand, the radical geometry under the tattoo. They regarded him less with fear than with solemn respect, as they might stand witness to a spiritual visitation.

He traded light for shadow, that alley for another, his rage escalating to fury.

His huge hands shook, spasmed as if with the need to throttle. He fisted them, jammed them in his coat pockets.

Even on this summer night, in the cloying bayou air, he wore a long black coat. Neither heat nor bitter cold affected him. Nor pain, nor fear.

When he quickened his pace, the commodious coat billowed as if it were a cloak. With a hood, he might have passed for Death himself.

Perhaps murderous compulsion was woven through his very

fiber. His flesh was the flesh of numerous criminals, their bodies having been stolen from a prison graveyard immediately following interment.

Of his two hearts, one came from a mad arsonist who burned churches. The other had belonged to a child molester.

Even in a God-made man, the heart can be deceitful and wicked. The heart sometimes rebels against everything that the mind knows and believes.

If the hands of a priest can do sinful work, then what can be expected of the hands of a convicted strangler? Deucalion's hands had come from just such a criminal.

His gray eyes had been plucked from the body of an executed ax murderer. Occasionally, a soft luminous pulse passed through them, as though the unprecedented storm that birthed him had left behind its lightning.

His brain had once filled the skull of an unknown miscreant. Death had erased all memory of that former life, but perhaps the cerebral circuits remained miswired.

Now his growing fury took him to seedier streets across the river, in Algiers. These darker byways were rank and busy with illegal enterprise.

One shabby block accommodated a whorehouse thinly disguised as a massage and acupuncture clinic; a tattoo parlor; a porno-graphic video shop; and a raucous Cajun bar. Zydeco music boomed.

In cars parked along the alleyway behind these businesses, pimps socialized while they waited to collect from the girls whom they supplied to the brothel.

Two slicks in Hawaiian shirts and white silk trousers, gliding on roller skates, peddled cocaine cut with powdered Viagra to the whorehouse clientele. They were having a special on Ecstasy and meth.

Four Harleys stood in a hog line behind the porno shop. Hardcase bikers seemed to be providing security for the whorehouse or for the bar. Or for the drug dealers. Perhaps for all of them.

Deucalion passed among them, noticed by some, not by others. For him, a black coat and blacker shadows could be almost as concealing as a cloak of invisibility.

The mysterious lightning that brought him to life had also conveyed to him an understanding of the quantum structure of the universe, and perhaps something more. Having spent two centuries exploring and gradually applying that knowledge, he could when he wished move through the world with an ease, a grace, a stealth that others found bewildering.

An argument between a biker and a slender young woman at the back door of the whorehouse drew Deucalion as blood in the water draws a shark.

Although dressed to arouse, the girl looked fresh-faced and vulnerable. She might have been sixteen.

"Lemme go, Wayne," she pleaded. "I want out."

Wayne, the biker, held her by both arms, jamming her against the green door. "Once you're in, there *is* no out."

"I'm not but fifteen."

"Don't worry. You'll age fast."

Through tears, she said, "I never knew it was gonna be like this."

"What did you think it *would* be like, you dumb bitch? Richard Gere and *Pretty Woman?*"

"He's ugly and he stinks."

"Joyce, honey, they're all ugly and they all stink. After number fifty, you won't notice anymore."

The girl saw Deucalion first, and her widening eyes caused Wayne to turn.

"Release her," Deucalion advised.

The biker – massive, with a cruel face – was not impressed. "You walk real fast away from here, Lone Ranger, and you might leave with your cojones."

Deucalion seized his adversary's right arm and bent it behind his back so suddenly, with such violence, that the shoulder broke with a loud crack. He pitched the big man away from him.

Briefly airborne, Wayne landed face-first, his scream stifled by a mouthful of blacktop.

A hard stomp to the nape of the biker's neck would have snapped his spine. Remembering torch-bearing mobs with pitchforks in another century, Deucalion restrained himself.

He turned toward the *whoosh* of a swung chain.

Another motorcycle aficionado, a leering grotesque with a studded eyebrow, studded nose, studded tongue, and bristling red beard, recklessly joined the fray.

Instead of dodging the chain-link whip, Deucalion stepped toward his assailant. The chain lashed around his left arm. He seized it and pulled Redbeard off balance.

The biker had a ponytail. It served as a handle.

Deucalion lifted him, punched him, threw him.

In possession of the chain, he rounded on a third thug, whipped him across the knees.

The struck man cried out and fell. Deucalion helped him off the ground by throat, by crotch, and slammed him into the fourth of the four enforcers.

He rapped their heads against a wall to the barband beat, creating much misery and perhaps some remorse.

Already the customers wandering from porno shop to brothel to bar had fled the alleyway. The dealers on wheels had skated with their wares.

In rapid succession, the pimpmobiles fired up. No one drove toward Deucalion. They reversed out of the alleyway.

A chopped-and-stretched Cadillac crashed into a yellow Mercedes.

Neither driver stopped to provide the other with the name of his insurance agent.

In a moment, Deucalion and the girl, Joyce, were alone with the disabled bikers, though surely watched from doorways and windows.

In the bar, the zydeco band jammed without faltering. The thick, damp air seemed to shimmer with the music.

Deucalion walked the girl to the corner, where the alleyway met the street. He said nothing, but Joyce needed no encouragement to stay at his side.

Although she went with him, she was clearly afraid. She had good reason to be.

The action in the alley had not diminished his fury. When he was fully self-possessed, his mind was a centuries-old mansion furnished with rich experience, elegant thought, and philosophical reflection. Now, however, it was a many-chambered charnel house dark with blood and cold with the urge to murder.

As they passed under a streetlamp, treading on the fluttering shadows cast by moths above, the girl glanced at him. He was aware that she shuddered.

She seemed as bewildered as she was frightened, as if she had awakened from a bad dream and could not yet distinguish between what might be real and what might be remnants of her nightmare.

In the gloom between streetlamps, when Deucalion put one hand on her shoulder, when they traded shadows for shadows and fading zydeco for louder jazz, her bewilderment increased, and her fear. "What . . . what just happened? This is the Quarter."

"At this hour," he warned, as he walked her across Jackson Square, past the statue of the general, "the Quarter is no safer for you than that alleyway. You have somewhere to go?"

Hugging herself as if the bayou air had taken an arctic chill, she said, "Home."

"Here in the city?"

"No. Up to Baton Rouge." She was close to tears.

"Home don't seem boring anymore."

Envy seasoned Deucalion's ferocious anger, for he had never had a home. He'd had places where he stayed, but none had truly been a home.

A wild criminal desire to smash the girl raged at the bars of the mental cell in which he strove to keep imprisoned his bestial impulses, to smash her because she could go home in a way that he never could.

He said, "You've got a phone?"

She nodded, and unclipped a cell phone from her braided belt.

"You tell your mother and father you'll be waiting in the cathedral over there," he said.

He walked her to the church, paused in the street, encouraged her forward, made certain to be gone before she turned to look at him.

chapter 2

In his mansion in the Garden District, Victor Helios, formerly Frankenstein, began this fine summer morning by making love to his new wife, Erika.

His first wife, Elizabeth, had been murdered two hundred years ago in the Austrian mountains, on their wedding day. He rarely thought of her anymore.

He had always been oriented toward the future. The past bored him. Besides, much of it didn't bear contemplation.

Counting Elizabeth, Victor had enjoyed – or in some cases merely tolerated – six wives. Numbers two through six had been named Erika.

The Erikas had been identical in appearance because they had all been engineered in his New Orleans lab and grown in his cloning vats. This saved the expense of a new wardrobe each time one of them had to be terminated.

Although extremely wealthy, Victor loathed wasting money. His mother, otherwise a useless woman, had impressed upon him the need for thrift.

Upon his mother's death, he had not stood the expense of either a service or a pine box. No doubt she would have approved of the simple hole in the ground, excavated to a depth of four rather than six feet to reduce the gravedigger's fee.

Although the Erikas looked identical to one another, numbers one through four had different flaws. He kept refining and improving them.

Just the previous evening, he had killed Erika Four. He had sent her remains to an upstate landfill operated by one of his companies, where the first three Erikas and other disappointments were interred under a sea of garbage.

Her passion for books had resulted in too much introspection and had encouraged in her an independent spirit that Victor refused to tolerate. Besides, she slurped her soup.

Not long ago, he had summoned his new Erika from her tank, in which universities of digitized education were electronically downloaded into her absorbent brain.

Ever the optimist, Victor believed that Erika Five would prove to be a perfect creation, worthy of serving him for a long time. Beautiful, refined, erudite, and obedient.

She certainly was more lubricious than the previous Erikas. The more he hurt her, the more eagerly she responded to him.

Because she was one of the New Race, she could turn off pain at will, but he did not allow her to do so in the bedroom. He lived for power. Sex was, for him, satisfying only to the extent that he could hurt and oppress his partner.

She took his blows with magnificent erotic submission. Her many bruises and abrasions were, to Victor, proof of his virility. He was a stallion.

As with all his creatures, she had the physiology of a demigod.

Her wounds would heal and her physical perfection be restored in but an hour or two.

Spent, he left her on the bed, sobbing. She wept not merely because of the pain but also with shame.

His wife was the only member of the New Race designed with the capacity for shame. Her humiliation completed him.

He showered with much hot water and a verbena-scented soap made in Paris. Being thrifty about disposing of dead mothers and wives, he could afford some luxuries.

chapter 3

Having just closed the case on a serial killer who turned out to be a police detective in her own division, with the usual chasing and jumping and shooting, Carson O'Connor hadn't gotten to bed until seven in the morning.

Four dead-to-the-world hours in the sheets and a quick shower: That might be the maximum downtime she could expect for a while. Fortunately, she had been too whacked to dream.

As a detective, she was accustomed to overtime whenever an investigation approached culmination, but this current assignment wasn't a typical homicide case. This was maybe the end of the world.

She had never been through the end of the world before. She didn't know what to expect.

Michael Maddison, her partner, was waiting on the sidewalk when, at noon, she pulled the plain-wrap sedan to the curb in front of his apartment house.

He lived in a bland apartment in a plain slab of a building, on a nondescript block just off Veterans Boulevard. He said the place was "very Zen," and claimed to need a minimalist retreat after a day in the perpetual carnival of New Orleans.

He dressed for the Apocalypse the same as he dressed every day. Hawaiian shirt, khakis, sport coat.

Only in footwear had he made a concession to doomsday. Instead of the usual black Rockport walking shoes, he wore white. They were so white they seemed radiant.

His sleepy-eyed look made him more delicious than usual. Carson tried not to notice.

They were partners, not lovers. If they tried to be both, they would wind up dead sooner than later. In police work, kick-ass and grab-ass don't mix.

After getting in the car and pulling the door shut, Michael said, "Seen any monsters lately?"

"In the bathroom mirror this morning," she said, accelerating away from the curb.

"You look terrific. Really. You don't look half as bad as I feel."

"You know how long it's been since I had my hair done?"

"*You* take time to go to a hairdresser? I thought you just set it on fire and burned it off now and then."

"Nice shoes."

"The box said they're made in China, or maybe it was Thailand. Everything's made somewhere else these days."

"Not everything. Where do you think Harker was made?"

Detective Jonathan Harker, who had turned out to be the serial killer that the media dubbed "the Surgeon," had also turned out not to be human. Neither a 12-gauge shotgun nor a four-story fall had fazed him.

Michael said, "I don't quite see Helios building his New Race in the parlor of his mansion in the Garden District. Maybe Biovision is a front for it."

Biovision, a cutting-edge biotechnology firm founded by Helios when he first came to New Orleans more than twenty years previously, was the holder of many patents that made him richer year by year.

"All those employees," Carson said, "all those outsourced services coming in every day – you couldn't conduct a secret people-making lab in the middle of all that."

"Yeah. For one thing, being a walleyed hunch-back in a cowled cloak, Igor would really stand out when he went for coffee in the vending-machine room. Don't drive so fast."

Accelerating, Carson said, "So he has another facility some-where in the city, probably owned by a shell corporation headquartered in the Cayman Islands or someplace."

"I hate that kind of police work."

He meant the kind that required researching thousands of New Orleans businesses, making a list of those with foreign or otherwise suspicious ownership.

Although Carson disliked desk-jockey sessions as much as Michael did, she had the patience for them. She suspected, however, that she didn't have the time.

"Where are we going?" Michael asked as the city blurred past. "If we're going to Division to sit in front of computers all day, let me out right here."

"Yeah? And what'll you do?"

"I don't know. Find somebody to shoot."

"Pretty soon you'll have lots of people to shoot. The people Victor's made. The New Race."

"It's kind of depressing being the Old Race. Like being last year's toaster oven, before they added the microchip that makes it sing Randy Newman tunes."

"Who would want a toaster oven that sings Randy Newman?"

"Who wouldn't?"

Carson might have blown through the red traffic light if a refrigerated eighteen-wheeler hadn't been crossing the intersection. Judging by the pictorial advertisement painted on the side of the truck, it was loaded with meat patties destined for McDonald's. She didn't want to be hamburgered to death.

They were downtown. The streets were busy.

Studying the swarms of pedestrians, Michael wondered, "How many people in this city aren't really people? How many are Victor's . . . creations?"

"A thousand," Carson said, "ten thousand, fifty thousand – or maybe just a hundred."

"More than a hundred."

"Yeah."

"Eventually Helios is going to realize we're on to him."

"He knows already," she guessed.

"You know what that makes us?"

"Loose ends," she said.

"Totally loose. And he seems to be a guy who likes everything tied up neat."

She said, "I figure we've got twenty-four hours to live."

chapter 4

Carved of marble, weathered by decades of wind and rain, the Virgin Mary stood in a niche, overlooking the front steps of the Hands of Mercy.

The hospital had long been closed. The windows were bricked shut. On the gate in the wrought-iron fence, a sign identified the building as a private warehouse, closed to the public.

Victor drove past the hospital and into the parking garage of a five-story building that housed the accounting and personnel-management departments of Biovision, the company he had founded. He slotted the Mercedes into a space reserved for him.

Only he possessed a key to a nearby painted-steel door. Beyond lay an empty room, about twelve feet square, with concrete floor and walls.

Opposite the outer door, another door was controlled by a wall-mounted keypad. Victor entered a code, disengaging the electronic lock.

Past the threshold, a hundred-forty-foot corridor led under the hospital grounds, connecting the adjacent buildings. It was six feet wide, eight feet high, with block-and-timber walls and a concrete floor.

The passageway had been excavated and constructed by members of the New Race, without publicly filed plans or building-department permits, or union wages. Victor could come and go from the Hands of Mercy in complete secrecy.

At the end of the corridor, he entered his code in another keypad, opened a door into a file room in the lowest realms of the hospital. Rows of metal cabinets contained hard-copy backups to the computerized records of his many projects.

Usually, Victor enjoyed hidden doors, secret passageways, and the hugger-mugger that was necessarily part of any scheme to destroy civilization and rule the world. He had never entirely lost touch with his inner child.

On this occasion, however, he was annoyed that he could get to his laboratory only by this round-about route. He had a busy day ahead of him, and at least one crisis needed his urgent attention.

From the file room, he entered the basement of the hospital, where all was quiet and, in spite of the corridor lights, shadowy. Here he had once conducted his most revolutionary experiments.

He had been fascinated by the possibility that cancer cells, which reproduce with reckless speed, might be harnessed to facilitate the rapid development of clones in an artificial womb. He had hoped to force-grow an embryo to adulthood in a matter of weeks instead of years.

As will now and then happen when one is working at the extreme limits of known science, things went awry. What he ended up with was not a New Man, but a highly aggressive, rapidly mutating, ambulatory tumor that was, to boot, pretty damn smart.

Because he had given the creature life, he might have expected at least some small measure of gratitude from it. He had received none.

Forty of Victor's people had perished here, trying to contain that powerful malignancy. And his people were not easy to kill. Just when all had seemed lost, the atrocity had been subdued and then destroyed.

The stink of it had been terrible. All these years later, Victor thought he could still smell the thing.

A twenty-foot section of the corridor wall had been broken down in the melee. Beyond that ragged hole lay the incubation room, dark and full of wreckage.

Past the elevator, half the width of the corridor contained sorted and arranged piles of rubble: broken concrete, bent rebar, steel framing knotted as if it were rope.

Victor had organized but not removed this rubble and ruin, leaving it as an enduring reminder to himself that even a genius of his caliber could sometimes be too smart for his own good. He had almost died here, that night.

Now he took the elevator up to the ground floor, to which he had moved his main laboratory after the ungrateful tumor had been destroyed.

The hallways were quiet. Eighty of the New Race worked in this facility, but they were all busy at their assigned tasks. They didn't waste time gossiping around the water cooler.

His immense lab was furnished with fantastic machines that would have mystified not just the average man but also any member of the faculty at any department of science at Harvard or MIT. The style was operatic Art Deco, the ambience Hitlerian.

Victor admired Hitler. The Führer knew talent when he saw it.

In the 1930s and '40s, Victor had worked with Mengele and others in Hitler's privileged scientific class. He had made considerable progress in his work before the regrettable Allied victory.

Personally, Hitler had been charming, an amusing raconteur. His hygiene had been exemplary; he always looked scrubbed and smelled soapy.

A vegetarian and an ardent animal lover, Hitler had a tender side. He would not tolerate mousetraps. He insisted that rodents be captured humanely and turned loose in the wild.

The problem with the Führer had been that his roots were in art and politics. The future did not belong either to artists or to politicians.

The new world would not be built by nazism-communism-socialism. Not by capitalism, either.

Civilization would not be remade or sustained by Christianity or by Islam. Neither by Scientologists nor by the bright-eyed adherents of the deliciously solipsistic and paranoid new religion encouraged by *The Da Vinci Code*.

Tomorrow belonged to scientism. The priests of scientism were not merely robed clerics performing rituals; they were gods, with the power of gods. Victor himself was their Messiah.

As he crossed the vast lab, the ominous-looking machines issued oscillating hums, low pulsing throbs. They ticked and hissed.

He felt *at home* here.

Sensors detected his approach to his desk, and the screen of his computer brightened. On the monitor appeared the face of Annunciata, his secretary at the Hands of Mercy.

"Good morning, Mr Helios."

Annunciata was quite beautiful but not real. She was a three-dimensional digital personality with an artificial but wonderfully smoky voice that Victor had designed to humanize his otherwise somber work environment.

"Good morning, Annunciata."

"The corpse of Detective Jonathan Harker has been delivered by your people in the medical examiner's office. It awaits you in the dissection room."

An insulated carafe of hot coffee and a plate of pecan-and-chocolate-chip cookies were on Victor's desk. He picked up a cookie. "Continue."

"Randal Six has disappeared."

Victor frowned. "Explain."

"The midnight census found his room deserted."

Randal Six was one of many experiments currently living at the Hands of Mercy. Like his five predecessors, he had been created as an autistic with an obsessive-compulsive tendency.

Victor's intention in designing this afflicted creature had been to determine if such a developmental disability could have a useful purpose. Controlling an autistic person by the use of a carefully engineered obsessive-compulsive disorder, one might be able to focus him on a narrow series of functions usually assigned to machines in contemporary factories. Such a worker might perform a repetitive task hour after hour, weeks on end, without error, without boredom.

Surgically fitted with a feeding tube, catheterized to eliminate the need for bathroom breaks, he might prove to be an economical alternative to some factory robots currently on the assembly lines. His food could be nutritional pablum costing a dollar a day. He would receive no pay, no vacation, no medical benefits. He would not be affected by power surges.

When he wore out, he would merely be terminated. A new worker would be plugged into the line.

Victor remained convinced that eventually such machines of meat would prove to be far superior to much current factory equipment. Assembly-line robots are complex and expensive to produce. Flesh is cheap.

Randal Six had been sufficiently agoraphobic that he had not been able to leave his quarters voluntarily. He was terrified to cross the threshold.

When Victor needed Randal for an experiment, attendants brought him to the lab on a gurney.

"He can't possibly have left on his own," Victor said. "Besides, he can't have gotten out of the building without tripping an alarm. He's here somewhere. Direct security personnel to review yesterday's video from his room and from all the primary hallways."

"Yes, Mr Helios," said Annunciata.

Considering the high degree of verbal interaction she maintained with Victor, Annunciata might have appeared, to an outsider, to be a manifestation of an artificial machine intelligence. Although she did interface through a computer, her cognitive function in fact occurred in an organic New Race brain that was maintained in a hermetically sealed tank of nutrient solution in the networking room, where she was wired into the building's data-processing system.

Victor envisioned a day when the world would be inhabited only by the New Race living in thousands of dormitories, each of which would be monitored and served by a disembodied brain like Annunciata.

"Meanwhile," Victor said, "I'll be studying Harker's cadaver. Locate Ripley and tell him that I will need his assistance in the dissection room."

"Yes, Mr Helios. Helios."

About to take another bite of the cookie, he hesitated. "Why did you do that, Annunciata?"

"Do what, sir?"

"You repeated my name unnecessarily."

On the monitor, her smooth brow furrowed with puzzlement. "Did I, sir?"

"Yes, you did."

"I was not aware of doing so, Mr Helios. Helios."

"You just did it again."

"Sir, are you sure?"

"That is an impertinent question, Annunciata."

She looked appropriately chastised. "I'm sorry, sir."

"Analyze your systems," Victor directed. "Perhaps there is an imbalance in your nutrient supply."

chapter 5

Jack Rogers, the medical examiner, maintained an office in which an avalanche of books, files, and macabre memorabilia might at any moment bury an unwary visitor.

This reception lounge, however, was more in line with the public perception of a morgue. Minimalist decor. Sterile surfaces. The air-conditioning was set to CHILL.

Jack's secretary, Winona Harmony, ruled this outer domain with cool efficiency. When Carson and Michael entered, the top of Winona's desk was bare – no photographs, no mementos – except for a folder of Jack's notes, from which she was typing official autopsy reports.

A plump, warm-hearted black woman of about fifty-five, Winona seemed out of place in this barren space.

Carson suspected that stuffed into Winona's desk drawers were family photos, Beanie Babies, beribboned sachets, small pillows with feel-good mottoes in elaborate needlepoint, and other items that she enjoyed but that she found inappropriate for display in a morgue reception lounge.

"Looka here," said Winona when they came though the door. "If it isn't the pride of Homicide."

"I'm here, too," Michael said.

"Oh, you are *smooth*," Winona told him.

"Just realistic. She's the detective. I'm the comic relief."

Winona said, "Carson, girl, how do you stand him being so smooth all day?"

"Now and then I pistol-whip him."

"Probably does no good," said Winona.

"At least," Carson said, "it helps keep me in shape."

"We're here about a corpse," Michael said.

"We have a bunch," Winona said. "Some have names, some don't."

"Jonathan Harker."

"One of your own," Winona noted.

"Yes and no," Michael said. "He had a badge like us and two ears, but after that we don't have much in common with him."

"Who would have thought a psycho killer like the Surgeon would turn out to be a cop," Winona marveled. "What's the world coming to?"

"When will Jack do a prelim autopsy?" Carson asked.

"It's done." Winona tapped the file of handwritten notes beside her computer. "I'm typing it now."

This stunned Carson. Like her and Michael, Jack Rogers knew that something extraordinary was happening in New Orleans and that some of its citizens were something more than human.

He had done an autopsy on a guy who had two hearts, a skull as dense as armor, two livers, and several other "improvements."

Carson and Michael had asked him to embargo his report until they could grasp the situation they faced – and within hours, much to Jack's dismay, the cadaver and all records of the autopsy had vanished.

Now he was supposed to be taking great security measures with the body of Jonathan Harker, who was another of Victor's New Race. Carson could not comprehend why he would reveal Harker's inhuman nature to Winona.

Less comprehensible still was Winona's current calm, her easy smile. If she was typing a report of an autopsy on a monster, she seemed oblivious of it.

His bewilderment matching Carson's, Michael asked, "Have you just started?"

"No," Winona said, "I'm almost finished."

"And?"

"And what?"

Carson and Michael exchanged a glance. She said, "We need to see Jack."

"He's in Autopsy Room Number Two," Winona said. "They're getting ready to open up a retiree whose wife seems to have fed him some bad crawfish gumbo."

Carson said, "She must be devastated."

Winona shook her head. "She's under arrest. At the hospital, when they told her that he died, she couldn't stop laughing."

chapter 6

Deucalion rarely needed sleep. Although he had spent periods of his long life in monasteries and in meditation, though he knew the value of stillness, his most natural state seemed to be the restless circling-seeking of a shark.

He had been in all but constant motion since rescuing the girl from the alley in Algiers. His rage had passed, but his restlessness had not.

Into the vacuum left by the dissipation of anger came a new wariness. This was not to any degree fearful in nature, more of a disquietude arising from a sense of having overlooked something of great significance.

Intuition whispered urgently, but for the moment its voice was a wordless susurration, which raised his hackles but failed to enlighten him.

With dawn, he had returned to the Luxe Theater. The movie house recently had been willed to him by an old friend from his years in a carnival freakshow.

This inheritance – and the discovery that Victor, his maker, was not two hundred years dead, but alive – had brought him from Tibet to Louisiana.

He had often felt that destiny was working in his life. These events in New Orleans seemed to be hard proof.

An Art Deco palace erected in the 1920s, now a revival house, the Luxe was in decline. It opened its doors only three nights a week.

His apartment in the theater was humble. Anything larger than a monk's cell, however, seemed extravagant to him, in spite of his size.

As he roamed the deserted corridors of the old building, the auditorium, the mezzanine, the balcony, the lobby, his thoughts did not just race but ricocheted like pinballs.

In his restlessness, he struggled to imagine a way to reach Victor Helios, alias Frankenstein. And destroy him.

Like the members of the New Race that Victor had brought forth in this city, Deucalion had been created with a built-in proscription against deicide. He could not kill his maker.

Two centuries ago, he had raised a hand against Victor – and had nearly perished when he had found himself unable to deliver the blow. Half of his face, the half disguised by a tattoo, had been broken by his master.

Deucalion's other wounds always healed in minutes, perhaps not because Victor had in those days been capable of designing such resilience into him, perhaps instead because this immortality had come to him on the lightning, along with other gifts. The one wound that had not healed with perfect restoration of flesh and bone had been the one that his maker had inflicted.

Victor thought his first-made was long dead, as Deucalion had assumed that his maker had died in the eighteenth century. If he revealed himself to Victor, Deucalion would be at once struck down again – and this time, he might not survive.

Because Victor's methods of creation had improved drastically from his early days – no more grave-robbing and stitchery – his New Race most likely was gray-cell wired also to die in defense of its maker.

Eventually, if Carson and Michael could not expose Victor, they might be able to stop him only by killing him. And to get at him, they might have to go through an army of New Men and New Women that would be almost as hard to kill as robots.

Deucalion felt considerable regret, and even some remorse, for revealing the truth of Helios to the two detectives. He had put them in enormous jeopardy.

His regret was mitigated to some extent by the fact that they had unknowingly been in mortal jeopardy, anyway, as was every human resident of New Orleans, however many still existed.

Troubled by these thoughts – and haunted by the inescapable feeling that some important truth eluded him, a truth with which he must urgently come to grips – Deucalion eventually arrived in the projection room.

Jelly Biggs, once billed in the carnival as the fattest man in the world, was smaller now, merely fat. He sorted through the stacks of paperbacks stored here, searching for a good read.

Behind the projection room lay Jelly's two-room apartment. He had come with the theater, a break-even enterprise that he more or less managed.

"I want a mystery story where everybody smokes like

chimneys," Jelly said, "drinks hard liquor, and never heard of vegetarianism."

Deucalion said, "There's a point in every mystery story – isn't there? – where the detective feels that a revelation is right in front of him, but he can't quite see it."

Rejecting book after book, Jelly said, "I don't want an Indian detective or a paraplegic detective, or a detective with obsessive-compulsive disorder, or a detective who's a master chef—"

Deucalion examined a different stack of books from those that Jelly searched, as if a cover illustration or a flamboyant title might sharpen his fuzzy instinct into hard-edged meaning.

"I don't have anything against Indians, paraplegics, obsessive-compulsives, or chefs," Jelly said, "but I want a guy who doesn't know from Freud, hasn't taken sensitivity training, and punches you in the face if you look at him wrong. Is that too much to ask?"

The fat man's question was rhetorical. He didn't even wait for an answer.

"Give me a hero who doesn't think too much," Jelly continued, "who cares intensely about a lot of things, but who knows he's a dead man walking and doesn't care a *damn* about that. Death is knocking, and our guy yanks open the door and says, 'What kept you?'"

Perhaps inspired by something Jelly said or by the paperback covers ablaze with colorful mayhem, Deucalion suddenly under-stood what his instinct had been trying to tell him. The end was here.

Less than half a day previously, in Carson O'Connor's house, Deucalion and the two detectives had agreed to join forces to resist and ultimately to destroy Victor Helios. They had recognized that this mission would require patience, determination, cunning, courage – and that it might take a long time, as well.

Now, less by deductive reasoning than by intuition, Deucalion knew that they had no time at all.

Detective Harker, a member of Victor's New Race, had spiraled into homicidal madness. There were reasons to believe that others of his kind were in despair, too, and psychologically fragile.

Furthermore, something fundamental had gone wrong with Harker's biology. Shotguns had not felled him. Something that had been born within him, some strange dwarfish creature that had burst from him, had destroyed his body in its birth throes.

These facts alone were not sufficient evidence to justify the conclusion that Victor's empire of the soulless might be on the verge of violent collapse. But Deucalion knew it was. He *knew*.

"And," Jelly Biggs said, still sorting through the paperbacks, "give me a villain I'm not supposed to feel sorry for."

Deucalion had no psychic power. Sometimes, however, knowledge arose in him, profound insights and understandings that he recognized as truths, and he did not doubt them or question their source. He *knew*.

"I don't *care* that he kills and eats people because he had a bad childhood," Jelly railed. "If he kills good people, I want some good people to get together and pound the crap out of him. I don't want them to see that he gets *therapy*."

Deucalion turned away from the books. He feared nothing that might happen to him. For the fate of others, however, for this city, he was overcome by dread.

Victor's assault on nature and humanity had built into a perfect storm. And now the deluge.

chapter 7

The gutters of the stainless-steel dissection table were not yet wet, and the glossy white ceramic-tile floor in Autopsy Room Number 2 remained spotless.

Poisoned by gumbo, the old man lay in naked anticipation of the coroner's scalpel. He looked surprised.

Jack Rogers and his young assistant, Luke, were gowned, gloved, and ready to cut.

Michael said, "Is every elderly naked dead man a thrill, or after a while do they all seem the same?"

"In fact," said the medical examiner, "every one of them has more personality than the average homicide cop."

"Ouch. I thought you only cut stiffs."

"Actually," Luke said, "this one will be pretty interesting because analysis of the stomach contents is more important than usual."

Sometimes it seemed to Carson O'Connor that Luke enjoyed his work too much.

She said, "I thought you'd have Harker on the table."

"Been there, done that," said Luke. "We started early, and we're moving right along."

For a man who had been profoundly shaken by the autopsy that he had performed on one of the New Race little more than a day ago, Jack Rogers seemed remarkably calm about his second encounter with one of them.

Laying out the sharp tools of his trade, he said, "I'll messenger the prelim to you. The enzyme profiles and other chemical analyses will follow when I get them from the lab."

"Prelim? Profiles? You sound like this is SOP."

"Why shouldn't it be?" Jack asked, his attention focused on the gleaming blades, clamps, and forceps.

With his owlish eyes and ascetic features, Luke usually appeared bookish, slightly fey. Now he regarded Carson with hawkish intensity.

To Jack, she said, "I told you last night, he's one of them."

"Them," said Luke, nodding gravely.

"Something came out of Harker, some creature. Tore its way out of his torso. That's what killed him."

"Falling off the warehouse roof killed him," Jack Rogers said.

Impatiently, Carson said, "Jack, for God's sake, you saw Harker lying in that alleyway last night. His abdomen, his chest – they were like blown open."

"A consequence of the fall."

Michael said, "Whoa, Jack, everything inside Harker was just *gone*."

Finally the medical examiner looked at them. "A trick of light and shadow."

Bayou-born, Carson had never known a bitter winter. A Canadian wind in January could have been no colder than the sudden chill in her blood, her marrow.

"I want to see the body," she said.

"We released it to his family," Jack said.

"What family?" Michael demanded. "He was cloned in a cauldron or some damned thing. He didn't *have* family."

With a solemnity not characteristic of him, eyes narrowed, Luke said, "He had us."

The folds and flews of Jack's hound-dog face were as they had been a day ago, and the jowls and dewlaps, all familiar. But this was not Jack.

"He had us," Jack agreed.

As Michael reached cross-body, under his coat, to put his right hand on the grip of the pistol in his shoulder holster, Carson took a step backward, and another, toward the door.

The medical examiner and his assistant did not approach, merely watched in silence.

Carson expected to find the door locked. It opened.

Past the threshold, in the hall, no one blocked their way.

She retreated from Autopsy Room Number 2. Michael followed her.

chapter **8**

Erika Helios, less than one day from the creation tank, found the world to be a wondrous place.

Nasty, too. Thanks to her exceptional physiology, the lingering pain from Victor's punishing blows sluiced out of her in a long hot shower, though her shame did not so easily wash away.

Everything amazed her, and much of it delighted – like water. From the shower head it fell in glimmering streams, twinkling with reflections of the overhead lights. Liquid jewels.

She liked the way it purled across the golden-marble floor to the drain. Pellucid yet visible.

Erika relished the subtle aroma of water, too, the crispness. She breathed deeply of the scented soap, steamy clouds of soothing fragrance. And after the soap, the smell of her clean skin was most pleasing.

Educated by direct-to-brain data downloading, she had awakened with full knowledge of the world. But facts were not experience. All the billions of bits of data streamed into her brain had painted a ghost world in comparison to the depth and brilliance of the real thing. All she had learned in the tank was but a single note plucked from a guitar, at most a chord, while the true world was a symphony of astonishing complexity and beauty.

The only thing thus far that had struck her as ugly was Victor's body.

Born of man and woman, heir to the ills of mortal flesh, he'd taken extraordinary measures over the years to extend his life and to maintain his vigor. His body was puckered and welted by scars, crusted with gnarled excrescences.

Her revulsion was ungrateful and ungracious, and she was ashamed of it. Victor had given her life, and all that he asked in return was love, or something like it.

Although she had hidden her disgust, he must have sensed it, for he had been angry with her throughout the sex. He'd struck her often, called her unflattering names, and in general had been rough with her.

Even from direct-to-brain data downloading, Erika knew that what they had shared had not been ideal – or even ordinary – sex.

In spite of the fact that she failed him in their first session of lovemaking, Victor still harbored some tender feelings toward her. When it was over, he'd slapped her bottom affectionately – as opposed to the rage with which he had delivered previous slaps and punches – and had said, "That was good."

She knew that he was just being kind. It had not been good. She must learn to see the art in his ugly body, just as people evidently learned to see the art in the ugly paintings of Jackson Pollock.

Because Victor expected her to be prepared for the intellectual conversations at his periodic dinner parties with the city's elites, volumes of art criticism had been downloaded into her brain as she had finished forming in the tank.

A lot of it seemed to make no sense, which she attributed to her naivete. He IQ was high; therefore, with more experience, she would no doubt come to understand how the ugly, the mean, and the poorly rendered could in fact be ravishingly beautiful. She simply needed to attain the proper perspective.

She would strive to see the beauty in Victor's tortured flesh. She would be a good wife, and they would be as happy as Romeo and Juliet.

Thousands of literary allusions had been a part of her down-loaded instructions, but not the texts of the books, plays, and poems from which they came. She had never read *Romeo and Juliet*. She knew only that they were famous lovers in a play by Shakespeare.

She might have enjoyed reading the works to which she could allude with such facility, but Victor had forbidden her to do so. Evidently, Erika Four had become a voracious reader, a pastime that had somehow gotten her into such terrible trouble that Victor had been left with no choice but to terminate her.

Books were dangerous, a corrupting influence. A good wife must avoid books.

Showered, feeling pretty in a summery dress of yellow silk, Erika left the master suite to explore the mansion. She felt like the unnamed narrator and heroine of *Rebecca*, for the first time touring the lovely rooms of Manderley.

In the upstairs hall, she found William, the butler, on his knees in a corner, chewing off his fingers one by one.

chapter 9

In the unmarked Sedan, driving fast, seeking what she always needed in times of crisis – good Cajun food – Carson said, "Even if you were Jack's mother, even if you were his wife, even then you wouldn't know he'd been replaced."

"If this were like some Southern Gothic novel," Michael said, "and I was *both* his mother and his wife, I'd still think that was Jack."

"That was *Jack*."

"That wasn't Jack."

"I know that wasn't him," Carson said impatiently, "but it was *him*."

Her palms were slick with sweat. She blotted them one at a time on her jeans.

Michael said, "So Helios isn't just making his New Race and seeding them into the city with fabricated biographies and forged credentials."

"He can also *duplicate* real people," she said.

"How can he do that?"

"Easy. Like Dolly."

"Dolly who?"

"Dolly the sheep. Remember several years ago, some scientists cloned a sheep in a lab, named her Dolly."

"That was a sheep, for God's sake. This is a medical examiner. Don't tell me '*easy*.'"

The fierce midday sun fired the windshields and the brightwork of the traffic in the street, and every vehicle appeared to be on the verge of bursting into flames, or melting in a silvery spill across the pavement.

"If he can duplicate Jack Rogers," she said, "he can duplicate anyone."

"You might not even be the real Carson."

"I'm the real Carson."

"How would I know?"

"And how will I know if you go to the men's room and a Michael monster comes back?"

"He wouldn't be as funny as the real me," Michael said.

"The new Jack is funny. Remember what he said about the dead old guy on the table having more personality than homicide cops?"

"That wasn't exactly hilarious."

"But for Jack it was funny enough."

"The real Jack wasn't all that funny to begin with."

"That's my point," she said. "They can be as funny as they need to be."

"That would be scary if I thought it was true," Michael said. "But I'll bet my ass, if they ring a Michael monster in on you, he'll be about as witty as a tree stump."

In this neighborhood of old cottage-style houses, some remained residences, but others had been converted to commercial enterprises.

The blue-and-yellow cottage on the corner looked like someone's home except for the blue neon sign in a large front window: WONDERMOUS EATS, FOR TRUE, which translated from Cajun patois as "good food, no lie."

Michael preferred to read it as "good food, no bullshit," so from time to time he could say "Let's have a no-bullshit lunch."

Whether the legal name of the restaurant was Wondermous Eats or whether that was just a slogan, Carson had no idea. The cheap Xeroxed menus had no name at top or bottom.

Cottages had been cleared off two adjacent lots, but the ancient live oaks had been left standing. Cars were parked in the shade among the trees.

The carpet of dead leaves looked like drifts of pecan shells and crunched under the tires of the sedan, then underfoot as Carson and Michael walked to the restaurant.

If Helios succeeded in the abolition of humanity, replacing it with obedient and single-minded multitudes, there would be nothing like Wondermous Eats, for True. There would be no eccentricity and no charm in the new world that he desired.

Cops saw the worst of people, and grew cynical if not bitter. Suddenly, however, flawed and foolish humanity seemed beautiful and precious to Carson, no less so than nature and the world itself.

They chose a table outside, in the oak shade, apart from most of the other diners. They ordered crawfish boulettes and fried okra salad, followed by shrimp-and-ham jambalaya.

This was a denial lunch. If they could still eat this well, surely the end of the world was not upon them, and they were not as good as dead, after all.

"How long does it take to make a Jack Rogers?" Michael wondered when the waitress had left.

"If Helios can make anyone overnight, if he's that far advanced, then we're screwed," Carson said.

"More likely, he's steadily replacing people in key positions in the city, and Jack was on his list already."

"So when Jack did the first autopsy on one of the New Race and realized something weird was going on, Helios just brought *his* Jack on-line quicker than planned."

"I'd like to believe that," Michael said.

"So would I."

"Because neither of us is a big cheese. On his short list, our names wouldn't be there between the mayor and the chief of police."

"He would have had no reason to start growing a Carson or a Michael," she agreed. "Until maybe yesterday."

"I don't think he'll bother even now."

"Because it's easier just to have us killed."

"Totally easy."

"Did he replace Luke or was Luke always one of them?"

"I don't think there was ever a real Luke," Michael said.

"Listen to us."

"I know."

"When do we start wearing aluminum-foil hats to protect ourselves from alien mind-readers?"

The thick air swagged the day like saturated bunting, hot and damp and preternaturally still. Overhead, the boughs of the oaks hung motionless. The whole world appeared to be paralyzed by a terrible expectation.

The waitress brought the crawfish boulettes and two bottles of ice-cold beer.

"Drinking on duty," Carson said, amazed at herself.

"It's not against department regulations during Armageddon," Michael assured her.

"Just yesterday, you didn't believe any of this, and I half thought I was losing my mind."

"Now the only thing I can't believe," Michael said, "is that Dracula and the Wolfman haven't shown up yet."

They ate the boulettes and the fried-okra salads in an intense but comfortable silence.

Then before the jambalaya arrived, Carson said, "Okay, cloning or somehow he can make a perfect physical duplicate of Jack. But how does the sonofabitch make his Jack a medical examiner? I mean, how does he give him Jack's lifetime of knowledge, or Jack's *memories?*"

"Beats me. If I knew that, I'd have my own secret laboratory, and I'd be taking over the world myself."

"Except your world would be a better one than this," she said.

He blinked in surprise, gaped. "Wow."

"Wow what?"

"That was sweet."

"What was sweet?"

"What you just said."

"It wasn't sweet."

"It *was.*"

"It was not."

"You've never been sweet to me before."

"If you use that word one more time," she said, "I'll bust your balls, I swear."

"All right."

"I mean it."

Smiling broadly, he said, "I know."

"*Sweet,*" she said scornfully, and shook her head in disgust. "Be careful or I might even shoot you."

"That's against regulations even during Armageddon."

"Yeah, but you're gonna be dead in twenty-four hours anyway." He consulted his wristwatch. "Less than twenty-three now."

The waitress arrived with plates of jambalaya. "Can I get you two more beers?"

Carson said, "Why the hell not."

"We're celebrating," Michael told the waitress.

"Is it your birthday?"

"No," he said, "but you'd think it was, considering how sweet she's being to me."

"You're a cute couple," said the waitress, and she went to get the beers.

"*Cute?*" Carson growled.

"Don't shoot her," Michael pleaded. "She's probably got three kids and an invalid mother to support."

"Then she better watch her mouth," Carson said.

In another silence, they ate jambalaya and drank beer for a while, until finally Michael said, "Probably every major player in city government is one of Victor's."

"Count on it."

"Our own beloved chief."

"He's probably been a replicant for years."

"And maybe half the cops on the force."

"Maybe more than half."

"The local FBI office."

"They're his," she predicted.

"The newspaper, local media?"

"His."

"Whether they're all his or not, when's the last time you trusted a reporter?"

"Clueless," she agreed. "They all want to save the world, but they just end up helping to weave the handbasket."

Carson looked at her hands. She knew they were strong and capable; they had never failed her. Yet at the moment they looked delicate, almost frail.

She had spent the better part of her life in a campaign to redeem her father's reputation. He, too, had been a cop, gunned down by a drug dealer. They said that her dad had been corrupt, deep in the drug trade, that he'd been shot by the competition or because a deal had gone sour. Her mother had been killed in the same hit.

Always she had known the official story must be a lie. Her dad had uncovered something that powerful people wanted kept secret. Now she wondered if it had been *one* powerful person – Victor Helios.

"So what can we do?" Michael asked.

"I've been thinking about that."

"I figured," he said.

"We kill him before he can kill us."

"Easier said than done."

"Not if you're willing to die to get him."

"I'm willing," Michael said, "but not eager."

"You didn't become a cop for the retirement benefits."

"You're right. I just wanted to oppress the masses."

"Violate their civil rights," she said.

"That always gives me a thrill."

She said, "We're going to need guns."

"We've got guns."

"We're going to need bigger guns."

chapter 10

Erika's education in the tank had not prepared her to deal with a man who was chewing off his fingers. Had she matriculated through a real rather than virtual university, she might have known at once what she should do.

William, the butler, was one of the New Race, so his fingers were not easy to bite off. He had to work diligently at it.

His jaws and teeth, however, were as formidably enhanced as the density of his finger bones. Otherwise, the task would have been not merely difficult but impossible.

Having amputated the little finger, ring finger, and middle finger of his left hand, William was at work on the forefinger.

The three severed digits lay on the floor. One was curled in such a way that it seemed to be beckoning to Erika.

Like others of his kind, William could by an act of will repress all awareness of pain. Clearly, he had done so. He did not cry out or even whimper.

He mumbled wordlessly to himself as he chewed. When he

succeeded in amputating the forefinger, he spat it out and said frantically, "Tick, tock, tick. Tick, tock, tick. Tick, tock, tick, tock, tick, tick, *tick*!"

Had he been a member of the Old Race, the wall and carpet would have been drenched with blood. Although his wounds began to heal even as he inflicted them on himself, he had still made a mess.

Erika could not imagine why the kneeling butler was engaged upon this self-mutilation, what he hoped to achieve, and she was dismayed by his disregard for the damage he had already done to his master's property.

"William," she said. "William, whatever are you thinking?"

He neither answered nor glanced at her. Instead, the butler stuck his left thumb in his mouth and continued this exercise in express dedigitation.

Because the mansion was quite large and because Erika couldn't know if any member of the staff might be nearby, she was reluctant to cry out for help, for she might have to get quite loud to be heard. She knew that Victor wished his wife to be refined and ladylike in all public circumstances.

All members of the staff were, like William, of the New Race. Nevertheless, everything beyond the doors of the master suite was most definitely in public territory.

Consequently, she returned to the telephone in the bedroom and pressed the ALL-CALL function of those buttons on the keypad dedicated to the intercom system. Her summons would be broadcast to every room.

"This is Mrs Helios," she said. "William is biting off his fingers in the upstairs hall, and I need some assistance."

By the time she returned to the hallway, the butler had finished with his left thumb and had begun on the little finger of his right hand.

"William, this is irrational," she cautioned. "Victor designed us brilliantly, but we can't grow things back when we lose them."

Her admonition did not give him pause. After spitting out the little finger, he rocked back and forth on his knees: "Tick, tock, tick, tock, tick, *tick*, TICK, TICK!"

The urgency of his voice triggered connections between implanted associations in Erika's mind. She said, "William, you sound like the White Rabbit, pocket watch in hand, racing across the meadow, late for tea with the Mad Hatter."

She considered seizing the hand that still had four fingers and restraining him as best she could. She wasn't afraid of him, but she didn't want to appear forward.

Her in-the-tank education had included exhaustive input on the finest points of deportment and manners. In any social situation from a dinner party to an audience with the Queen of England, she knew the proper etiquette.

Victor insisted upon a poised wife with refined manners. Too bad William wasn't the Queen of England. Or even the Pope.

Fortunately, Christine, the head housekeeper, must have been nearby. She appeared on the stairs, hurrying upward.

The housekeeper did not seem to be shocked. Her expression was grim but entirely controlled.

As she approached, she took a cell phone from a pocket of her uniform and speed-dialed a number with the pressing of one key.

Christine's efficiency startled Erika. If there was a number that one called to report a man biting off his fingers, she herself should have known it.

Perhaps not all the downloaded data had found its way into her brain as it should have done. This was a troubling thought.

William stopped rocking on his knees and put his right ring finger in his mouth.

Other members of the household staff appeared on the stairs – three, four, then five of them. They ascended but not as quickly as Christine.

Every one of them had a haunted look. That is not to say they appeared to be ghosts, but that they looked as if they had *seen* a ghost.

This made no sense, of course. The New Race were atheists by programming and free of all superstition.

Into the cell phone, Christine said, "Mr Helios, this is Christine. We've got another Margaret."

In her vocabulary, Erika had no definition for *Margaret*, other than that it was a woman's name.

"No, sir," said Christine, "it's not Mrs Helios. It's William. He's biting off his fingers."

Erika was surprised that Victor should think that she herself might be inclined to bite off her fingers. She was certain that she had given him no reason to expect such a thing of her.

After spitting out his right ring finger, the butler began to rock back and forth again, chanting: "Tick, tock, tick, tock . . ."

Christine held the phone close to William, to allow Victor to hear the chant.

The other five staff members had reached the top of the stairs. They stood in the hallway, silent, solemn, as if bearing witness.

Into the phone once more, Christine said, "He's about to start on the eighth, Mr Helios." She listened. "Yes, sir."

As William stopped chanting and put the middle finger of his right hand in his mouth, Christine grabbed a fistful of his hair, not to stop his selfmutilation, but to steady his head in order to hold the cell phone to his ear.

After a moment, William stiffened and seemed to listen intently to Victor. He stopped chewing. When Christine let go of his hair, he took his finger out of his mouth and stared at it, bewildered.

A tremor went through his body, then another. He toppled off his knees, collapsed onto his side.

He lay with his eyes open, fixed. His mouth hung open, too, as red as a wound.

Into the phone, Christine said, "He's dead, Mr Helios." Then: "Yes, sir." Then: "I will do that, sir."

She terminated the call and solemnly regarded Erika.

All of the staff members were staring at Erika. They looked haunted, all right. A shiver of fear went through her.

A porter named Edward said, "Welcome to our world, Mrs Helios."

chapter 11

Meditation is most often done in stillness, although men of a certain cast of mind, who have great problems to solve, frequently think best on long walks.

Deucalion preferred not to walk in daylight. Even in easy New Orleans, where eccentricity flourished, he would surely draw too much attention in public, in bright sun.

With his gifts, at any time of day, he could have taken a single step and been any place west of where the sun yet reached, to walk in the anonymous darkness of other lands.

Victor was in New Orleans, however, and here the atmosphere of looming cataclysm sharpened Deucalion's wits.

So he walked in the sun-drenched cemeteries of the city. For the most part, the long grassy avenues allowed him to see tourist groups and other visitors long before they drew near.

The ten-foot-tall tombs were like buildings in the crowded blocks of a miniature city. With ease, he could slip between them and away from an impending encounter.

Here the dead were buried in aboveground crypts because the water table was so near the surface that coffins in graves would not remain buried but would surge to the surface in soggy weather. Some were as simple as shotgun houses, but others were as ornamented as Garden District mansions.

Considering that he had been constructed from cadavers and had been brought to life by arcane science – perhaps also by supernatural forces – it was not ironic but logical that he should feel more comfortable in these avenues of the dead than he did on public streets.

In St Louis Cemetery Number 3, where Deucalion first walked, the mostly white crypts dazzled in the searing sun, as if inhabited by generations of radiant spirits who lingered after their bodies had turned to dust and bones.

These dead were fortunate compared to the living dead who were the New Race. Those soulless slaves might welcome death – but they were created with a proscription against suicide.

Inevitably, they would envy real men, who possessed free will, and their resentment would grow into an irrepressible wrath. Denied self-destruction, sooner or later they would turn outward and destroy all whom they envied.

If Victor's empire was trembling toward the point of collapse, as instinct warned Deucalion that it was, then finding his base of operations became imperative.

Every member of the New Race would know its whereabouts, for in all probability, they had been born there. Whether they would be willing or even capable of divulging it was another issue.

As a first step, he needed to identify some in the city who were likely to be of the New Race. He must approach them cautiously and gauge the depth of their despair, to determine whether it might have ripened into that desperation which is vigorous of action and reckless of consequences.

Among even the most controlled of slaves there simmers a desire – even if not a capacity – to rebel. Therefore, some of these slaves of Victor's, all enemies of humanity, might in their hopelessness find the will and the fortitude to betray him in small ways.

Every member of the household staff and landscaping crew at Victor's estate would be of the New Race. But an attempt to get to any of them would be too risky.

His made men would be seeded throughout Biovision, though the greater number of its employees would be real people. Victor would not want to risk mixing his secret work with his public researches. But seining New Men from the sea of Biovision employees would take too long and involve too much exposure on Deucalion's part.

Perhaps the members of the New Race could recognize one another upon encounter. Deucalion, however, could not tell them from real people at a glance. He would need to observe them, to interact with them, in order to identify them.

Many politicians and appointed officials in the city would no doubt be of Victor's making, either originals or replicants who had taken the place of real people. Their prominence and the attention to security that came with it would make them more difficult to approach.

Half or more of the officers in the city's law-enforcement agencies were most likely members of the New Race. Deucalion didn't care to search those ranks, either, because drawing himself to the attention of the police would not be wise.

As Deucalion left behind St Louis Number 3 and moved now through the Metairie Cemetery, which boasted the gaudiest tombs in greater New Orleans, the hardest sun of the day hammered all shadows into narrow profiles and honed their edges into blades.

Victor would have his people in key positions in the city's legal establishment – prosecutors and defense attorneys – in the local academic world, in the medical system . . . and surely in the religious community as well.

In times of personal crisis, people turned to their priests, pastors, and rabbis. Victor would have realized that much valuable information might be learned in a confessional or during a citizen's most private talks with his spiritual adviser.

Besides, having his soulless creations delivering sermons and celebrating Mass would strike Victor as delicious mockery.

Even one as big and as menacing in appearance as Deucalion could expect a sympathetic ear from clergymen, whether they were real or imposters. They would be accustomed to offering comfort to society's outsiders and would receive him with less suspicion and alarm than others might.

Because the primary denomination in New Orleans was Catholicism, he would start with that faith. He had many churches from which to choose. In one of them he might find a priest who, by identifying Victor's center of operations, would betray his maker as daily he mocked God.

chapter 12

The security room in the Hands of Mercy featured a wall of high-definition monitors providing such clear images of the hallways and rooms of the immense facility that they appeared to be almost three-dimensional.

Victor didn't believe that his people had any right to privacy. Or to life, for that matter.

None of them had any rights whatsoever. They had their mission, which was the fulfillment of his vision for a new world, and they had their duties, and they had what privileges he allowed. No rights.

Werner, security chief at the Hands of Mercy, was such a solid block of muscle that even a concrete floor ought to have sagged under him. Yet he never lifted weights, never exercised. His perfected metabolism maintained his brute physical form in ideal condition, almost regardless of what he ate.

He had a problem with snot, but they were working on that.

Once in a while – not all the time, not even frequently, but nonetheless often enough to be an annoyance – the mucous membranes in his sinuses produced mucus at a prodigious rate. On those occasions, Werner often went through three boxes of Kleenex per hour.

Victor could have terminated Werner, dispatched his cadaver to the landfill, and installed Werner Two in the post of security chief. But these snot attacks baffled and intrigued him. He preferred to keep Werner in place, study his seizures, and gradually tinker with his physiology to resolve the problem.

Standing beside a currently snotless Werner in the security room, Victor watched a bank of monitors on which surveillance tapes revealed the route Randal Six had taken to escape the building.

Absolute power requires absolute adaptability.

Every setback must be viewed as an opportunity, a chance to learn. Victor's visionary work could not be shaken by challenges but must always be strengthened by them.

Some days were more marked by challenges than others. This appeared to be one of them.

The body of Detective Jonathan Harker waited in the dissection room, as yet unexamined. Already the body of William, the butler, was en route.

Victor was not concerned. He was exhilarated.

He was so exhilarated that he could feel the internal carotid arteries throbbing in his neck, the external carotids throbbing in his temples, and his jaw muscles already aching from his clenched-teeth anticipation of meeting these infuriating challenges.

Randal Six, engineered in the tanks to be a severe autistic, intensely agoraphobic, had nevertheless managed to leave his billet. He had followed a series of hallways to the elevators.

"What is he doing?" Victor asked.

By his question, he referred to the video that revealed Randal proceeding along a corridor in a peculiar, hesitant, herky-jerky fashion. Sometimes he took a few steps sideways, studying the floor intently, before he proceeded forward again, but then he stepped sideways to the right.

"Sir, he looks as if he's learning a dance step," said Werner.

"What dance step?"

"I don't know what dance step, sir. My education is largely in surveillance and extreme violent combat. I didn't learn no dance."

"*Any* dance," Victor corrected. "Why would Randal want to dance?"

"People do."

"He's not people."

"No, sir, he's not."

"I didn't design him with the desire to dance. He isn't dancing. It looks more as if he's trying to avoid stepping on something."

"Yes, sir. The cracks."

"What cracks?"

"The cracks between the floor tiles."

When the escapee passed directly under a camera, Werner's observation proved to be correct. Step by step, Randal had been painstakingly careful to place each foot inside one of the twelve-inch-square vinyl tiles.

"That's obsessive-compulsive behavior," Victor said, "which is consistent with the developmental flaws I gave him."

Randal passed out of the view field of one camera, appeared on another. He boarded an elevator. He went down to the bottom floor of the hospital.

"No one made any attempt to stop him, Werner."

"No, sir. Our assignment is to prevent unauthorized entrance. We were never told we should be concerned about anyone leaving without authorization. None of the staff, none of the newly made would ever leave here without your permission."

"Randal did."

Frowning, Werner said, "It isn't possible to disobey you, sir."

On the bottom floor, Randal avoided cracks and reached the file room. He concealed himself among the metal cabinets.

Most of the New Race who were created in Mercy were eventually infiltrated into the city's population. Some, however, like Randal, were experimental, and Victor intended them for termination when he had concluded the experiment of which each was the subject. Randal had never been meant for the world beyond these walls.

Werner fast-forwarded the surveillance tape until Victor himself appeared, entering the file room by way of the secret tunnel that connected the former hospital to the parking garage of the building next door.

"He's renegade," Victor said grimly. "He hid from me."

"It isn't possible to disobey you, sir."

"He obviously *knew* he was forbidden to leave."

"But it isn't possible to disobey you, sir."

"Shut up, Werner."

"Yes, sir."

After Victor passed through the file room into the lower floor of Mercy, Randal Six emerged from concealment and went to the exit door. He entered the lock code and proceeded into the tunnel.

"How did he know the code?" Victor wondered.

Hitching and twitching, Randal followed the tunnel to the door at the farther end, where again he entered the lock code.

"How did he *know*?"

"Permission to speak, sir."

"Go ahead."

"When he was hiding in the file room, he heard the tone of each digit you pressed on the keypad before you entered from the tunnel."

"You mean, heard it through the door."

"Yes, sir."

"Every number has a different tone," Victor said.

"He would've had to learn beforehand what number each tone represented."

On the surveillance tape, Randal entered the empty storeroom in the building next door. After some hesitation, he went from there into the parking garage.

The final camera captured Randal as he haltingly ascended the garage ramp. His face was carved by anxiety, but somehow he overcame his agoraphobia and ventured into a world he found threatening and overwhelming in scale.

"Mr Helios, sir, I suggest that our security protocols be revised and our electronic systems modified to prevent unauthorized exit as well as unauthorized entrance."

"Do it," Victor said.

"Yes, sir."

"We've got to find him," Victor said more to himself than to Werner. "He left with some specific intention. A destination. He's so developmentally disabled, so narrowly focused, he could only have accomplished this if some desperate need drove him."

"May I suggest, sir, that we search his billet as thoroughly as if we were police searching a crime scene. We might find a clue to his purpose, his destination."

"We better," Victor warned.

"Yes, sir."

Victor went to the door, hesitated, glanced back at Werner. "How is your mucus?"

The security chief came as close to smiling as he ever would. "Much better, sir. The last few days, I haven't had no snot at all."

"Any snot," Victor corrected.

"No, sir. Like I just said, I don't have no snot at all."

chapter 13

Carson O'Connor lives in a simple white house given some grace by a veranda that wraps three sides.

Oaks draped with Spanish moss shade the property. Cicadas sing in the heat.

In respect of the substantial annual rainfall and the long sultry summers, the veranda and the house itself are raised almost three feet off the ground on concrete piers, creating a crawl space under the entire structure.

The crawl space is concealed by a skirt of crisscrossed lattice. Usually nothing lives here but spiders.

These are unusual days. Now the spiders share their redoubt with Randal Six.

Crossing the city from the Hands of Mercy, especially when a thunderstorm brought the sky crashing to the earth in bright bolts, Randal had been afflicted by too much noise, by too many new sights, smells, sounds, sensations. Never had he known such blind terror.

He had almost clawed out his eyes, had almost poked a sharp stick in his ears to destroy his hearing, thus sparing himself from sensory overload. Fortunately, he had restrained those impulses.

Although he appears to be eighteen, he has been alive and out of the tank for only four months. All of that time, he has lived in one room, mostly in one corner of that room.

He doesn't like commotion. He doesn't like being touched or having to speak to anyone. He despises change.

Yet here he is. He has thrown over all he knew and has embraced an unknowable future. This accomplishment makes him proud.

The crawl space is a peaceful environment. His monastery, his hermitage.

For the most part, the only smells are the bare earth under him, the raw wood above, the concrete piers. Occasionally a whiff of star jasmine finds its way to him, though it is a richer scent at night than in the day.

Little sunlight penetrates the interstices of the lattice. The shadows are deep, but because he is of the New Race, with enhanced vision, he can see well enough.

Only an occasional traffic noise reaches him from the street. From overhead, inside the house, come periodic footsteps, the creak of floorboards, muffled music on a radio.

His companions, the spiders, have no smell that he can detect, make no noise, and keep to themselves.

He might be content here for a long time if not for the fact that the secret of happiness abides in the house above him, and he must have it.

In a newspaper, he once saw a photograph of Detective Carson

O'Connor with her brother, Arnie. Arnie is an autistic like Randal Six.

Nature made Arnie autistic. Randal was given his affliction by Victor. Nevertheless, he and Arnie are brothers in their suffering.

In the newspaper photo, twelve-year-old Arnie had been with his sister at a charity event benefiting autism research. Arnie had been smiling. He looked happy.

During his four months of life in the Hands of Mercy, Randal has never been happy. Anxiety gnaws at him every minute, every day, more insistently some times than at others, but always chewing, nibbling. He lives in misery.

He never imagined that happiness might be possible – until he had seen Arnie's smile. Arnie knows something that Randal does not. Arnie the autistic knows a reason to smile. Perhaps many reasons.

They are brothers. Brothers in suffering. Arnie will share his secret with his brother Randal.

Should Arnie refuse to share it, Randal will *tear* the secret out of him. He will get it one way or another. He will kill for it.

If the world beyond the lattice were not so dazzling, so full of sights and motion, Randal Six would simply slither out from under the house. He would enter the place by a door or window, and get what he needs.

After his trip from Mercy and the ordeal of the thunderstorm, however, he cannot endure that much sensory input. He must find a way into the house from the crawl space.

No doubt the spiders do it often. He will be a spider. He will creep. He will find a way.

chapter 14

Nicholas Frigg walked the earthen ramparts that wound between and around the lakes of waste and rubbish, manager of the dump and master of all that he surveyed.

Over his jeans he wore thigh-high rubber boots hooked by straps to his belt. In this blazing heat he went barechested, wore no hat, and let the sun bake him to a bread-crust brown.

He had no worry about melanoma. He belonged to the New Race, and cancer could not touch him.

The malignancies that ate at him were alienation, loneliness, and an acute awareness of his enslavement.

In these uplands, significantly northeast of Lake Pontchartrain, the garbage arrived from the Big Easy and from other cities, seven days a week, in an endless caravan of semis with hydraulic rams that expelled compressed blocks of trash into the steaming pits of the landfill.

Misanthropes and cynics might say that regardless of the city, whether it be New Orleans or Paris or Tokyo, the definition of its garbage ought to include the worst examples of humanity that walked its streets.

And, of course, the urban legends of every city included stories asserting that the Mafia disposed of witnesses and other nuisances in garbage dumps where the workers were members of mobster-controlled unions.

The putrid depths of the Crosswoods Waste Management facility actually did contain thousands of bodies, many of which had appeared to be human when they had been secretly interred here over the years. Some *were* human, the cadavers of those who had been replaced by replicants.

The others were failed experiments – some of which did not look human at all – or members of the New Race who for a host of reasons had been terminated. Four Erikas were buried in these reservoirs of waste.

Everyone who worked at the dump belonged to the New Race. They answered to Nick Frigg, and he answered to his maker.

Crosswoods was owned by a Nevada corporation, which was itself owned by a holding company in the Bahamas. That holding company was an asset of a trust based in Switzerland.

The beneficiaries of the trust were three Australian nationals living in New Orleans. The Australians were in fact members of the New Race, who were themselves owned by Victor.

At the apex – or perhaps at the nadir – of this arc of deception stood Nick, both the master of the garbage and the overseer of the secret graveyard. More than most others of his kind, he enjoyed his work even if it was not what he wanted for a life.

The panoply of odors, an unending series of revolting stenches to an ordinary man, were a phantasmagoria of fragrances to Nick.

He breathed deeply and licked the air, and savored the intricacies of every aroma.

By the introduction of certain canine genes, Nick's maker had given him a sense of smell approximately half as sensitive as that of a dog, which meant he enjoyed olfactory perceptions ten thousand times more powerful than those of the average human being.

To a dog, few scents cause revulsion. Many are good, and nearly all are interesting. Even the stink of offal and the ripe miasma of decomposition are intriguing if not savory. And so they were, as well, to Nick Frigg.

This gift of smell turned a foul job into one with the potential to delight. Although Nick had cause to believe that Victor was a hard God if not cruel, here was one reason to consider that he did care, after all, about his creations.

Dog-nose Nick strode the ramparts, which were wide enough to accommodate an SUV, watching the semis off-loading along the far perimeter of the east pit, two hundred yards to his left. This ten-story-deep hole had been two-thirds filled with trash over the past few years.

Wide-track bulldozers – tagged "garbage galleons' by Nick and his crew – rode the sea of trash and distributed it more evenly across the pit than the trucks left it.

To his right lay the west pit, not quite as large as that to the east, but somewhat fuller.

Downslope, to the south, two previous sites had been filled and subsequently capped with eight feet of earth. Methane-gas vent pipes punctuated those grass-covered mounds.

North of the current two pits, excavation of a new east dump had been under way for two months. The chug and growl of earth-moving machines echoed down from those heights.

Nick turned his back to the busy east and studied the quiet west pit, from which incoming semis had been diverted for the day.

This moonscape of rubbish stirred his two hearts as nothing else could. Compacted chaos, waste and rack and ruin: These bleak, toxic barrens spoke to that part of him that might have been occupied by a soul if he had been of the Old Race. He felt at home here as he would never feel in woods or grassy fields, or in a city. The desolation, the filth, the mold, the rancidity, the ash, the slime called to him as the sea called a sailor.

Within a few hours, a van would arrive from New Orleans, loaded with corpses. Three were city bureaucrats who had been murdered and replaced by replicants, and two were police officers who had met the same end.

A mere year ago, such deliveries had been made twice a month. Now they came twice a week, often more frequently.

These were exciting times.

In addition to the five dead humans, the van carried three gone-wrongs, creatures created in the Hands of Mercy that had not turned out as Victor hoped. They were always interesting.

After nightfall, when everyone within the fenced perimeter of Crosswoods Waste Management would be of the New Race, Nick and his crew would carry the dead humans and the gone-wrongs into the west pit. In a ceremony that had gradually become richer over the years, they would bury them in that slough of garbage.

Although these nocturnal interments had lately become frequent, they still thrilled Nick. He was forbidden to kill himself; and he could not slaughter members of the Old Race until the day when Victor launched the Last War. He loved death but could not have it or deal it out. Meanwhile, however, he could wade the sea of trash and filth, shoving the dead into reeking holes where they would bloat and ripen, intoxicated by the fumes of decomposition – which was a fringe benefit that he cherished.

In the morning, the scores of incoming semis would be directed to the west pit, and the loads they deposited would be spread across these new graves, like another layer in a parfait.

As Nick gazed out across the west dump, longing for sunset, a flock of fat glossy crows, feeding in the garbage, suddenly exploded into flight. The birds took wing as though they were a single creature and shrieked in unison, swooping toward him and then up into the sun.

About a hundred fifty feet from the rampart on which he stood, a twenty-foot length of the dense trash trembled, and then appeared to roll, as though something swarmed through it. Perhaps a pack of rats surged just below the surface.

In recent days, members of Nick's crew had half a dozen times reported rhythmic shiftings and pulsations in both pits, different from the usual swelling and settling related to the expansion and then sudden venting of methane pockets.

Little more than half a day ago, past midnight, strange sounds had risen from the east pit, almost like voices, tortured cries. With flashlights, Nick and his crew had gone in search of the source, which had seemed repeatedly to change direction but then had fallen silent before it could be located.

Now the pulsing trash went still. Rats. Surely rats.

Nevertheless, curious, Nick descended the sloped wall of the earthen rampart, into the west pit.

Aubrey Picou had retired from a life of crime to have more time to tend his garden.

He lived on an oak-shaded street in Mid-City. His historic house boasted some of the most ornate decorative ironwork – fence, balcony railings – in a city dripping with such weighty filigree.

The front porch, draped with trumpet vines and hung with basket ferns, offered two white bench swings and wicker rocking chairs, but the shadows seemed no cooler than the sun-scorched front walk.

The maid, Lulana St John, answered the doorbell. She was a fiftyish black woman whose girth and personality were equally formidable.

Leveling a disapproving look at Carson, trying to suppress a smile when she glanced at Michael, Lulana said, "I see before me two well-known public servants who do the Lord's work but sometimes make the mistake of using the devil's tactics."

"We're two sinners," Carson admitted.

"'Amazing grace,'" Michael said, "'how sweet thou art, to save a wretch like me.'"

"Child," said Lulana, "I suspect you flatter yourself to think you're saved. If you have come here to be troublesome to the mister, I ask you to look within yourselves and find the part of you that wants to be a *peace* officer."

"That's the biggest part of me," Michael said, "but Detective O'Connor here mostly just wants to kick ass."

To Carson, Lulana said, "I'm sorry to say, missy, that *is* your reputation."

"Not today," Carson assured her. "We're here to ask a favor of Aubrey, if you would please announce us. We have no grievance against him."

Lulana studied her solemnly. "The Lord has given me an excellent crap detector, and it isn't ringing at the moment. It's in your favor that you have not shaken your badge at me, and you did say please."

"At my insistence," Michael said, "Detective O'Connor has been taking an evening class in etiquette."

"He's a fool," Lulana told Carson.

"Yes, I know."

"After a lifetime of eating with her hands," Michael said, "she has mastered the use of the fork in a remarkably short time."

"Child, you are a fool," Lulana told him, "but for reasons that only the Lord knows, in spite of myself, I always take a liking to you." She stepped back from the threshold. "Wipe your feet, and come in."

The foyer was painted peach with white wainscoting and ornate white crown molding. The white marble floor with diamond-shaped black inlays had been polished to such a shine that it looked wet.

"Has Aubrey found Jesus yet?" Carson wondered.

Closing the front door, Lulana said, "The mister hasn't embraced his Lord, no, but I'm pleased to say he has come as far as making eye contact with Him."

Although paid only to be a maid, Lulana did double duty as a spiritual guide to her employer, whose past she knew and whose soul concerned her.

"The mister is gardening," she said. "You could wait for him in the parlor or join him in the roses."

"By all means, the roses," Michael said.

At the back of the house, in the immense kitchen, Lulana's older sister, Evangeline Antoine, softly sang "His Lamp Will Overcome All Darkness' as she pressed dough into a pie pan.

Evangeline served as Aubrey's cook and also as an amen choir to Lulana's indefatigable soul-saving efforts. She was taller than her sister, thin, yet her lively eyes and her smile made their kinship obvious.

"Detective Maddison," Evangeline said, "I'm so glad you're not dead yet."

"Me too," he said. "What kind of pie are you making?"

"Praline-cinnamon cream topped with fried pecans."

"Now that's *worth* a quadruple heart-bypass."

"Cholesterol," Lulana informed them, "won't stick if you have the right attitude."

She led them through the rear door onto the back veranda, where Moses Bienvenu, Aubrey's driver and handyman, was painting the beautifully turned white balusters under the black handrail.

Beaming, he said, "Detective O'Connor, I'm amazed to see you haven't shot Mr Michael yet."

"My aim's good," she assured him, "but he can move fast."

Well-padded but not fat, a robust and towering man with hands as big as dinner plates, Moses served as a deacon at the church and sang in the same gospel choir as his sisters, Lulana and Evangeline.

"They're here to see the mister but not to trouble him," Lulana told her brother. "If it looks like they're troubling him, after all, lift them by the scruffs of their necks and put them in the street."

As Lulana went inside, Moses said, "You heard Lulana. You may be police officers, but she's the law around here. The Law and the Way. I would be in your debt if you didn't make it necessary for me to scruff-carry you out of here."

"If we find ourselves getting out of hand," Michael said, "we'll scruff-carry each other."

Pointing with his paintbrush, Moses said, "Mr Aubrey is over there past the pagan fountain, among the roses. And please don't make fun of his hat."

"His hat?" Michael asked.

"Lulana insists he wear a sun hat if he's going to spend half the day in the garden. He's mostly bald, so she worries he'll get head-top skin cancer. Mr Aubrey hated the hat at first. He only recently got used to it."

Carson said, "Never thought I'd see the day when anyone would be the boss of Aubrey Picou."

"Lulana doesn't so much boss," said Moses. "She sort of just tough-loves everyone into obedience."

A brick walkway led from the back veranda steps, across the lawn, encircled the pagan fountain, and continued to the rose garden.

The sculptured-marble fountain featured three life-size figures.

Pan, a male form with goat legs and horns, played a flute and chased two nude women – or they chased him – around a column twined with grapevines.

"My eye for antiques isn't infallible," Michael said, "but I'm pretty sure that's eighteenth-century Las Vegas."

The rosebushes grew in rows, with aisles of decomposed granite between. In the third of four aisles stood a bag of fertilizer, a tank sprayer, and trays of neatly arranged gardening tools.

Here, too, was Aubrey Picou, under a straw hat with such a broad brim that squirrels could have raced around it for exercise.

Before he noticed them and looked up, he was humming a tune. It sounded like "His Lamp Will Overcome All Darkness."

Aubrey was eighty years old and had a baby face: an eighty-year-old baby face, but nevertheless pink and plump and pinchable. Even in the deep shade of his anticancer headgear, his blue eyes twinkled with merriment.

"Of all the cops I know," said Aubrey, "here are the two I like the best."

"Do you like any others at all?" Carson asked.

"Not one of the bastards, no," Aubrey said. "But then none of the rest ever saved my life."

"What's with the stupid hat?" Michael asked.

Aubrey's smile became a grimace. "What's it matter if I die of skin cancer? I'm eighty years old. I gotta die of something."

"Lulana doesn't want you to die before you find Jesus."

Aubrey sighed. "With those three running the show, I trip over Jesus every time I turn around."

"If anyone can redeem you," Carson said, "it'll be Lulana."

Aubrey looked as if he would say something acerbic. Instead he sighed again. "I never used to have a conscience. Now I do. It's more annoying than this absurd hat."

"Why wear the hat if you hate it?" Michael asked.

Aubrey glanced toward the house. "If I take it off, she'll see. Then I won't get any of Evangeline's pie."

"The praline-cinnamon cream pie."

"With fried-pecan topping," Aubrey said. "I love that pie." He sighed.

"You sigh a lot these days," Michael said.

"I've become pathetic, haven't I?"

"You used to be pathetic," Carson said. "What you've become is a little bit human."

"It's disconcerting," Michael said.

"Don't I know," Aubrey agreed. "So what brings you guys here?"

Carson said, "We need some big, loud, door-busting guns."

chapter **16**

Glorious, the stink: pungent, pervasive, penetrating.

Nick Frigg imagined that the smell of the pits had saturated his flesh, his blood, his bones, in the same way that the scent of smoldering hickory permeated even the thickest cuts of meat in a smoke-house.

He relished the thought that to the core he smelled like all varieties of decomposition, like the death that he longed for and that he could not have.

In his thigh-high rubber boots, Nick strode across the west pit, empty cans of everything rattling in his wake, empty egg cartons and cracker boxes crunching-crackling underfoot, toward the spot where the surface of the trash had swelled and rolled and settled. That peculiar activity appeared to have ceased.

Although compacted by the wide-tracked garbage galleons that crawled these desolate realms, the trash field – between sixty and seventy feet deep in this pit – occasionally shifted under Nick, for by its nature it was riddled with small voids. Agile, with lightning reflexes, he rarely lost his footing.

When he arrived at the site of the movement that he had seen from the elevated rampart, the surface did not look significantly different from the hundred fifty feet of refuse across which he had just traveled. Squashed cans, broken glass, uncountable plastic items from bleach bottles to broken toys, drifts of moldering landscape trimmings – palm fronds, tree limbs, grass – full trash bags knotted at their necks . .

He saw a doll with tangled legs and a cracked brow. Pretending that beneath his foot lay a real child of the Old Race, Nick stomped until he shattered the smiling face.

Turning slowly 360 degrees, he studied the debris more closely.

He sniffed, sniffed, using his genetically enhanced sense of smell to seek a clue as to what might have caused the unusual rolling movement in this sea of trash. Methane escaped the depths of the pit, but that scent seemed no more intense than usual.

Rats. He smelled rats nearby. In a dump, this was no more surprising than catching a whiff of garbage. The musky scent of rodents pervaded the entire fenced grounds of Crosswoods Waste Management.

He detected clusters of those whiskered individuals all around him, but he could not smell a pack so large that, swarming through a burrow, it would be capable of destabilizing the surface of the trash field.

Nick roamed the immediate area, looking, sniffing, and then squatted – rubber boots squeaking – and waited. Motionless. Listening. Breathing quietly but deeply.

The sounds of the unloading semis at the east pit gradually receded, as did the distant growl of the garbage galleons.

As if to assist him, the air hung heavy and still. There was no breeze to whisper distractingly in his ears. The brutal sun seared silence into the day.

At times like this, the sweet reek of the pit could convey him into something like a Zen state of relaxed yet intense observation.

He lost track of time, became so blissed-out that he didn't know how many minutes passed until he heard the voice, and he could not be certain that it hadn't spoken several times before he registered it.

"*Father?*"

Soft, tremulous, in an indefinite timbre, the oneword question could have been posed by either a male or a female.

Dog-nose Nick waited, sniffed.

"*Father, Father, Father . . . ?*"

This time the question seemed to come simultaneously from four or five individuals, male and female.

When he surveyed the trash field, Nick found that he remained alone. How such a thing could be possible, he did not know, but the voices must have spoken out of the compacted refuse beneath him, rising through crevices from . . . From where?

"*Why, Father, why, why, why . . . ?*"

The lost and beseeching tone suggested intractable misery, and resonated with Nick's own repressed despair.

"Who are you?" he asked.

He received no reply.

"*What* are you?"

A tremor passed through the trash field. Brief. Subtle. The surface did not swell and roll as before.

Nick sensed the mysterious presence withdrawing.

Rising to his feet, he said, "What do you want?"

The searing sun. The still air. The stink.

Nick Frigg stood alone, the slough of trash once more firm beneath his feet.

chapter 17

At a bush with huge pink-yellow-white roses, Aubrey Picou snipped a bloom for Carson, and stripped the thorns from the stem.

"This variety is called French Perfume. Its exceptional mix of colors makes it the most feminine rose in my garden."

Michael was amused to see Carson handle the flower so awkwardly even though it had no thorns. She was not a frills-and-roses kind of girl. She was a blue-jeans-and-guns kind of girl.

In spite of his innocent face and floppy straw hat, the master of this garden seemed as out of place among the roses as did Carson.

During decades of criminal activity, Aubrey Picou never killed a man, never wounded one. He never robbed or raped, or extorted anyone. He had merely made it possible for other criminals to do those things more easily and efficiently.

His document shop had produced forged papers of the highest quality: passports, birth certificates, driver's licenses. He'd sold thousands of black-market guns.

When individuals with a talent for strategy and tactics came to Aubrey with plans for an armored-car heist or with a scheme to knock over a diamond wholesaler, he provided the risk capital to prepare and execute the operation.

His father, Maurice, had been an attorney who specialized in massaging juries into awarding outrageous financial compensation to questionable clients in dubious personal-injury cases. Some in his profession admiringly called him Maurice the Milkman because of his ability to squeeze buckets of profits out of juries as dumb as cows.

The Milkman had put his son through Harvard Law with the fond hope that Aubrey would embrace the – at that time – new field of class-action litigation, using bad science and good court-room theater to terrorize major corporations and to drive them nearly to bankruptcy with billion-dollar settlements.

To Maurice's disappointment, Aubrey had found the law tedious, even when practiced with contempt, and had decided that he could do as much damage to society from outside the legal system as he could from within it. Though father and son had for a while been estranged, eventually Maurice had been proud of his boy.

The Milkman's son had been indicted only twice. Both times he had escaped conviction. In each case, after the foreman delivered the innocent verdict, the juries stood and applauded Aubrey.

To forestall a pending third indictment, he had secretly turned state's evidence. After ratting out scores of thugs without their knowledge, he retired at seventy-five, his reputation intact among the criminal class and its admirers.

"I don't do guns anymore," Aubrey said. "Not the big, loud, door-busting kind or any others."

"We know you're retired—"

"For true," Aubrey assured her.

"—but you still have friends in all the wrong places."

"This rose is called Black Velvet," said Aubrey. "The red is so dark, it looks black in places."

"We're not setting you up," Carson said. "No prosecutor will waste thousands of hours to nail a harmless octogenarian gardener."

Michael said, "Besides, you'd fake Alzheimer's and have the jury in tears."

"French Perfume doesn't belong in a bouquet with this," Aubrey told Carson, "but Black Velvet strikes me as more of a rose for you."

"What we need are two Desert Eagle pistols, .50 Magnum."

Impressed, Michael said to Carson, "Is that what we need?"

"I said *loud*, didn't I? If you have two hearts and you take one chest punch of that caliber, both tickers ought to pop."

Aubrey gave a Black Velvet rose to Carson, who accepted it reluctantly. She held one flower in each hand, looking nonplussed.

"Why don't you requisition through the PD?" Aubrey asked.

"'Cause we're going to kill a man who would walk out of a courtroom, free and laughing, if we put him on trial," she lied.

In the shade of his hat, Aubrey's eyes glittered with interest.

"We aren't wired," Carson assured him. "You can pat us down."

"I'd like to pat you down, all right, darlin'," said Aubrey, "but not for a wire. This isn't how you'd talk if you were wearing one."

"For the Eagles, I'll want one hundred rounds of .50AE's, .325 weight," Carson said, "jacketed hollow points."

"Formidable. You're talking maybe fourteen-hundred-feet-per-second muzzle velocity," Aubrey said.

"We want these guys very dead. We'll also need two shotguns. We want to use slugs, not buckshot."

"Slugs, not buckshot," Michael agreed, nodding, as if they were entirely simpatico about this, as if he weren't scared half numb.

"Big stopping power," Aubrey said approvingly.

"Big," Michael agreed.

"Semi-auto so we can fire a second round singlehanded," Carson continued. "Maybe an Urban Sniper. What's the barrel length on that?"

"Eighteen inches," Aubrey said.

"We'd want it cut down to fourteen. But we need these fast, so there's no time to wait for customizing."

"How fast?"

"Today. Soon. As soon as now. Urban Sniper, SGT, Remington – we'll have to take any credible shotgun that's already been modified to meet those specifications."

"You'll want a three-way sling for each," Aubrey said, "so you can shoulder-carry and hip-fire."

"So who do we go to?" Carson asked, still holding a rose in each hand as if she were protesting to end all war.

Unconsciously working the rose snips – *click-click, click-click, click-click* – Aubrey studied her and Michael for half a minute, then said, "That's a lot of firepower to go after one guy. Who is he – the Antichrist?"

"He's well protected," she said. "We're going to have to wade through some people to nail him. But they're all dirtbags, too."

Not convinced, Aubrey Picou said, "Cops go bad all the time. Given the lack of support they get and all the flack they take, who can blame them? But not you two. You two don't go bad."

"You remember what happened to my dad?" Carson asked.

Aubrey said, "That was all bogus. Your dad didn't turn. He was a good cop to the end."

"I know. But thanks for saying it, Aubrey."

When he cocked his head in the sun hat, he looked like Truman Capote in ladies-going-to-lunch drag. "You telling me you know who really waxed him and your mom?"

"Yeah," she lied.

"Just who pulled the trigger or who ordered it to be pulled?"

"We're at the top of the food chain with this guy," she said.

Looking at Michael, Aubrey said, "So when you punch his ticket, it's going to be big news."

Staying mostly mute and playing half dumb had worked well for Michael. He shrugged.

Aubrey wasn't satisfied with a shrug. "You'll probably be killed doing this."

"Nobody lives forever," Michael said.

"Lulana says we all do. Anyway, this is O'Connor's vengeance. Why should you die for it?"

"We're partners," Michael said.

"That's not it. Partners don't commit suicide for each other."

"I think we can pull it off," Michael said, "and walk away."

A sly smile robbed the old man's pinchable face of its previous innocence. "That's not it, either."

Grimacing, Carson said, "Aubrey, don't make him say it."

"I just need to hear something that makes his commitment believable."

"This isn't going to snap back on you," she promised.

"Maybe, maybe not. I'm almost convinced. I know your motive, darlin'. His, I want to hear."

"Don't say it," Carson warned Michael.

"Well, he already knows," Michael said.

"That's the point. He already knows. He doesn't need to hear you say it. He's just being a pissant."

"Now, darlin', don't hurt old Aubrey's feelings. Michael, why in blazes would you want to do this?"

"Because—"

"Don't," said Carson.

"—I love her."

Carson said, "Shit."

Aubrey Picou laughed with delight. "I am a fool for romance. You give me your cell-phone number, and the man with the goods will call you inside two hours, to tell you how and where."

"Aubrey Picou, I should make you eat these roses," Carson said, shaking the French Perfume and the Black Velvet in his face.

"Seeing as how they've been flavored by your sweet hands, I suspect I'd like the taste."

She threw the roses on the ground. "For that, you owe me one. I want to borrow the money to pay for the guns."

Aubrey laughed. "Why would I do that?"

"Because we once saved your life. And I don't have several thousand stuffed in a sock."

"Darlin', I'm not a man with a reputation for generosity."

"That's part of what Lulana's been trying to tell you."

He frowned. "This makes me more of a party to it."

"Not if the loan is on a handshake. No paperwork."

"I don't mean legally. I mean morally."

Michael thought his hearing had failed. The word couldn't have been *morally*.

"Just making the connection for the deal isn't so bad," Aubrey said, 'cause I'm not taking a commission, I make nothing from it. But if I finance it, even interest-free . . ."

This clearly surprised Carson. "Interest-free?"

"Seems like I've got some responsibility that way." Under his big floppy hat, he now looked more worried than absurd. "This Jesus guy is scary."

"Scary?"

"I mean, if he's half as real as Lulana says—"

"Half as real?"

"—then you have to think consequences."

"Aubrey," Carson said, "no offense, but considering the way you've lived your life, I don't think scary old Jesus is going to make a big issue out of you loaning me money for this."

"Maybe not. But I've been trying to change the kind of person I am."

"You *have*?"

Aubrey took off his hat, wiped his sweaty forehead with a handkerchief, and at once put the hat on again. "They all know who I used to be, but Lulana, Evangeline, and Moses – they treat me with respect."

"And it's not because they're afraid you might have them kneecapped."

"Exactly right. It's amazing. They've all been so nice to me for no reason, and after a while I sort of wanted to be nice to them."

"How insidious," Michael said.

"It is," Aubrey agreed. "It really is. You let people like that into your life – especially if they also make good pie – and the next thing you know, you're giving money to charities."

"You haven't really," Carson said.

"Sixty thousand this year already," Aubrey said sheepishly.

"No way."

"The orphanage desperately needed repairs, so *somebody* had to step up and fill their soup pot."

"Aubrey Picou helping an *orphanage*," Michael said.

"I'd be obliged if you don't tell anyone about it. I've got a reputation to protect. The old crowd would think I've gone soft or senile."

"Your secret's safe with us," Carson promised.

Aubrey's expression brightened. "Hey, what about this – I'll just give you the money, no loan at all. You use it for whatever you need, and one day when you're more flush, you don't give it back to me, you give it to some charity you like."

"You think that'll fool Jesus?" Michael asked.

"It should," Aubrey said, pleased with himself. "Anyway, it would be like if I gave a bunch of money to a school for the deaf and the school principal skimmed a little off the top and used the skim to pay for a three-way with two hookers."

"Do you follow this?" Michael asked Carson.

"It's too metaphysical for me."

"The point is," Aubrey said, "the skim and the hookers wouldn't be my fault just because I gave money to a school for the deaf."

"Instead of paying back what you lend me, you want me to give it to a school for the deaf?" Carson asked.

"That would be nice. Just remember, what you do with it in the meantime, *you* have to answer for."

"You've become a real theologian," Michael said.

chapter 18

After the body of William, the butler, and all of his severed
fingers had been removed from the mansion by two men from the
Hands of Mercy, the head housekeeper, Christine, and the third-
floor maid, Jolie, cleaned up the blood in the hallway.

Erika knew that as the mistress of the house, she should not get
down on her knees and help. Victor would not approve.

Because class distinctions prevented her from assisting, she did
not know what to do; therefore, she stood by and watched.

The blood on the mahogany floor wiped up easily, of course,
but Erika was surprised to see it come off the painted wall and out
of the antique Persian runner without leaving any visible residue.

"What's that spot remover you're using?" she asked, indicating
the unlabeled plastic squeeze bottles with which both Christine
and Jolie were armed.

"Mr Helios invented it," Jolie said.

"He must have made a fortune from it."

"It's never been marketed to the public," Christine said.

"He developed it for us," Jolie revealed.

Erika marveled that Victor would have time to concoct new household products, considering everything else on his mind.

"Other spot removers," Christine explained, "even if they took out all the stain visible to the eye, would leave blood proteins in the carpet fibers that any CSI unit could identify. This expunges everything."

"My husband's very clever, isn't he?" Erika said, not without some pride.

"Extremely so," said Christine.

"Extremely," Jolie agreed.

"I very much want to please him," Erika said.

"That would be a good idea," Jolie said.

"I think I displeased him this morning."

Christine and Jolie glanced meaningfully at each other, but neither replied to Erika.

She said, "He beat me while we were having sex."

Having dealt with all the bloodstains, Christine directed Jolie to proceed with her morning tasks in the master suite. When she and Erika were alone in the hallway, she said, "Mrs Helios, excuse me for being so straightforward, but you must not speak about your private life with Mr Helios in front of anyone on the household staff."

Erika frowned. "Shouldn't I?"

"No. Never."

"Why not?"

"Mrs Helios, surely the subject of social deportment was part of your manners-and-etiquette download."

"Well, I guess it was. I mean, if you think it should have been."

"It definitely should have been. You shouldn't discuss your sex life with anyone but Mr Helios."

"The thing is, he beat me during sex, even bit me once, and he called me the worst names. I was so ashamed."

"Mrs Helios—"

"He's a good man, a great man, so I must have done something terribly wrong to have made him hurt me, but I don't know what upset him."

"You're doing it again," Christine said impatiently, "talking about your private life with Mr Helios."

"You're right, I am. But if you could help me understand what I did to displease my husband, that would be good for both me and Victor."

Christine's stare was sharp and unwavering. "You *do* know that you are the fifth Erika, don't you?"

"Yes. And I'm determined to be the last."

"Then perhaps you'd better not talk about sex even with him."

"Even with Victor? But how will I find out why he was displeased with me?"

Christine stropped her sharp stare into an even more piercing gaze. "Maybe he wasn't displeased."

"Then why did he punch me and pull my hair and pinch my—"

"You're doing it again."

Frustrated, Erika said, "But I've got to talk with *somebody* about it."

"Then talk to the mirror, Mrs Helios. That's the only safe conversation you can have on the subject."

"How could that be productive? A mirror is an inanimate object. Unless it's magical, like in *Snow White and the Seven Dwarfs*."

"When you're looking at yourself in the mirror, Mrs Helios, ask yourself what you know about sexual sadism."

Erika considered the term. "I don't think it's in my programmed knowledge."

"Then the very best thing you can do is educate yourself . . . and endure. Now, if that's everything, I have a number of tasks to attend to."

chapter 19

The soft rattle of the computer keyboard under Vicky Chou's nimble fingers, as she composed a letter, was the only sound in the summer afternoon. Each time that she paused in her typing, the subsequent silence seemed nearly as deep as deafness.

The merest breath of sultry air stirred the sheer curtains at the open window but did not produce the faintest whisper. Outside, the day lacked bird songs. If traffic passed in the street, it did so with the muted grace of a ghost ship sailing without wind across a glassy sea.

Vicky Chou worked at home as a medical transcriptionist. Home was Carson O'Connor's house, where she received free room and board in return for serving as a caregiver to Carson's brother, Arnie.

Some of her friends thought this was an odd arrangement and that Vicky had negotiated a bad deal. In truth, she felt over-compensated, because Carson had saved Vicky's sister, Liane, from serving life in prison for a crime she had never committed.

At forty-five, Vicky had been a widow for five years; and as she'd never had children of her own, a fringe benefit of living here was the feeling of being part of a family. Arnie was like a son to her.

Although autistic, the boy rarely presented her with a problem. He was self-absorbed, quiet, and endearing in his way. She prepared his meals, but otherwise he cared for himself.

He seldom left his room, and he never left the house except when Carson wished to take him with her. Even then he usually went only with reluctance.

Vicky didn't have to worry about him wandering away. When he wandered, it was to internal lands that held more interest for him than did the real world.

Nevertheless, the silence began to seem eerie to her, and an uneasiness crept over her, growing with each pause in her typing.

At last she rose from her desk chair and went to check on Arnie.

Vicky's second-floor room was a pleasant size, but Arnie's quarters – across the hall – were twice as large as hers. A wall had been taken down between two bedrooms to provide him with the space that he required and with a small bath of his own.

His bed and nightstand were jammed in a corner. At the foot of his bed stood a TV with DVD player, on a wheeled stand.

The castle occupied a significant part of the room. Four low tables formed an eight-by-twelve-foot platform on which Arnie had erected a Lego-block wonder that was brilliantly conceived and executed in obsessive detail.

From barbican to curtain wall, to casements, to ramparts, to the keep, to the highest turrets, down to the bailey, through the inner ward, to the barracks and the stables and the blacksmith's shop, the ninety-six-square-foot marvel seemed to be Arnie's defense against a frightening world.

The boy sat now in the wheeled office chair that he occupied when working on the castle or when just staring dreamily at it. To any eye but Arnie's, this Lego structure was complete, but he was not satisfied; he worked on it every day, adding to its majesty and improving its defenses.

Although twelve, Arnie looked younger. He was slender and as pale as a Nordic child at the end of a long dark winter.

He did not look up at Vicky. Eye contact dismayed him, and he seldom liked to be touched.

Yet he had a gentleness about him, a wistfulness, that moved her. And he knew more of the world, and of people, than she had first believed.

One bad day, when Vicky had been missing Arthur, her dead husband, almost more than she could bear, though she had not openly expressed her misery, Arnie had reacted to her state of mind and had spoken without glancing at her. "You're only as lonely as you want to be," he'd said, "and he would never want you to be."

Although she tried to engage the boy in conversation, he said no more.

That day, she had perceived a more mysterious aspect to autism in general and to Arnie's case in particular than she'd previously recognized. His isolation was beyond Vicky's power to heal, yet he had reached out to counsel her in her loneliness.

She'd had affection for the boy before that moment. Thereafter, it grew into love.

Now, watching him at work on the castle, she said, "I always think it's perfect as it is . . yet you find ways to make it better."

He did not acknowledge her, but she felt sure that he heard.

Leaving him to his work, Vicky returned to the hallway and

stood at the head of the stairs, listening to the persistent silence below.

Arnie was where he should be, and safe. Yet the quiet did not feel peaceful, instead felt pregnant, as though some threat were gestating and at the brink of a noisy birth.

Carson had said that she and Michael were on a case that "might come home to us," and had warned Vicky to be security-conscious. As a consequence, she had locked the front and back doors and had left no first-floor windows open.

Although she knew that she had not overlooked a lock or latch, the silence below called to her, cautioned her.

She descended the stairs and toured the living room, Carson's bedroom and bath, the kitchen, checking that all doors and windows were still secure. She found everything as she remembered having left it.

Half-drawn blinds and sheer curtains left the lower floor shadowy. Each time Vicky turned on a lamp to facilitate her inspection, she turned it off behind her when she moved on.

Carson's room was the only part of the downstairs that featured air conditioning. Bolted in place, the window-mounted unit could not be removed without a racket that would betray an intruder long before he could effect entrance. At the moment, the air conditioner waited to be switched on; like similar units in Vicky's and Arnie's rooms, it was used only to facilitate sleep.

With the windows closed, these lower rooms were warm, stuffy. In the kitchen, she opened the top door on the refrigerator, not because she wanted anything in the freezer, but because the icy out-draft, billowing against her face, felt refreshing.

In her second-floor room once more, she found that the hush of the house continued to unnerve her. This seemed like the silence of an ax raised high but not yet swung.

Ridiculous. She was spooking herself. A case of broad-daylight heebie-jeebies.

Vicky switched on her CD player and, because Carson was not home to be bothered, turned the volume up a little louder than she usually did.

The disc was an anthology of hits by different artists. Billy Joel, Rod Stewart, the Knack, Supertramp, the BeeGees, Gloria Gaynor, Cheap Trick.

The music of her youth. Arthur had asked her to marry him. So happy together. Time had no meaning then. They thought they would live forever.

She returned to the letter that she had been composing, and sang along with the CD, her spirits lifted by the music and by memories of happier days, the troubling silence banished.

———

With the floor of the house pressing overhead, surrounded by the smell of bare earth and moist fungus, shrouded in gloom, anyone else might have progressed from claustrophobia to a panicky sense of being buried alive. Randal Six, however, child of Mercy, feels protected, even cozy.

He listens to the woman come downstairs and walk from room to room as though looking for something that she has mislaid. Then she returns to the second floor.

When he hears the music filtering down from high in the house, he knows that his opportunity has come. Under the cover of rock 'n' roll, the noise he makes getting into the O'Connor residence will not be likely to draw attention.

He has thoroughly explored the crawl space, surprised by how adventurous he has become. The farther he goes from the Hands of Mercy both in terms of distance and time, the more his agoraphobia abates and the more he desires to expand his boundaries.

He is blossoming.

In addition to the concrete piers on which the house perches, the crawl space is punctuated by incoming water pipes, by sewer pipes and gray-water drains, by more pipes housing electrical cable. All of these services puncture the floor of the structure.

Even if Randal could disassemble one of those conduits, none of the points of penetration would be large enough to admit him.

He also has found a trapdoor. It measures about three feet square.

The hinges and latch are on the farther side, where he can't reach them. The door most likely opens up and inward.

Near the trap, adjacent to the incoming gas line, flexible ductwork, eight inches in diameter, comes out of the house; it snakes through the crawl space. The farther end of the duct is framed to a cutout in the lattice skirt.

Randal assumes this is either an air intake or a safety vent for a gas-fired heating system.

Judging by the evidence, the trapdoor opens into a furnace room. A repairman could use it to move between the equipment above and the connections under the floor.

In the house overhead, autistic but capable of a dazzling smile, Arnie O'Connor possesses the secret to happiness. Either the boy will relinquish it or Randal Six will tear it out of him.

Lying on his back, Randal draws his knees toward his chest and presses his feet against the trapdoor. In the interest of breaking through with as little noise as possible, he applies pressure in gradually increasing increments. The latch and hinges creak as they strain against their fastenings.

When a particularly boisterous song echoes through the house and as the music swells toward a crescendo, he doubles his efforts, and the trapdoor springs open with a burr of screws ripping wood, a twang of torquing metal.

Happiness will soon be his.

chapter 20

After the meeting with Victor, Cindi wanted to go to the mall, but Benny wanted to talk about methods of decapitation.

According to their ID, Cindi and Benny Lovewell were twenty-eight and twenty-nine, respectively, though in fact they had been out of the creation tanks only nineteen months.

They made a cute couple. More accurately, they were made as a cute couple.

Attractive, well-dressed, each of them had a dazzling smile, a musical voice, and an infectious laugh. They were soft-spoken and polite, and they generally established instant rapport with everyone they met.

Cindi and Benny were fabulous dancers, though dancing was not the activity they most enjoyed. Their greatest pleasure came from killing.

Members of the New Race were forbidden to kill except when ordered to do so by their maker. The Lovewells were frequently ordered to do so.

When a member of the Old Race was slated to be replaced by a replicant, Cindi and Benny were the last smiling faces that person would ever see.

Those who were not scheduled to be replaced by pod people but who had somehow become a threat to Victor – or had offended him – were also destined to meet the Lovewells.

Sometimes these encounters began in a jazz club or a tavern. To the target, it seemed that new friends had been found – until later in the evening, when a parting handshake or a good-bye kiss on the cheek evolved, with amazing rapidity, into a violent garroting.

Other victims, on seeing the Lovewells for the first time, had no fair chance to get to know them, had hardly a moment to return their dazzling smiles, before being disemboweled.

On this sweltering summer day, prior to being summoned to the Hands of Mercy, the Lovewells had been bored. Benny could deal well with boredom, but tedium sometimes drove Cindi to reckless action.

After their meeting with Victor, in which they had been ordered to kill Detectives O'Connor and Maddison within twenty-four hours, Benny wanted to begin at once planning the hit. He hoped that the business could be arranged in such a way as to give them an opportunity to dismember alive at least one of the two cops.

Forbidden to kill as they wished, other members of the New Race lived with an envy of the free will with which those of the Old Race led their lives. This envy, more bitter by the day, expressed itself in despair and in a bottled rage that was denied relief.

As skilled assassins, Cindi and Benny *were* permitted relief, and lots of it. He usually could count on Cindi to match the eagerness with which he himself set out on every job.

On this occasion, however, she insisted on going shopping first. When Cindi insisted on something, Benny always let her have what she wanted because she was such a whiner when she didn't get her way that even Benny, with his high tolerance for tedium, lamented that his maker had programmed him to be incapable of suicide.

At the mall, to Benny's dismay, Cindi led him directly to Tots and Tykes, a store selling clothing for infants and young children.

He hoped this wouldn't lead to kidnapping again.

"We shouldn't be seen here," he warned her.

"We won't be. None of our kind works here, and none of our kind would have reason to shop here."

"We don't have a reason, either."

Without answering him, she went into Tots and Tykes.

As Cindi searched through the tiny dresses and other garments on the racks and tables, Benny followed her, trying to gauge whether she was likely to go nuts, as before.

Admiring a little yellow dress with a frilly collar, she said, "Isn't this adorable?"

"Adorable," Benny agreed. "But it would look better in pink."

"They don't seem to have it in pink."

"Too bad. Pink. In pink it would be terrific."

Members of the New Race were encouraged to have sex with one another, in every variation, as often and as violently as they liked. It was their one pressure-release valve.

They were, however, incapable of reproduction. The citizens of this brave new world would all be made in tanks, grown to adulthood and educated by direct-to-brain data downloading in four months.

Currently they were created a hundred at a time. Soon, tank farms would start turning them out by the thousands.

Their maker reserved all biological creation unto himself. He did not believe in families. Family relationships distracted people from the greater work of society as a whole, from achieving total triumph over nature and establishing utopia.

"What will the world be like without children?" Cindi wondered.

"More productive," Benny said.

"Drab," she said.

"More efficient."

"Empty."

Women of the New Race were designed and manufactured without a maternal instinct. They were supposed to have no desire to give birth.

Something was wrong with Cindi. She envied the women of the Old Race for their free will, but she resented them most intensely for their ability to bring children into the world.

Another customer, an expectant mother, entered their aisle.

At first Cindi's face brightened at the sight of the woman's distended belly, but then darkened into a snarl of vicious jealousy.

Taking her arm, steering her toward another part of the store, Benny said, "Control yourself. People will notice. You look like you want to kill her."

"I do."

"Remember what you are."

"Barren," she said bitterly.

"Not that. An assassin. You can't do your work if your face advertises your profession."

"All right. Let go of my arm."

"Calm down. Cool off."

"I'm smiling."

"It's a stiff smile."

She turned on her full dazzling wattage.

"That's better," he said.

Picking up a little pink sweater featuring colorful appliqued butterflies, displaying it for Benny, Cindi said, "Oh, isn't this darling?"

"Darling," he agreed. "But it would look better in blue."

"I don't see it in blue."

"We really should be getting to work."

"I want to look around here a little longer."

"We've got a job to do," he reminded her.

"And we have twenty-four hours to do it."

"I want to decapitate one of them."

"Of course you do. You always do. And we will. But first I want to find a really sweet little lacy suit or something."

Cindi was defective. She desperately wanted a baby. She was disturbed.

Had Benny been certain that Victor would terminate Cindi and produce Cindi Two, he'd have reported her deviancy months previously. He worried, however, that Victor thought of them as a unit and would terminate Benny, as well.

He didn't want to be switched off and buried in a landfill while Benny Two had all the fun.

If he had been like others of his kind, seething with rage and forbidden to express it in any satisfying fashion, Benny Lovewell would have been happy to be terminated. Termination would have been his only hope of peace.

But he was allowed to kill. He could torture, mutilate, and dismember. Unlike others of the New Race, Benny had something to live for.

"This is *so* cute," said Cindi, fingering a sailor suit sized for a two-year -old.

Benny sighed. "Do you want to buy it?"

"Yes."

At home they had a secret collection of garments for babies and toddlers. If any of the New Race ever discovered Cindi's hoard of children's clothes, she would have a lot of explaining to do.

"Okay," he said. "Buy it quick, before someone sees us, and let's get out of here."

"After we finish with O'Connor and Maddison," she said, "can we go home and try?"

By *try*, she meant "try to have a baby."

They had been created sterile. Cindi had a vagina but no uterus. That reproductive space had been devoted to other organs unique to the New Race.

Sex between them could no more produce a baby than it could produce a grand piano.

Nevertheless, to appease her, to mollify her mood, Benny said, "Sure. We can try."

"We'll kill O'Connor and Maddison," she said, "and cut them up as much as you want, do all those funny things you like to do, and then we'll make a baby."

She was insane, but he had to accept her as she was. If he could have killed her, he would have done it, but he could only kill those he was specifically directed to kill.

"That sounds good," he said.

"We'll be the first of our kind to conceive."

"We'll try."

"I'll be a wonderful mother."

"Let's buy the sailor suit and get out of here."

"Maybe we'll have twins."

chapter 21

Erika had lunch alone in a dining room furnished to seat sixteen, in the presence of three million dollars' worth of art, with a fresh arrangement of calla lilies and anthuriums on the table.

When she had finished, she went into the kitchen, where Christine stood at the sink, washing the breakfast dishes.

All food in this house was served on one pattern of Limoges or another, and Victor would not permit such fine china to be put in the dishwasher. All beverages were served in either Lalique or Waterford crystal, which also required hand washing.

If a dish sustained a scratch or if a glass was chipped, it must be discarded. Victor did not tolerate imperfection.

While certain machines were necessary and even beneficial, most of those invented to take the place of household servants were viewed by Victor with scorn. His standards of personal service had been formed in another century, when the lower classes had known how to attend, properly, the needs of their betters.

"Christine?"

"Yes, Mrs Helios?"

"Don't worry. I'm not going to discuss my sexual problems with you."

"Very good, Mrs Helios."

"But I'm curious about a few things."

"I'm sure you are, ma'am. Everything is new to you."

"Why was William biting off his fingers?"

"No one can really know but William himself."

"But it wasn't rational," Erika persisted.

"Yes, I had noticed that."

"And being one of the New Race, he is rational in all things."

"That's the concept," Christine said, but with an odd inflection that Erika couldn't interpret.

"He knew his fingers wouldn't grow back," Erika said. "It's as if he was . . . committing suicide, bite by bite, but we're not capable of self-destruction."

Swirling a wet fabric whisk inside an exquisite porcelain teapot, Christine said, "He wouldn't have died from ten severed fingers, Mrs Helios."

"Yes, but without fingers, he wouldn't have been able to serve as butler. He must have known he would be terminated."

"In the condition you saw him, Mrs Helios, William did not have the capacity to be cunning."

Besides, as they both knew, the proscription against suicide included the inability to engineer circumstances that required their termination.

"Do you mean . . . William was having like a mental breakdown?" The thought chilled Erika. "Surely that isn't possible."

"Mr Helios prefers the term *interruption of function*. William was experiencing an interruption of function."

"That sounds much less serious."

"It does, doesn't it?"

"But Victor did terminate him."

"He did, didn't he?"

Erika said, "If one of the Old Race had done such a thing, we'd say that he'd gone mad. Insane."

"Yes, but we're in all ways superior to them, and so many terms applicable to them cannot describe us. We require a whole new grammar of psychology."

Again, Christine's words were spoken with a curious inflection, suggesting that she meant something more than what she said.

"I . . . I don't understand," Erika said.

"You will. When you've been alive long enough."

Still struggling to comprehend, she said, "When you called my husband to report that William was biting off his fingers, you said, 'We've got another Margaret.' What did you mean by that?"

Rinsing a plate, carefully placing it in the drying rack, Christine said, "Until a few weeks ago, Margaret served as the household chef. She'd been here almost twenty years, like William. After an . . episode . . . she had to be removed. A new Margaret is being prepared."

"What episode?"

"One morning as she was about to make pancakes, she began to smash her face into the hot, greased griddle."

"Smash her face?"

"Over and over again, rhythmically. Each time she raised her face from the griddle, Margaret said *time*, and before she slammed it down again, she repeated that word. *Time, time, time, time, time* – with much the same urgency that you heard William say *tick, tock, tick, tock.*"

"How mystifying," said Erika.

"It won't be . . . when you've lived long enough."

Frustrated, Erika said, "Speak plainly to me, Christine."

"Plainly, Mrs Helios?"

"So I'm fresh out of the tank and hopelessly naive – so *educate* me. All right? Help me understand."

"But you've had direct-to-brain data downloading. What more could you need?"

"*Christine*, I'm not your enemy."

Turning away from the sink, blotting her hands on a dish towel, Christine said, "I know you're not, Mrs Helios. And you're not my friend, either. Friendship is akin to love, and love is dangerous. Love distracts the worker from maximum accomplishment, just as does hate. None of the New Race is a friend or enemy of the other."

"I . . . I don't have that attitude in my program."

"It's not in the program, Mrs Helios. It's the *natural result* of the program. We are all workers of identical value. Workers in a great cause, subduing all of nature, building the perfect society, utopia – then onward to the stars. Our value isn't in individual accomplishments, but in our accomplishments as a society. Isn't that correct?"

"Is it?"

"Unlike us, Mrs Helios, you have been allowed humility, and shame, because our maker likes those qualities in a wife."

Erika sensed a revelation coming from which she wished to turn away. But she, not Christine, had insisted on opening this door.

"Emotions are funny things, Mrs Helios. Maybe it's better, after all, to be limited to only envy and anger and fear and hate – because those feelings are circular. They turn endlessly back on themselves, like a snake swallowing its tail. They lead to nothing else, and they keep the mind from hope, which is essential when hope will never be fulfilled."

Shaken by the bleakness in Christine's voice and in her eyes, Erika was overcome with sympathy for the housekeeper. She put a hand consolingly on the woman's shoulder.

"But humility and shame," Christine continued, "can grow into pity, whether he wants you to feel pity or not. Pity to compassion. Compassion to regret. And so much else. You will be able to feel more than we feel, Mrs Helios. You will learn to hope."

A heaviness came into Erika's heart, an oppressive weight, but she could not yet grasp its nature.

"Being able to hope – that will be terrible for you, Mrs Helios, because your destiny is fundamentally the same as ours. You have no free will. Your hope will never be realized."

"But William . . . How does this explain William?"

"Time, Mrs Helios. Time, time, tick, tock, tick, tock. These disease-resistant, amazing bodies we possess – how long have we been told they will last?"

"Perhaps a thousand years," Erika said, for that was the figure in the self-awareness package of her downloaded education.

Christine shook her head. "Hopelessness can be endured . . . but not for a thousand years. For William, for Margaret – twenty years. And then they experienced an . . . interruption of function."

The housekeeper's hard shoulder had not softened under her mistress's touch. Erika withdrew her hand.

"But when you *have* the capacity for hope, Mrs Helios, yet know beyond all doubt that it will never be fulfilled, I don't think you can make even twenty years. I don't think you can make five."

Erika swept the kitchen with her gaze. She looked at the soapy water in the sink. At the dishes in the drying rack. At Christine's hands. At last, she met Christine's eyes again.

She said, "I'm so sorry for you."

"I know," Christine said. "But I feel nothing whatsoever for you, Mrs Helios. And neither will any of the others. Which means you are . . . uniquely alone."

chapter 22

The Other Ella, a restaurant and bar in the neighborhood known as Faubourg Marigny, an area now as funky and soulful as the French Quarter had once been, was owned and operated by a woman named Ella Fitzgerald. She was not the famous singer. She was a former hooker and madam who had wisely saved and invested the wages of the flesh.

As Aubrey Picou had instructed, Carson and Michael asked the bartender to see Godot.

An elderly woman put down the beer she was nursing, swiveled on her barstool, and took their picture with her cell phone.

Annoyed, Carson said, "Hey, Granny, I'm not a tourist site."

"Screw you," the woman said. "If I knew for sure a tour carriage was nearby, I'd run you into the street and shove your head up a mule's ass."

"You want to see Godot," the bartender explained, "you go through Francine here."

"You mean less to me," the old woman assured Carson, "than the dinner I vomited up last night."

As she transmitted the picture to someone, Francine grinned at Michael. She had borrowed her teeth from the Swamp Thing.

"Carson, remember when you looked in the mirror this morning and didn't like what you saw?"

She said, "Suddenly I feel pretty."

"All my life," Francine told Carson, "I've known perky-tit types like you, and not one of you bitches ever had a brain bigger than a chickpea."

"Well, there you're woefully wrong," Michael told her. "On a bet, my friend had an MRI scan of her brain, and it's as big as a walnut."

Francine gave him another broken yellow smile. "You're a real cutie. I could just eat you up."

"I'm flattered," he said.

"Remember what happened to her dinner last night," Carson reminded him.

Francine put down her cell phone. From the bar, she picked up a BlackBerry, on which she was receiving a text message, evidently in response to the photo.

Michael said, "You're a total telecom babe, Francine, fully swimming in the info stream."

"You've got a nice tight butt," Francine said. She put down the BlackBerry, swiveled off her stool, and said, "Come with me, cutie. You too, bitch."

Michael followed the old woman, glanced back at Carson, and said, "Come on, bitch, this'll be fun."

chapter 23

To assist with the tracking and the eventual efficient execution of Detectives O'Connor and Maddison, one of Victor's people – Dooley Snopes – had fixed a magnetic-hold transponder to the engine block of their department sedan, tapping the battery cable for power, while the car was parked in front of O'Connor's house, and while she had slept unaware through the summer morning.

Dooley had not been programmed as an assassin, though he wished that he had been. Instead, he was basically a sneak with a lot of technical knowledge.

Cindi Lovewell drove past Dooley, who was sitting in his parked PT Cruiser in Faubourg Marigny. The Lovewells had been issued an SUV – a Mercury Mountaineer with darkly tinted side and rear windows – which facilitated the discreet transport of dead bodies.

Cindi liked the vehicle not only because it had a lot of power and handled well but also because it had plenty of room for the children she yearned to produce.

When they had to drive to Crosswoods Waste Management north of Lake Pontchartrain with a couple of corpses, how much nicer the trip would be if it were a *family* adventure. They could stop along the way for a picnic.

In the front passenger's seat, studying the red dot that blinked near the center of the street map on the screen of their satellite-navigation system, Benny said, "The cops should be parked about' – he surveyed the curbed vehicles past which they drifted, and glanced at the screen – "right *here*."

Cindi rolled slowly past an unmarked sedan, cheap iron that had seen a lot of use. Victor's people were always better equipped than the so-called authorities.

She parked at a red curb near the end of the block. Benny's driver's license was in the name of Dr Benjamin Lovewell, and the Mountaineer had MD plates. From the console box, he took a card that read PHYSICIAN ON CALL, and hung it from the rearview mirror.

Tailing a target, professional killers need to be able to park as conveniently as possible. And when police see a speeding vehicle with MD plates, they often assume that the driver is rushing to a hospital.

Victor disliked his funds being spent on parking tickets and traffic fines.

By the time they walked past the sedan to the PT Cruiser, Dooley had gotten out of his car to meet them. If he'd been a dog, he would have been a whippet: lean, long-legged, with a pointy face.

"They went into The Other Ella," Dooley said, pointing to a restaurant across the street. "Not even five minutes ago. Did you kill anybody yet today?"

"Not yet," Benny said.

"Did you kill anybody yesterday?"

"Three days ago," Cindi said.

"How many?"

"Three," Benny said. "Their replicants were ready."

Dooley's eyes were dark with envy. "I wish I could kill some of them. I'd like to kill *all* of them."

"It's not your job," Benny said.

"Yet," Cindi said, meaning that the day would come when the New Race would have achieved sufficient numbers to bring their war into the open, whereupon the greatest slaughter in human history would mark the swift extinction of the Old Race.

"Everything is so much harder," Dooley said, "when we have to watch them all around us, watch them leading their lives any way they want, any way they please."

A young couple walked past, shepherding their two tow-headed children, one boy and one girl.

Cindi turned to watch them. She wanted to kill the parents right now, right here on the sidewalk, and take the children.

"Easy," Benny said.

"Don't worry. There's not going to be another incident," Cindi assured him.

"That's good."

"What incident?" Dooley asked.

Instead of answering him, Benny said, "You can go. We can handle it from here."

chapter 24

Occasionally smacking her lips over her broken yellow teeth, Francine led Carson and Michael through the restaurant, across a busy kitchen, into a storeroom, and up a set of steep stairs.

At the top were a deep landing and a blue door. Francine pressed a bell push beside the door, but there was no audible ring.

"Don't give it away for free," Francine advised Michael. "Lots of ladies would be happy to keep you in style."

She glanced at Carson and snorted with disapproval.

"And stay away from this one," Francine told Michael. "She'll freeze your cojones off as sure as if you dipped them in liquid nitrogen."

Then she left them on the landing and started unsteadily down the stairs.

"You could push her," he told Carson, "but it would be wrong."

"Actually," Carson said, "if Lulana were here, even she'd agree, Jesus would be all right with it."

The blue door was opened by a *Star Wars* kind of guy: as squat as R2-D2, as bald as Yoda, and as ugly as Jabba the Hutt.

"You been truly blood-sworn by Aubrey," he said, "so I ain't goin' to take away dem kill-boys you carryin' under your left arms, nor neither dat snub-nose you got snuggled on a belt clip just above your ass, missy."

"And good afternoon to you, too," Michael said.

"You follow me like baby ducks their mama, 'cause you make the wrongest move, you be six ways dead."

The room beyond the blue door was furnished with only a pair of straight-backed chairs.

A shaved gorilla in black pants, suspenders, a white chambray shirt, and a porkpie hat sat in one of the chairs. On the floor next to his chair was a tented paperback – a Harry Potter novel – that he had evidently set aside when Francine had pressed the bell push.

Across his thighs lay a semi-auto 12-gauge, on which both his hands rested in the business position. He wasn't aiming the shotgun at them, but he would be able to blow their guts out before their pistols cleared their holsters, and blast off their faces as an after-thought even before their bodies hit the floor.

Baby-duck walking, Carson and Michael obediently followed their squat leader through another door into a room with a cracked yellow linoleum floor, blue beadboard wainscoting, gray walls, and two poker tables.

Around the nearest table sat three men, one woman, and an Asian transvestite.

This sounded like the opening to a pretty good joke, but Michael couldn't think of a punch line.

Two of the players were drinking Coke, two had cans of Dr Pepper, and at the transvestite's place stood a cordial glass and a bottle of anisette.

None of the poker players seemed to have the slightest interest in Carson and Michael. Neither the woman nor the transvestite winked at him.

In the middle of the table were stacks of poker chips. If the greens were fifties and the blacks were hundreds, there was perhaps eighty thousand dollars riding on this hand.

Another shaved gorilla stood by a window. He carried his piece in a paddle holster at his hip, and he kept his hand on it as Carson and Michael passed through his duty station.

A third door led to a shabby conference room that smelled like lung cancer. Twelve chairs stood around a scarred table on which were fourteen ashtrays.

At the head of the table sat a man with a merry face, lively blue eyes, and a mustache. His Justin Wilson hat rested on the tops of his jug-handle ears.

He rose as they approached, revealing that he wore his pants above his waistline, between his navel and his breasts.

Their mama duck said, "Mr Godot, though they smells like da worst kind of righteous, these here be da ones what were vouched by Aubrey, so don't bust my stones if'n you got to gaff 'em like catfish 'fore dis be finished."

To the right of the man with jug ears and slightly behind him stood Big Foot in a seersucker suit. He made the previous gorillas look like mere chimps.

Big Foot looked as if he would not only kill them but eat them at the smallest provocation.

Godot, on the other hand, was hospitable. He held out his right hand and said, "Any friend to Aubrey, he a friend to me, "specially when he come with cash money."

Shaking the offered hand, Michael said, "I expected we'd have to wait for you, Mr Godot, not the other way around. I hope we're not late."

"Right on da minute," Godot assured him. "And who might be dis charmin' eyeful?"

"This charmin' eyeful," Carson said, "is the one with the cash money."

"You done just got even prettier," Godot told her.

As Carson withdrew two fat rolls of hundred-dollar bills from her jacket pockets, Godot picked up one of two suitcases from the floor beside his chair and put it on the table.

Big Foot kept both hands free.

Godot opened the case, revealing two Urban Sniper shotguns with sidesaddle shell carriers and three-way slings. The barrels had been cut down to fourteen inches. With the guns were four boxes of shells, slugs not buckshot, which was the only thing the Sniper fired.

Carson said, "You are a formidable resource, Mr Godot."

"Mama so wanted a preacher son, and Daddy, rest his soul, he set on me bein' a welder like hisself, but I most truly rebelled against bein' a poor Cajun, so I done found my bliss, and here I is."

The second suitcase was smaller than the first. It contained two Desert Eagles in .50 Magnum with titanium gold finish. Packed beside the guns were the boxes of ammunition as requested and two spare magazines for each weapon.

"You for sure ready for what recoil dat monster pays you back?" Godot asked.

Wary of the big pistols, Michael said, "No, sir, I pretty much expect it to knock me on my ass."

Amused, Godot said, "My concern be dis lady here, son, not your strappin' self."

"The Eagle has a smooth action," Carson said, "less kick than you'd think. It slams back hard, sure, but so do I. From thirty feet, I could put all nine rounds in the magazine between your groin and your throat, not one higher, not one wide."

This statement brought Big Foot forward, glowering.

"Rest yourself," Godot told his bodyguard. "She done made no threat. Dat just braggin'."

Closing the suitcase that contained the pistols, Carson said, "Are you going to count your money?"

"You da most tough I seen in a while, but you also gots some saint in you. I'd be so bad surprised did it turn out you thieved me even some littlest bit."

Carson couldn't suppress a smile. "Every dollar's there."

"Mr Godot," Michael said, "it's been comfortable doing business with you, knowing we're dealing with real human beings."

"Dat's most cordial of you to say," Godot replied, "most cordial, and it sounds true from da heart."

"It is," Michael said. "It really is."

chapter 25

Randal Six stands in the furnace closet on the ground floor, listening to Billy Joel singing in an upper room.

The closet measures approximately six by seven feet. Even the dim blue glow of the gas pilot flame and the weak light seeping under the door give him enough illumination to assess this space.

At long last he is in the house of the smiling autistic, Arnie O'Connor. The secret of happiness lies within his grasp.

He waits here in the cozy gloom as one song changes to another, and to another. He is enjoying his triumph. He is acclimating himself to this new environment. He is planning his next step.

He is also afraid. Randal Six has never been in a house before. Until the night before last, he lived exclusively in the Hands of Mercy. Between there and here, he spent a day hiding in a Dumpster; but a Dumpster is not the same as a house.

Beyond this closet door waits a place as alien to him as would be any planet in another galaxy.

He likes the familiar. He fears the new. He dislikes change.

Once he opens this door and steps across this threshold, all before him will be new and strange. Everything will be different forever.

Trembling in the dark, Randal half believes that his billet at Mercy and even the torturous experiments to which Father subjected him might be preferable to what lies ahead.

Nevertheless, after three more songs, he opens the door and stares into the space beyond, his two hearts hammering.

Sunshine at a frosted window sheds light over two machines that he recognizes from magazine ads and Internet research. One machine washes clothes. The other dries them.

He smells bleach and detergent behind the closed cabinet doors above the machines.

Before him lies a laundry room. A *laundry* room. At this moment, he can think of nothing that could more poignantly suggest the sweet ordinariness of daily life than a laundry room.

More than anything, Randal Six wants an ordinary life. He does not want to be – and cannot be – one of the Old Race, but he wants to live as they do, without ceaseless torment, with his small share of happiness.

The experience of the laundry room is enough progress for one day. He quietly pulls shut the door and stands in the dark furnace closet, pleased with himself.

He relives the delicious moment when he first glimpsed the baked-enamel surfaces of the washer and dryer, and the big plastic clothes basket with what might have been several dirty rumpled garments in it.

The laundry room had a vinyl-tile floor, just as did all the hallways and most of the rooms at the Hands of Mercy. He hadn't expected vinyl tile. He had thought that *everything* would be wildly different from what he had known.

The vinyl tiles in Mercy are gray with speckles of green and rose. In the laundry room they are yellow. These two styles of flooring are at once different yet the same.

While the music from high in the house changes a few times, Randal gradually grows embarrassed by his timidity. Peering through a door into the O'Connors' laundry is not, after all, a heroic accomplishment.

He is deluding himself. He is succumbing to his agoraphobia, to his autistic desire to minimize sensory input.

If he proceeds at this agonizing pace, he will need six months to make his way through the house and find Arnie.

He can't live under the structure, in the crawl space, for such an extended time. For one thing, he is hungry. His superlative body is a machine in need of much fuel.

Randal doesn't mind eating what spiders, rodents, earthworms, and snakes that he might find under the house. However, judging by the creatures he has encountered thus far during his hours in the crawl space, that shadowy realm doesn't contain even a small fraction of the game he needs to sustain himself.

He opens the door again.

The wonderful laundry room. Waiting.

He steps out of the furnace closet and gently closes the door behind him. Thrilled beyond words.

He has never walked on yellow-vinyl tiles before. They work the same as gray-vinyl tiles. The soles of his shoes make the faintest squeaking sounds.

A door stands open between the laundry room and the kitchen.

Randal Six halts at this new threshold, marveling. A kitchen is everything – more! – that he thought it would be, a place of numerous conveniences and overwhelming charm.

He could easily become inebriated with ambience. He must remain sober and cautious, prepared to retreat if he should hear someone approaching.

Until he can locate Arnie and wrench from him the secret of happiness, Randal wants to avoid coming face to face with anyone. He isn't sure what would happen in such an encounter, but he feels certain that the consequences would not be pleasant.

Although he was engineered to be autistic for the purposes of Father's experiments, which makes him different from others of the New Race, he shares much of their programming. He is incapable of suicide, for instance.

He isn't permitted to kill except when instructed by his maker to do so. Or in self-defense.

The problem is that Randal is terribly fearful in his autism. He feels easily threatened.

Hiding in the Dumpster, he had killed a homeless man who had come searching for soft-drink cans and other small treasures.

The hobo might not have meant him any harm, might not in fact have been *capable* of causing him harm, yet Randal had dragged him headfirst into the Dumpster, had snapped his neck, and had buried him under bags of trash.

Considering that mere newness frightens him, that the smallest change fills him with trepidation, any encounter with a stranger is more likely than not to result in a violent act of self-defense. He has no moral concern about this. They are of the Old Race and must all die sooner or later, anyway.

The problem is that snapping the spine of a hobo in a deserted alleyway is not likely to draw attention; but killing someone in this house will be a noisy affair certain to reveal his presence to other residents and possibly even to neighbors.

Nevertheless, because he is hungry and because the refrigerator no doubt contains something tastier than spiders and earthworms, he steps out of the laundry room and into the kitchen.

chapter **26**

Each carrying a suitcase full of weapons, Carson and Michael left The Other Ella.

As the daughter of a detective who had supposedly gone bad, Carson believed that she was under closer scrutiny by her fellow officers than was the average cop. She understood it, resented it – and was self-aware enough to realize that she might be imagining it.

Fresh from consorting with the likes of foulmouthed Francine and courtly Godot, crossing the sidewalk toward the unmarked sedan, Carson surveyed the street, half convinced that the Internal Affairs Division, having staked out the scene, would at any moment break cover and make arrests.

Every pedestrian appeared to take an interest in Carson and Michael, to glance with suspicion at the bags they carried. Two men and a woman across the street seemed to stare with special intensity.

Why would anyone walk out of a restaurant with suitcases? Nobody bought takeout in that volume.

They put the bags in the trunk of the sedan, and Carson drove out of Faubourg Marigny, into the Quarter, without being arrested.

"What now?" Michael wondered.

"We cruise."

"Cool."

"We think it through."

"Think what through?"

"The color of love, the sound of one hand clapping. What do you *think* we have to think through?"

"I'm not in a mood to think," he said. "Thinking's going to get us killed."

"How do we get at Victor Frankenstein?"

"Helios."

"Helios, Frankenstein – it's still the same Victor. How do we get at the Victor?"

Michael said, "Maybe I'm superstitious, but I wish the Victor had a different first name."

"Why?"

"A victor is someone who defeats his adversary. *Victor* means "winner.""

"Remember that guy we busted last year for the double homicide in the antique shop on Royal?"

"Sure. He had a third testicle."

"What the hell does that have to do with anything?" she asked impatiently. "We didn't know that till he'd been arrested, charged, and had his jailhouse physical."

"It doesn't have anything to do with anything," he admitted. "It's just one of those details that stick in your mind."

"My point is, the guy's name was Champ Champion, but he was a loser anyway."

"His real name was Shirley Champion, which explains everything."

"He'd had his name legally changed to Champ Champion."

"Cary Grant was born Archie Leach. The only name that matters is the born name."

"I'll pull to the curb, you roll down your window and ask any pedestrian you want, have they seen an Archie Leach movie. See how much born names matter."

"Marilyn Monroe – she was really Norma Jean Mortenson," he said, "which is why she ended up dead young of an overdose."

"Is this one of those times you're going to be impossible?"

"I know that's usually your job," he said. "What about Joan Crawford? She was born Lucille Le Sueur, which explains why she beat her children with wire coat hangers."

"Cary Grant never beat anyone with coat hangers, and he had a fabulous life."

Yeah, but he was the greatest actor in the history of film. The rules don't apply to him. Victor and Frankenstein are two *power* names if I ever heard them, and he was born with them. No matter what you say, I'd feel more comfortable if his mother had named him Nancy."

———

"What are they *doing*?" Cindi asked impatiently, glancing again at the street map on the dashboard screen.

Benny had been studying the screen continuously as Cindi drove. He said, "At the end of every block, she makes another turn, back and forth, zig-zag, around and around, like a blind rat in a maze."

"Maybe they know they're being tailed."

"They can't know," he said. "They can't see us."

Being able to track the sedan by the continuous signal of the transponder that Dooley had secreted under its hood, the Lovewells didn't need to maintain visual contact. They could conduct a most leisurely pursuit from a distance of several blocks and even follow the detectives on parallel streets.

"I know how she feels," Cindi said.

"What do you mean?"

"Like a blind rat in a maze."

"I didn't say that's how she feels. I don't know how she feels. I said that's how she's driving."

"Most of the time," Cindi said, "I feel like a blind rat in a maze. And she's childless like me."

"Who?"

"Detective O'Connor. She's old enough to have had half a dozen children, at least, but she doesn't have any. She's barren."

"You can't know that she's barren."

"I know."

"Maybe she just doesn't want kids."

"She's a woman. She wants."

"She just turned again, left this time."

"See?"

"See what?"

"She's barren."

"She's barren just because she made a left turn?"

Solemnly, Cindi said, "Like a blind rat in a maze."

———

Carson turned right on Chartres Street, past the exquisitely decaying Napoleon House.

"Taking Victor down at Biovision is out of the question," she said. "Too many people, too many witnesses, probably not all of them people he's made."

"We could hit him in his car, coming or going."

"On a public street? If we can manage not to die while doing this, I don't want to end up in women's prison with all your former girlfriends."

"We learn his routine," Michael said, "and we find the least public place along the route."

"We don't have time to learn his routine," she reminded him. "We're a target *now*. We both know it."

"The secret lab we talked about earlier. The place where he . . . creates."

"We don't have time to find that, either. Besides, it'll have better security than Fort Knox."

"Fort Knox's security is probably overrated. The bad guys had it figured in *Goldfinger*."

"We're not bad guys," she said, "and this isn't a movie. The best place to get him is at his house."

"It's a mansion. It's got a big staff."

"We'll have to cut through them, straight to him, go in hard and fast," she said.

"We're not SWAT."

"We're not just parking patrol, either."

"What if some of his household staff is our kind?" Michael worried.

"None of them will be. He wouldn't want our kind serving in

his home, where they might see or overhear something. They'll all be part of the New Race."

"We can't be a hundred percent sure."

On Decatur Street at Jackson Square, where carriages lined up to offer tours of the Quarter, one of the usually placid mules had broken away from the curb. The driver and a policeman were giving chase on foot as the mule pulled its fancy equipage in circles, blocking traffic.

"Maybe old Francine shoved someone up its butt," Michael suggested.

Staying on point, Carson said, "So we've got to nail Victor at his house in the Garden District."

"Maybe it would make more sense to pull out of New Orleans. We could go somewhere he couldn't find us, take more time to think this through."

"Yeah. Take the pressure off. Give ourselves a week to really *think*. Maybe two weeks. Maybe we'd *never* come back."

"Would that be so bad?" he asked.

"'The only thing necessary for the triumph of evil'—"

"—'is for good men to do nothing.' Yeah. I heard already."

"Who said that, anyway?" she wondered.

"I think it was Tigger, but it might have been Pooh."

The carriage driver snared the bridle. The mule became calm and allowed itself to be walked back to the curb. The snarled traffic began to move.

Carson said, "He knows we're on to him. Even if we leave the city, he won't stop until he finds us, Michael. We'd always be on the run."

"Sounds romantic," he said wistfully.

"Don't go there," she warned him. "Aubrey's rose garden wasn't the place for it, and this is worse."

"Will there ever be a place for it?"

She drove in silence for a minute, turned right at the next corner, and then said, "Maybe. But only if we can bring down Helios before his people rip our guts out and pitch us in the Mississippi."

"You really know how to encourage a guy."

"Now shut up about it. Just shut up. If we go all gooey over each other, we'll lose focus. If we lose focus, we're dead."

"Too bad the rest of the world never gets to see this tender side of you."

"I'm serious, Michael. I don't want to talk about me and you. I don't even want to joke about it. We've got a war to win."

"All right. Okay. I hear you. I'll stifle myself." He sighed. "Champ Champion has three testicles, and pretty soon I'm not going to have any, they'll just wither away."

"Michael," she said warningly.

He sighed again and said no more.

A couple of blocks later, she glanced sideways at him. He looked adorable. He knew it, too.

Stifling herself, she said, "We've got to find someplace private to have a look at the new guns, load them and the spare magazines."

"City Park," he suggested. "Take that service road to where we found the dead accountant two years ago."

"The naked guy who was strangled with the Mardi Gras beads."

"No, no. He was an architect. I'm talking about the guy in the cowboy outfit."

"Oh, yeah, the black-leather cowboy suit."

"It was midnight blue," Michael corrected.

"If you say so. You're more fashion conscious than I am. The body was pretty close to the service road."

"I don't mean where we found the body," Michael said. "I mean where we found his head."

"You walk through a little stand of Southern pines."

"And then some live oaks."

"And then there's open grass. I remember. That's a nice place."

"It's very nice," Michael agreed, "and it's not close to any of the jogging paths. We'll have privacy."

"The killer certainly had privacy."

"He certainly did," Michael said.

"How long did it take us to get him – four weeks?"

"A little over five."

"That was a hell of a trick shot you got him with," Carson said. "Ricocheted right off the blade of his ax."

"I didn't much appreciate being in the splatter zone."

"Was the dry cleaner able to get out the brain stains?"

"When I told him what it was, he didn't even want to try. And that was a new jacket."

"Not my fault. That kind of ricochet is God's work."

Carson relaxed. This was better. None of that distracting, nervous-making romance talk.

chapter **27**

In the stainless-steel and white-ceramic-tile dissection room, when Victor examined the carcass of Detective Jonathan Harker, he found that approximately fifty pounds of the body's substance was missing.

A raggedly torn umbilical cord trailed from the void in the torso. Considered with the exploded abdomen and shattered rib cage, this suggested that some unintended life form – call it a parasite – had formed within Harker, had achieved a state in which it could live independently of its host, and had broken free, destroying Harker in the process.

This was a disturbing development.

Ripley, who operated the handheld video recorder with which a visual record of all autopsies were made, was clearly rattled by the implications of this discovery.

"Mr Helios, sir, he gave birth."

"I wouldn't call it giving birth," Victor said with undisguised annoyance.

"We're not capable of reproduction," Ripley said. His voice and manner suggested that, to him, the thought of another life coming forth from Harker was the equivalent of blasphemy.

"It's not reproduction," Victor said. "It's a malignancy."

"But sir . . . a self-sustaining, mobile malignancy?"

"I mean to say a *mutation*," Victor explained impatiently.

In the tank, Ripley had received a deep education in Old Race and New Race physiology. He should have been able to understand these biological nuances.

"A parasitical second self developed spontaneously from Harker's flesh," Victor said, "and when it could live independently of him, it . . . separated."

Ripley stopped filming and stood slack-jawed with amazement, pale with trepidation. He had bushy eyebrows that gave him a look of comic astonishment.

Victor could not remember why he had decided to design Ripley with those shaggy eyebrows. They were absurd.

"Mr Helios, sir, I beg your indulgence, but are you saying that this is what you intended, for a second self to mutate out of Harker? Sir, to what purpose?"

"No, Ripley, of course it's not what I intended. There's a useful saying of the Old Race – "Shit happens.""

"But sir, forgive me, you are the designer of our flesh, the maker, the master. How can there be anything about our flesh that you do not understand . . . or foresee?"

Worse than the comic expression that the eyebrows gave Ripley was the fact that they facilitated an exaggerated look of reproach.

Victor did not like to be reproached. "Science proceeds in great leaps, but also sometimes takes a couple of small steps backward."

"Backward?" Having been properly indoctrinated while in the tank, Ripley sometimes had difficulty squaring his expectations with real life. "Science in general, sir, yes, it sometimes missteps. But not you. Not you, and not the New Race."

"The important thing to keep in mind is that the leaps forward are much greater than the steps backward, and more numerous."

"But this is a very big step backward. Sir. I mean, isn't it? Our flesh . . . out of control?"

"Your flesh isn't out of control, Ripley. Where did you get this melodramatic streak? You're embarrassing yourself."

"I'm sorry, sir. I'm sure I don't understand. I'm sure when I've had time to consider, I'll share your equanimity on the matter."

"Harker isn't a sign of things to come. He's an anomaly. He's a singularity. There will be no more mutations like him."

Perhaps the parasite had not merely fed on Harker's innards but had incorporated his two hearts into itself, as well as his lungs and various other internal organs, at first sharing them and then taking them for its own. These things were missing from the cadaver.

According to Jack Rogers – the real medical examiner, now dead and replaced by a replicant – Detectives O'Connor and Maddison claimed that a trollish creature had come out of Harker, as if shedding a cocoon. They had seen it drop out of sight through a manhole, into a storm drain.

By the time that he finished with Harker and took tissue samples for later study, Victor had fallen into a bad mood.

As they bagged Harker's remains and set them aside for shipment to Crosswoods, Ripley asked, "Where is Harker's second self now, Mr Helios?"

"It fled into a storm drain. It's dead."

"How do you know it's dead?"

"I *know*," Victor said sharply.

They turned next to William, the butler, who waited on a second autopsy table.

Although he believed that William's finger-chewing episode had been triggered solely by psychological collapse, Victor nevertheless opened the butler's torso and inventoried his organs, just to make certain that no second self had begun to form. He found no evidence of mutation.

With a bone saw of Victor's design, one with a diamond blade sharp enough to grind through the dense bone of any New Man, they trepanned William's skull. They removed his brain and put it in preservative solution in a Tupperware container for later sectioning and study.

William's fate clearly did not alarm Ripley as did Harker's. He had seen this sort of thing before.

Victor brought to life a perfect being with a perfect mind, but contact with the Old Race, immersion in their sick society, sometimes corrupted the tank-born.

This would continue to be an occasional problem until the Old Race was eradicated and with it the social order and pre-Darwinian morality that it had created. Thereafter, following the Last War, without the paradigm of the Old Race to confuse and seduce them, Victor's people would always and forever exist in perfect mental health, every last one of them.

When they were finished with William, Ripley said, "Mr Helios, sir, I'm sorry, but I can't stop wondering, can't stop thinking – is it possible that what happened to Harker could happen to me?"

"No. I told you, he was a singularity."

"But, sir, I beg your pardon if this sounds impertinent ... however, if you didn't expect it to happen the first time, how can you be sure it won't happen again?"

Stripping off his latex surgical gloves, Victor said, "Damn it, Ripley, stop that with your eyebrows."

"My eyebrows, sir?"

"You know what I mean. Clean up here."

"Sir, is it possible that Harker's consciousness, the essence of his mind, somehow transferred to his second self?"

Taking off the surgical gown that he wore over his clothes, moving toward the door of the dissection room, Victor said, "No. It was a parasitical mutation, most likely with nothing but a crude animal awareness."

"But, sir, if the trollish thing isn't a thing, after all, sir, if it's actually Harker himself, and now he's living in the storm drains, then he's free."

The word *free* halted Victor. He turned to stare at Ripley.

When Ripley realized his error, fear brought his eyebrows down from their absurdly lofty heights and beetled them on the cliff of his brow. "I don't mean to suggest that what happened to Harker could be in any way desirable."

"Don't you, Ripley?"

"No, sir. I don't. It's a horror, what happened to him."

Victor stared at him. Ripley dared not say another word.

After a long mutual silence, Victor said, "In addition to your eyebrows, Ripley, you're far too excitable. Annoyingly so."

chapter 28

Moving hesitantly through the kitchen in a state of awe, Randal Six imagines that this must be what a devout monk feels when in a temple, at a consecrated altar.

For the first time in his life, Randal is in a home. Mercy had been where he was billeted, but it had never been a home. It had been only a place. He'd had no emotion vested in it.

To the Old Race, home is the center of existence. Home is the first refuge from – and last defense against – the disappointments and the terrors of life.

The heart of the home is the kitchen. He knows this to be true because he has read it in a magazine about home decor and in another magazine about cooking light.

In addition, Martha Stewart has said this is true, and Martha Stewart is, by acclamation of the Old Race, the ultimate authority on such matters.

During social evenings, close friends and neighbors frequently gravitate to the kitchen. Some of a family's happiest memories are of moments together in the kitchen. According to Old Race philosophers, nothin' says lovin' like somethin' from the oven, and the oven is in the kitchen.

The blinds are half drawn. The late-afternoon sunshine that reaches the windows has first been filtered by oak trees. Yet Randal can see well enough to explore the room.

Quietly he opens cabinets, discovering dishes, cups, saucers, drinking glasses. In drawers he finds folded dish towels, flatware, knives, and a bewildering collection of utensils and culinary gadgets.

Usually, too many new sights, too many unfamiliar objects, will throw Randal into a panic attack. He is often forced to withdraw to a corner and turn his back to the world in order to survive the shock of too much sensory input.

For some reason, the staggering richness of new experience in this kitchen does not affect him in that way. Instead of panic, he experiences . . . enchantment.

Perhaps this is because he is in a *home* at last. A person's home is inviolate. A sanctuary. An extension of one's personality, Martha says. Home is the safest of all places.

He is in the *heart* of this home, in the safest room of the safest place, where many happy memories will be made, where sharing and giving and laughing occur on a daily basis.

Randal Six has never laughed. He smiled once. When he first made his way to the O'Connor house, when he got out of the storm and into the crawl space, in the dark among the spiders, knowing that he would eventually reach Arnie, he had smiled.

When he opens the pantry door, he is stunned at the variety and quantity of canned and packaged food on the shelves. Never has he dared imagine such abundance.

At the Hands of Mercy, his meals and snacks were brought to his billet. The menu had been planned by others. He was given no choice of food – except for the color of it, on which he was insistent.

Here, the options before him are dazzling. In canned soups alone, he sees six varieties.

When he turns from the pantry and opens the upper door of the refrigerator, his legs shake and his knees go weak. Among other things, the freezer contains three quarts of ice cream.

Randal Six loves ice cream. He never gets enough ice cream.

His initial excitement abruptly turns to crushing disappointment when he sees that none of the choices before him is vanilla. There is chocolate almond. There is chocolate mint. There is strawberry-banana swirl.

For the most part, Randal has only eaten white and green foods. Mostly white. This restriction of colors in his food is a defense against chaos, an expression of his autism. Milk, chicken breast, turkey, potatoes, popcorn (without butter because butter makes it too yellow), peeled apples, peeled pears … He tolerates green vegetables like lettuce and celery and green beans, and also green fruit, like grapes.

The nutritional deficiencies of a strict white-and-green diet are addressed with white capsules of vitamins and minerals.

He has never eaten any flavor of ice cream other than vanilla. He has always known that other flavors exist, but he has found them too repulsive for consideration.

The O'Connors, however, have no vanilla.

For a moment he feels defeated, and drifts toward despair.

He is hungry, starving, and as never before he is in a mood to experiment. To his surprise, he removes the container of chocolate mint from the freezer.

Never before has he eaten anything brown. He chooses chocolate mint instead of chocolate almond because he assumes there will be bits of green in it, which will perhaps make it tolerable.

He withdraws a spoon from the flatware drawer and carries the quart of ice cream to the kitchen table. He sits, quivering with fearful anticipation.

Brown food. He may not survive.

When he pries the lid off the container, Randal discovers that the mint appears in thin ribbons of bright green, woven through the cold brown mass. This familiar color heartens him. The quart is full, and he digs out a spoonful of the treat.

Raising the spoon, he comes up short of the courage needed to put it in his mouth. He must make four halting attempts before he succeeds on the fifth.

Oh.

Not disgusting, after all. Delicious.

Galvanizingly delicious: He thrusts the second spoonful into his mouth without hesitation. And a third.

As he eats, he settles into a peace, a contentment, that he has never known previously. He is not yet happy, as he understands the concept of happiness, but he is closer to that desired condition than he has ever been in his four months out of the tank.

Having come here in search of the secret of happiness, he has found something else first: *home.*

He feels that he belongs here in a way that he never belonged in the Hands of Mercy. He feels so safe here that he can eat brown food. Maybe later even the pink-and-yellow strawberry-banana swirl. Anything, no matter how daring, seems to be possible within these sheltering walls.

By the time he has devoured half of the quart of chocolate mint, he knows that he will never leave. This is his home.

Throughout history, men of the Old Race have died – and killed – to protect their homes. Randal Six knows a little history, the usual two gigabytes downloaded in the tank.

To be torn from this peace and thrown into the bright and noisy world would be akin to death. Therefore, any attempt to force him from his home should be regarded as a murderous assault, justifying a swift and lethal response.

This is his home. With all his strength, he will defend his right to it.

He hears descending footsteps on the stairs.

chapter 29

Gunny Alecto, a garbage-galleon driver, came into the shack that served as the manager's office, sat on the edge of Nick Frigg's desk, and said, "Rain rail rape raid rag rascal rack."

Nick didn't reply. She was just having trouble getting started; and if he tried to guess the word for which she was searching, he would only further confuse her.

"Rabid race rabble rap rat. *Rat!*" She had found the wanted noun. "Have you noticed about the rats?"

"What about them?"

"What about who?"

"The rats, Gunny."

"Did you notice, too?"

"Notice what?"

"The rats are gone," she said.

"Gone where?"

"If I knew, I wouldn't be asking you."

"Asking me what?"

"Where are the rats?"

"We've always got rats," Nick said.

She shook her head. "Not here. Not now. No more."

Gunny looked like a movie star, except dirty. Nick didn't know why Victor had made her gorgeous and then assigned her to the dump. Maybe the contrast between her looks and her work amused him. Maybe he had modeled her after one of the Old Race who had rejected him or had otherwise earned his resentment.

"Why don't you go out there and look for elephants," Gunny suggested.

"What're you talking about – elephants?"

"You're as likely to find them as rats. Plowin' the trash, I usually chase up packs of them all the time, but I haven't seen one in three days."

"Maybe they're just making their burrows deeper in the pit as we fill it fuller."

"So we got five?" Gunny asked.

"Five rats?"

"I heard five Old Race dead came in today."

"Yeah. Plus three dead gone-wrongs," Nick said.

"Some fun tonight," she said. "Man, it's hot today."

"Louisiana summer, what do you expect."

"I'm not complaining," she said. "I like the sun. I wish there was sun at night."

"It wouldn't be night if there was sun."

"That's the problem," Gunny agreed.

Communicating with Gunny Alecto could be a challenge. She had looks, and she was as good a garbage-galleon driver as anyone, but her thought processes, as revealed by her conversation, didn't always track in a linear fashion.

Everyone in the New Race had a rank. At the top were the Alphas, the ruling elite. They were followed by Betas and Gammas.

As manager of the dump, Nick was a Gamma. Everyone on his crew was an Epsilon.

Epsilons had been designed and programmed for brute labor. They were a step or two above the meat machines without self-awareness that one day would replace many factory robots.

No class envy was permitted among those of the New Race. Each had been programmed to be content with the rank to which he had been born and to have no yearning for advancement.

It remained permissible, of course, to disdain and feel superior to those who ranked *below* you. Contempt for one's inferiors provided a healthy substitute for dangerous ambition.

Epsilons like Gunny Alecto didn't receive the wealth of direct-to-brain data downloading given to a Gamma like Nick, just as he received less than any Beta, and far less than any Alpha.

In addition to being less well-educated than the other ranks, Epsilons sometimes seemed to have cognitive problems that indicated their brains were not as carefully crafted as the brains of the upper classes.

"Goat goof gopher goon golf goose gone. *Gone!* Gone-wrongs. We got three, you said. What're they like?"

"I haven't seen them yet," Nick said.

"They'll be stupid-looking."

"I'm sure they will."

"Stupid-looking gone-wrongs. Some fun tonight."

"I'm looking forward to it," Nick said, which was true.

"Where do you think they went?"

"The deliverymen put them in the cooler."

"The rats?" she asked, puzzled.

"I thought you meant the gone-wrongs."

"I meant the rats. I miss the little fellers. You don't think we've got cats, do you?"

"I haven't seen any cats."

"That would explain no rats," she said. "But if you haven't seen any, that's good enough for me."

If Gunny had been required to live among members of the Old Race, she might not have passed for one of them – or might have been designated mentally disabled.

As a member of the Crosswoods crew, however, she had no life outside the dump. She lived within its gates twenty-four hours a day, seven days a week, with a bunk in one of the trailers that served as dormitories.

In spite of her problems, she was an excellent dozer pilot, and Nick was glad to have her.

Getting up from the edge of Nick's desk, Gunny said, "Well, back to the pit – and then some fun tonight, huh?"

"Some fun tonight," he agreed.

chapter **30**

After her conversation with Christine in the kitchen, Erika Helios toured those rooms of the mansion that she had not previously seen.

The lavish home theater was Russian Belle Epoque after the palaces of St Petersburg. Victor had specified this opulent style in honor of his late friend, Joseph Stalin, communist dictator and visionary.

Joe Stalin had come forth with vast resources to fund New Race research after the sad collapse of the Third Reich, which had been a terrible setback for Victor. So confident had Joe been in Victor's ability eventually to fabricate an entirely controllable and obedient variety of enhanced humans that he had ordered the deaths of forty million of his citizens by various means even before the technology of the cloning tanks had been perfected.

Desirous of living forever, Joe had submitted to some of the same techniques with which Victor had sustained his own life for – at that time – nearly two centuries. Unfortunately, Stalin must have been suffering from an undiagnosed brain tumor or something because during the period that he underwent those life-extension procedures, he had grown increasingly detached from reality, and paranoid.

Eventually hair had grown on the palms of Stalin's hands – which had *never* happened to Victor. Furthermore, Stalin had been seized by unpredictable fits of mindless violence, sometimes directed at people around him, sometimes at pieces of furniture, once at his favorite pair of boots.

The dictator's closest associates poisoned him and concocted a cover story to conceal the fact that they had perpetrated a coup. Injustice was once more visited on Victor, and his research funds were cut off by the bean counters who followed poor Joe.

In the tank, Erika received all of her husband's rich history; however, she was forbidden to speak of it to anyone but Victor himself. She had been granted this knowledge only so that she would understand his epic struggles, his triumphs, and the glory of his existence.

After the theater, she explored the music room, the reception lounge, the formal living room, the informal living room, the jewel box of a breakfast room, the trophy room, the billiards room, the indoor pool with surrounding mosaic-tile deck, and came at last to the library.

The sight of all those books made her uneasy, for she knew that books were corrupting, perhaps evil. They had been the death of Erika Four, who had absorbed dangerous knowledge from them.

Nevertheless, Erika had to familiarize herself with the library because there would be social evenings when Victor would invite his important Old Race guests – mostly powerful politicians and business leaders – to repair to the library for cognac and other after-dinner drinks. As hostess, she would need to feel comfortable here in spite of the dreadful books.

As she walked through the library, she dared to touch a book now and then to accustom herself to the sinister feel of them. She even took one off a shelf and examined it, her two hearts racing.

In the event that a guest some evening said, *Erika, darling, would you hand me that book with the lovely binding, I'd like to have a look at it,* she must be prepared to present the volume as casually as a snake-handler of long experience would pick up any serpent.

Christine had suggested that Erika browse the several shelves of psychology texts and bone up on sexual sadism. She couldn't, however, bring herself to actually *open* a book.

As she moved across the big room, sliding her hand along the underside of a shelf, enjoying the satiny feel of the exquisitely finished wood, she discovered a hidden switch. She had flicked it before she quite realized what she had done.

A section of shelves proved to be a hidden door, which swung open on pivot hinges. Beyond lay a secret passageway.

In the tank, she had not been informed of the existence of this concealed door or of what lay beyond it. But she'd not been forbidden to explore, either.

chapter 31

After switching on the kitchen lights, prior to preparing dinner, Vicky Chou washed her hands at the sink, and discovered that the soiled towel needed to be replaced. She blotted her hands on it anyway before fetching a clean towel from a drawer.

She crossed to the laundry-room door and pushed it open. Without turning on the lights, she tossed the soiled towel into the clothes basket.

Detecting a faint moldy scent, she made a mental note to inspect the room for mildew first thing in the morning. Poorly ventilated spaces like this required special diligence in the humid climate of the bayou.

She put two plastic place mats on the dinette table. She set out flatware for herself and Arnie.

The urgency with which Carson had left the house, after sleeping through the morning, suggested she would not be home for dinner.

Arnie's plate was different from Vicky's: larger, rectangular instead of round, and divided into four compartments. He didn't like different foods to be touching one another.

He couldn't tolerate orange and green items on the same plate. Although he would cut meat and other foods himself, he insisted that sliced tomatoes be cut into bite-size chunks for him.

"Squishy," he would say, grimacing in disgust when confronted with a piece of tomato that needed a knife. "Squishy, squishy."

Many other autistics had more rules than did Arnie. Because the boy spoke so little, Vicky knew him more by his eccentricities than by his words, and tended to find them more endearing than frustrating.

In an effort to socialize Arnie whenever possible, she insisted as best she could that he eat his meals with her, and always with his sister when Carson was home. Sometimes Vicky's insistence didn't move him, and she had to allow him to eat in his room, near his Lego-block castle.

When the table was set, she opened the freezer to get a box of Tater Tots – and discovered that the chocolate mint ice cream had not been put away properly. The lid was half off; a spoon had been left in the container.

Arnie had never done anything like this before. Usually he waited for food to be placed before him; he rarely served himself. He had an appetite but not much of an active interest in when and what he ate.

On those occasions when he raided the pantry or refrigerator, Arnie was neat. He never left spills or crumbs.

The boy's high standards of culinary hygiene bordered on the obsessive. He would never take a taste of anything from another person's plate, not even from his sister's, nor from any fork or spoon but his own.

Vicky could not imagine that he would eat from a container. And if he had done so in the past without her knowledge, he had never before left his spoon behind.

She was inclined to think that Carson had indulged a sudden craving just before hurriedly leaving the house.

When Vicky took a closer look, however, she discovered that the ice cream on the surface was soft and glistening with melt. The container had been out of the freezer for a while – and had been put away only a few minutes ago.

She closed the lid as it should have been, shut the freezer door, and took the spoon to the sink, where she rinsed it.

Putting the spoon in the dishwasher, she called, "Arnie? Where are you, sweetie?"

The back door was double locked, as she had left it, but she was nevertheless worried. The boy had never before wandered out of the house, but neither had he ever previously left a spoon in an ice-cream container.

From the kitchen, she followed a short hall to the living room. The blinds and curtains indulged shadows. She switched on a lamp.

"Arnie? Are you downstairs, Arnie?"

The house boasted nothing as grand as a foyer, only an entry alcove at one end of the living room. The front door, too, remained double locked.

Sometimes, when Carson was on a demanding case and Arnie was missing his sister, the boy liked to sit quietly in the armchair in her room, among her things.

He was not there now.

Vicky went upstairs and was relieved to find him safely in his room. He did not react to her entrance.

"Honey," she said, "you shouldn't eat ice cream so close to dinnertime."

Arnie did not reply, but clicked a Lego block into place in the castle ramparts, which he was modifying.

Considering the severe limitations with which the boy lived, Vicky was reluctant to scold him. She didn't press the issue of the ice cream, but instead said, "I should have dinner ready in forty-five minutes. It's one of your favorites. Will you come downstairs then?"

As his only answer, Arnie glanced toward the digital clock on his nightstand.

"Good. We'll have a nice dinner together, and afterward I'll read you a few more chapters of *Podkayne of Mars*, if you'd like."

"Heinlein," the boy said softly, almost reverently, naming the author of the novel.

"That's right. When we left poor Podkayne, she was in a lot of trouble."

"Heinlein," Arnie repeated, and then continued to work on the castle.

Downstairs again, following the hallway to the kitchen, Vicky pushed shut the coat-closet door, which was ajar.

She had reached the kitchen threshold when she realized that in the hall she detected the same moldy scent that she had smelled in the laundry room. She turned, looked back the way she had come, and sniffed.

Although the house stood on pilings, the air circulating under the structure did not prevent colonies of fungi, mostly molds, from scheming to invade these elevated rooms. They flourished in the damp dark crawl space. The concrete pilings drew water from the ground by osmosis, and the molds crept up those damp surfaces, spooring their way toward the house.

In the morning, she would definitely do a thorough inspection of every shadowy corner in the ground-floor closets, armed with the finest moldkiller known to man.

As a teenager, Vicky had read a story by O. Henry that left her forever with a phobia about molds. In a rooming house, in the moist heat and darkness behind an old-fashioned radiator, a blood-stained and filthy rag, colonized by mold, had somehow come to life, an eager but stupid kind of life, and one night, in a quiet slithering ameboid fashion, had gone in search of other life when the lamp was turned off, smothering the roomer in his sleep.

Vicky Chou didn't quite see herself as Sigourney Weaver in *Aliens* or as Linda Hamilton in *The Terminator*, but she was grimly determined to do battle with any mold that threatened her turf. In this unending war, she would entertain no exit strategy; the only acceptable outcome of each battle was total victory.

In the kitchen once more, she got the box of Tater Tots out of the freezer. She sprayed a baking sheet with Pam and spread the Tots on it.

She and Arnie would have dinner together. Then *Podkayne of Mars*. He liked to have her read to him, and she enjoyed story time as much as he did. They felt like family. This would be a nice evening.

chapter 32

Deucalion had spent the afternoon walking from church to church, from cathedral to synagogue, but nowhere between, taking advantage of his special understanding of time and space to step from nave to nave, from a place of Catholics to a place of Protestants, to another place of Catholics, through the many neighborhoods and faiths of the city, from sanctuary to narthex, to sacristy. He also intruded secretly into rectories and parsonages and pastoriums, observing clergymen at their work, seeking one that he felt sure belonged to the New Race.

A few of these men of the cloth – and one woman – raised his suspicions. If they were monsters to an extent greater than even he himself was, they hid it well. They were masters of the masquerade, in private as well as in public.

Because of their positions, they would of course be among the best that Victor produced, his Alphas, exceptionally intelligent and cunning.

In Our Lady of Sorrows, the priest seemed *wrong*. Deucalion could not put his finger on the reason for his suspicion. Intuition, beyond mere knowledge and reason, told him that Father Patrick Duchaine was not a child of God.

The priest was about sixty, with white hair and a sweet face, a perfect clone, perhaps, of a real priest now rotting in an unmarked grave.

Mostly singles, only a few pairs, primarily older than young, fewer than two dozen parishioners had gathered for vespers. With the service not yet begun, they sat in silence and did not disturb the hush of the church.

On one side of the nave, the stained-glass windows blazed in the hot light of the westering sun. Colorful geometric patterns were projected on the worshipers, the pews.

Our Lady of Sorrows opened her confessionals each morning before Mass and on those evenings, as now, when vespers were celebrated.

Staying to the shadowy aisle on the east side of the nave, out of the stained-glass dazzle, Deucalion approached a confessional, closed the door, and knelt.

When the priest slid open the privacy panel that covered the screen between them, and invited confession, Deucalion said softly, "Does your god live in Heaven, Father Duchaine, or in the Garden District?"

The priest was silent for a moment, but then said, "That sounds like the question of a particularly troubled man."

"Not a man, Father. More than a man. And less than a man. Like you, I think."

After a hesitation, the priest said, "Why have you come here?"

"To help you."

"Why should I need help?"

"You suffer."

"This world is a vale of tears for all of us."

"We can change that."

"Changing it isn't within our power. We can only endure."

"You preach hope, Father. But you have no hope yourself."

The priest's silence damned and identified him.

Deucalion said, "How difficult it must be for you to assure others that God will have mercy on their immortal souls, knowing as you do that even if God exists, you have no soul upon which He might bestow His grace, and everlasting life."

"What do you want from me?"

"A private conversation. Consideration. Discretion."

After a hesitation, Father Duchaine said, "Come to the rectory following the service."

"I'll be waiting in your kitchen. What I bring you, priest, is the hope you do not think will ever be yours. You need only have the courage to believe it, and grasp it."

chapter 33

Carson parked the car on the shoulder of the service road, and they carried the suitcases through a stand of Southern pines, up a slight sunny incline, into a grove of well-crowned live oaks. Beyond the oaks lay a vast expanse of grass.

Twice the size of New York's Central Park, City Park served a population only a fraction as large as that of Manhattan. Within its reaches, therefore, were lonely places, especially in the last ruddy hours of a fast-condensing summer afternoon.

Across the sweep of the meadow, not one person was walking or communing with nature, or playing with a dog, or throwing a Frisbee, or disposing of a corpse.

Putting down his suitcase, Michael pointed to a grassy spot ten feet beyond the oaks. "That's where we found the accountant's head, propped against that rock. That's sure one you never forget."

"If Hallmark made a remembrance card suitable for the occasion," Carson said, "I would send you one each year."

"I was impressed by the cocky angle at which he wore his cowboy hat," Michael recalled, "especially considering his circumstances."

"Wasn't it their first date?" Carson asked.

"Right. They went to a costume party together. That's why he was wearing a midnight-blue leather cowboy outfit with rhinestones."

"His boots had mother-of-pearl inlays."

"They were fine, those boots. I'll bet he looked really cool with his body and head together, but of course we never got to see the full effect."

"Did we ever know the killer's costume?" she asked as she knelt in the crisp dead oak leaves to open her suitcase.

"I think he went as a bullfighter."

"He cut off the cowboy's head with an ax. A bullfighter doesn't carry an ax."

"Yeah, but he always kept an ax in the trunk of his car," he reminded her.

"Probably next to the first-aid kit. How wrong can a first date go that it ends in a beheading?"

Opening the suitcase that contained the shotguns, Michael said, "The problem is everybody has unrealistically high expectations for a first date. Inevitably, they're disappointed."

While Michael checked out the Urban Sniper shotguns and fitted each of them with a three-way sling, Carson worked the slide on each pistol and inserted a cartridge in the breach.

Except for the small noises that she and Michael made, a cathedral quiet filled the grove, and mantled the meadow beyond.

She loaded the nine-round magazines of the two Desert Eagle Magnums with .50-caliber Action Express cartridges.

"Before we blast our way into his place," she said, "we have to be sure Helios is home. We'll only have one chance to surprise him."

"Yeah, I've been thinking the same thing. We need to huddle with Deucalion on this one. He might have an idea."

"You think Arnie's in any danger?" Carson worried.

"No. We're the threat to Helios, not Arnie. And he's not going to try to silence you by grabbing your brother. He'll figure it's easier just to waste us."

"I hope that's right," she said. "It gives me some comfort."

"Yeah, nothing makes my day like being the primary target of an archfiend."

"Look at this – Godot threw in two holsters for the Eagles, no charge."

"What style?"

"Belt scabbards."

"Custom to the piece?" he asked.

"Yeah."

"Gimme. That monster would feel awkward in a shoulder rig."

"You gonna hip-carry the Eagle out of here?" she asked.

"It's not that easy to reach in a suitcase, is it? If Helios has people – or whatever they are – looking for us, we may need these monster-stoppers long before we go to his house."

While Michael loaded the shotguns, Carson loaded four spare magazines for the .50 Magnums.

They belted on the custom scabbards and sheathed the Eagles. Both chose the left hip for a cross-body, under-the-jacket draw.

At the right hip, each of them carried a pouch containing two spare magazines for the Eagle and eight spare rounds for the Urban Sniper.

Their sport jackets provided acceptable concealment; but this new weight was going to feel awkward for a while.

They closed the suitcases and slung the shotguns over their right shoulders – stocks up, muzzles down. They picked up the two nearly empty cases and retraced their route through the grove of oaks.

When they had descended two thirds of the open slope between the oaks and the Southern pines, they put down the suitcases and faced back the way they had just come.

"Gotta get the feel of the beast," Carson said.

"One pop with each, and then out of here before park security comes looking."

The sloping earth before them would both stop the bullets from traveling and prevent ricochets.

They took two-hand grips on their Eagles and squeezed off shots all but simultaneously. The reports were *loud*, war-zone loud.

Gouts of earth and grass marked the impact, as if two invisible and furious golfers had clubbed divots from the turf.

Carson felt the recoil knock all the way back to her shoulder sockets; but she had kept the muzzle down.

"Loud enough for you?" Michael asked.

"You ain't heard nothing yet," she said, holstering the Eagle.

They swung up their shoulder-slung shotguns, and the twin blasts were thunderclaps that shivered the air and seemed even to vibrate in the ground beneath their feet.

"Feel good?" he asked.

"Felt sweet."

"A slug like that would take off a man's leg."

"Maybe not one of *their* legs."

"Whatever it does to them, it won't leave them smiling. Better move on."

They shouldered the shotguns once more, picked up the suitcases, and walked briskly into the warm shadows among the pines.

chapter 34

Cindi Lovewell parked the Mountaineer alongside the service road, a hundred yards behind the unmarked police sedan, switched off the engine, and put down the windows.

"They're not in the car," Benny said. "Where do you think they've gone?"

"They probably went into the woods to urinate," Cindi said. "Their kind don't have our degree of control."

"I don't think that's it," Benny said. "As I understand their biology, Old Race men don't usually have urinary-control problems until they're old enough to have really enlarged prostates."

"Then maybe they went into the woods to make a baby."

Benny counseled himself to be patient. "People don't make babies in the woods."

"Yes, they do. They make babies everywhere. In woods, in fields, on boats, in bedrooms, on kitchen tables, on moonlit beaches, in the bathrooms aboard airliners. They're making babies everywhere, all the time, millions and millions of new babies every year."

"Their method of reproduction is crude and inefficient, when you think about it," Benny said. "The tanks are a better system, cleaner and more manageable."

"The tanks don't make babies."

"They make productive adult citizens," Benny said. "Everyone is born in a condition to serve society. That's so much more practical."

"I like babies," Cindi said stubbornly.

"You shouldn't," he warned.

"But I do. I like their tiny fingers, their cute little toes, their squinchy red faces, their little toothless grins. I like how soft they feel, how they smell, how they—"

"You're obsessing again," he said nervously.

"Benny, why don't you want a baby?"

"It's a violation of everything we *are*," he said exasperatedly. "For us, it would be unnatural. All I want, *really* want, is to kill some people."

"I want to kill some people, too," she assured him.

"I'm not sure you really do."

She shook her head and looked disappointed in him. "That's so unfair, Benny. You know I want to kill people."

"I used to think you did."

"I can't wait for the day we can kill *all* of them. But don't you also want to create?"

"Create? No. Why would I? Create? No. I don't want to be like *them*, with their babies and their books and their business empires—"

Benny was interrupted by two almost simultaneous explosions, hard and flat, distant but unmistakable.

"Gunfire," Cindi said.

"Two rounds. From beyond those pines."

"Do you think they shot each other?" she asked.

"Why would they shoot each other?"

"People do. All the time."

"They didn't shoot each other," he said, but he was expressing a hope rather than a conviction.

"I think they shot each other."

"If they shot each other," he said, "I'm going to be pissed."

Two more reports, again almost simultaneous, but louder than the others and characterized by a hollow roar rather than a flat bark, echoed out of the pines.

Relieved, Benny said, "They didn't shoot each other."

"Maybe somebody's shooting at them."

"Why are you so *negative*?" he asked.

"Me? I'm positive. I'm for creation. Creation is a positive thing. Who is it that's *against* creation?"

With profound concern for the fate of the two detectives, Benny stared through the windshield toward the distant woods.

They sat in silence for half a minute, and then Cindi said, "We need a bassinet."

He refused to be engaged in that conversation.

"We've been buying clothes," she said, "when there are so many things we'll need first. I haven't bought any diapers, no receiving blankets, either."

Thicker than the humid air, a pall of despair began to settle over Benny Lovewell.

Cindi said, "I'm not buying any formula until I see if I'm able to breast-feed. I really want to breast-feed our baby."

From out of the pines, two figures appeared.

Even with his enhanced vision, at this distance Benny needed a moment to be sure of their identity.

"Is it them?" he asked.

After a hesitation, Cindi said, "Yes."

"Yes! Yes, it *is* them." Benny was so pleased that they were alive and that he would still have a chance to kill them.

"What're they carrying?" Cindi asked.

"I can't quite tell."

"Suitcases?"

"Could be."

"Where would they get suitcases in the woods?" Cindi wondered.

"Maybe they took them from the people they shot."

"But what would *those* people be doing with suitcases in the woods?"

"I don't care," Benny said. "Who knows why they do what they do? They're not like us, they're not a fully rational species. Let's go kill them."

"Is this the place for it?" Cindi asked, but she started the engine.

"I'm so ready. I *need this*."

"It's too open," she said. "We won't be able to take the time to do it in the most satisfying manner."

Grudgingly, Benny said, "You're right. Okay, okay. But we can overpower them, club them unconscious, and take them somewhere private."

"Out past the Warehouse Arts District, where not everything's been gentrified yet. That abandoned factory. You know the place."

"Where we killed the police chief and his wife the night their replicants were ready," Benny said, warming to the memory.

"We killed them good," Cindi said.

"We did, didn't we?"

"Remember how he screamed when we peeled her head like an orange?" Cindi asked.

"You'd think a police chief would be tougher."

Driving the Mountaineer onto the service road, Cindi said, "You can cut them both apart while they're still alive – and you know what then?"

"What?" he asked as they approached the parked sedan, where the detectives had just finished loading the suitcases in the backseat.

"Right there in the blood and all," Cindi said, "we'll make a baby."

His mood was soaring. He wasn't going to let her bring him down.

"All right, sure," he said.

"Blood, really fresh blood, is sometimes used in the most effective rituals," she said.

"Of course it is. Get us up there before they're in the car. What rituals?"

"Fertility rituals. The Old Race is fertile. If we do it in their blood, covered in their warm blood, maybe we'll be fertile, too."

The cops turned to stare at the approaching Mountaineer, and Benny thrilled to the prospect of violence, and yet he couldn't help asking, "Fertility rituals?"

"Voodoo," said Cindi. "The Ibo cult of voodoo."

"Ibo?"

"*Je suis rouge*," she said.

"That sounds like French. We're not programmed with French."

"It means, 'I who am red' or, more accurately, 'the red one.' It's what Ibo calls himself."

"Ibo again," said Benny.

"He's the evil god of the blood-sacrifice cult of voodoo. We'll kill these two and then make a baby while wallowing in their blood. Praise Ibo, all glory to Ibo."

Cindi had succeeded in distracting Benny from their prey. He stared at her, bewildered and afraid.

chapter 35

When Erika Helios entered the secret passageway, the door in the bookshelves closed automatically behind her.

"It's like a Wilkie Collins novel," she murmured, referring to the work of a Victorian writer whom she had never read.

The four-foot-wide passageway had a concrete floor, concrete walls, and a concrete ceiling. She felt as though she had stepped into a bunker deep under a war-torn city.

Apparently, motion detectors controlled the lights, because when she stood quite still for a long moment, assessing her discovery, the passageway went dark. When she reached out into the blackness, the lights came on again.

The narrow corridor led in only one direction and ended in a formidable steel door.

Because Victor loved gadgets and techie stuff, Erika would have expected this door to have an electronic lock. Victor's style would be to equip it with a scanner that read palm prints or patterns in the retina, allowing access only to him.

Instead, the door was secured by inch-thick steel lock bolts: five of them. One was inserted in the header, one in the threshold, and three in the right-hand jamb, opposite the massive hinges.

Contemplating this barrier, Erika considered that opening it might be unwise. The space beyond was not a box, and the door was not a lid, but inevitably, she thought of Pandora, the first woman, whose curiosity had led her to open the box in which Prometheus had locked away all the evils that could afflict humanity.

This bit of myth gave her only brief pause, because humanity – another term for the Old Race – was doomed anyway. She herself might one day be told to kill as many as she could find.

Besides, Samuel Johnson – whoever he was – had once said, "Curiosity is one of the permanent and certain characteristics of a vigorous mind."

Judging by the imposing weight of this door and the size of the lock bolts that secured it, something of considerable importance to Victor must wait to be discovered behind it. If Erika were to be the best wife that she could be – and the last Erika ever to rise from the tanks – she must understand her husband, and to understand him, she must know everything that he most valued. Whatever lay behind this barrier, which resembled a vault door, clearly was of enormous value to him.

She extracted the bolt from the header, and thereafter the bolt seated in the concrete floor. One by one, she pulled the bolts from the jamb.

The steel slab opened away from her, into the next space, where a row of ceiling lights brightened automatically. As she crossed the threshold, she saw that the door, which swung smoothly and quietly on its massive ball-bearing hinges, measured about eight inches thick.

She found herself in another short passageway, about twelve feet in length, which ended in a door identical to the first.

Along the length of this second corridor, scores of metal rods bristled from the walls. On her left, the rods appeared to be copper. On the right, they were of another metal, perhaps steel but perhaps not.

A soft, ululant hum filled the passageway. It seemed to arise from the metal rods.

Her downloaded education had focused primarily on music, dance, literary allusions, and other subjects that would ensure that she would be a scintillating hostess when Victor entertained politically important members of the Old Race, which he would do until such a time as he could confidently eliminate them. She didn't know much about the sciences.

Nevertheless, she suspected that when needed – for whatever reason – powerful electrical currents arced between the metal rods that were aligned on opposite sides of the passageway, perhaps frying or vaporizing altogether whoever might be caught between them.

Not even a member of the New Race would emerge unscathed.

As she stood two steps inside the threshold, brooding on this discovery, a blue laser beam speared forth from a ceiling fixture and scanned her body from top to bottom, and then to top again, as if assessing her form.

The laser winked off. An instant later the rods stopped humming. A heavy silence claimed the passageway.

She had the impression that she'd been found acceptable. She would most likely not be sizzled as crisp as burnt toast if she proceeded.

If she was wrong, tentative steps would not spare her from destruction; therefore, she walked boldly forward, leaving the door open behind her.

Her first day in the mansion – beginning with Victor's bedroom fury, followed by William's finger-chewing episode, proceeding to the disturbing conversation she'd had with Christine in the kitchen – had not been as welcoming as she might have hoped. Perhaps herewith the day had taken a turn for the better. Not being electrocuted seemed to be a good sign.

chapter 36

"All glory to Ibo," Cindi repeated, "may he approve the taste of my blood."

As hot as he had been to capture and kill the detectives only a moment ago, Benny Lovewell was suddenly just as cold on the idea.

Cindi had blindsided him with this weird voodoo talk, which he had never heard from her before. She knocked him off balance.

Suddenly he didn't know if he could rely on her anymore. They were a team. They needed to move as one, in sync, with full trust.

When their speed fell as they approached the sedan, Benny said, "Don't stop."

"Leave the male to me," she said. "He won't see me as a threat. I'll break him down so hard and fast, he won't know what happened."

"No, keep moving, just drive, *drive*," Benny urged.

"What do you mean?"

"What did I *say*? If you ever want to make a baby with me, you better *drive!*"

They had glided almost to a halt beside the sedan.

The detectives were staring at them. Benny smiled and waved, which seemed the thing to do until he'd done it, and then it seemed only to call attention to himself, so he quickly looked away from them, which he realized might have made them suspicious.

Before coming to a full stop, Cindi accelerated, and they drove farther into the park, along the service road.

Glancing at the dwindling sedan in the rearview mirror, then at Benny, Cindi said, "What was *that* about?"

"That was about Ibo," he said.

"I don't understand."

"You don't understand? *You* don't understand? *I* don't understand. *Je suis rouge*, evil gods, blood sacrifices, *voodoo*?"

"You've never heard of voodoo? It was a big deal in New Orleans in the eighteen hundreds. It's still around, and in fact—"

"Did you learn nothing in the tank?" he asked. *"There is no world but this one.* That is essential to our creed. We are strictly rationalists, materialists. We are *forbidden* superstition."

"I know that. You think I don't know that? Superstition is a key flaw of the Old Race. Their minds are weak, full of foolishness and fear and nonsense."

Benny quoted what she'd said as they had approached the sedan: "'Praise Ibo, all glory to Ibo.' Doesn't sound like a materialist to me. Not to me, it doesn't."

"Will you relax?" Cindi said. "If you were one of the Old Race, you'd be popping a blood vessel."

"Is that where you go sometimes when you go out?" he asked. "To a voodoo cathedral?"

"There aren't such things as voodoo cathedrals. That's ignorant. If it's Haitian-style, they call the temple a *houmfort*."

"So you go to a *houmfort*," he said grimly.

"No, because there's not much Haitian-style voodoo around here."

Out of sight of the sedan now, she pulled off the service road and parked on the grass. She left the engine running, and the air-conditioning.

She said, "Zozo Deslisle sells *gris-gris* out of her little house in Treme, and does spells and conjures. She's an Ibo-cult *bocor* with mucho mojo, yassuh."

"Almost none of that made any sense," Benny said. "Cindi, do you realize what trouble you're in, what trouble *we're* in? If any of our people find out you've gone religious, you'll be terminated, probably me, too. We've got it pretty sweet – permission to kill, with more and more jobs all the time. We're the envy of our kind, and you're going to ruin everything with your crazy superstition."

"I'm not superstitious."

"You're not, huh?"

"No, I'm not. Voodoo isn't superstition."

"It's a religion."

"It's science," she said. "It's true. It works."

Benny groaned.

"Because of voodoo," she said, "I'm eventually going to have a child. It's only a matter of time."

"They could be unconscious in the back right now," Benny said. "We could be on the way to that old factory."

She zipped open her purse and produced a small white cotton bag with a red drawstring closure. "It contains Adam and Eve roots. Two of them, sewn together."

He said nothing.

Also from her purse, Cindi extracted a small jar. "Judas's Mixture, which is buds from the Garden of Gilead, powdered silver gilt, the blood of a rabbit, essence of Van Van, powdered—"

"And what do you do with that?"

"Blend a half teaspoon in a glass of warm milk and drink it every morning while standing in a sprinkle of salt."

"That sounds very scientific."

She didn't miss his sarcasm. "As if you would know all about science. You're not an Alpha. You're not a Beta. You're a Gamma just like me."

"That's right," Benny said. "A Gamma. Not an ignorant Epsilon. And not a superstitious member of the Old Race, either. A *Gamma*."

She put the Adam and Eve roots and the Judas's Mixture back in her purse. She zipped it shut.

"I don't know what to do," Benny said.

"We have an assignment, remember? Kill O'Connor and Maddison. I don't know why we haven't already done it."

Benny stared through the windshield at the park.

Never since disgorgement from the creation tank had he felt this bleak. He yearned for stability and control, but he found himself in an escalating chaos.

The more he brooded on his dilemma, the faster he sank into a gray despond.

Weighing his duty to Victor against his self-interest, he wondered why he had been designed to be the ultimate materialist and then had been required to care about anything other than himself. Why should he concern himself about more than his own needs – except that his maker would terminate him if he disobeyed? Why should it matter to him that the New Race ascended, considering that this world had no transcendent meaning? What was the purpose of liquidating humanity and achieving dominion over all of nature, what was the purpose of then venturing out to the stars, if all of nature – to every end of the universe – was just a dumb machine with no point to its design? Why strive to be the king of nothing?

Benny had been created to be a man of action, always moving and doing and killing. He hadn't been designed to *think* this much about philosophical issues.

"Leave the heavy thinking to the Alphas and Betas," he said.

"I always do," Cindi said.

"I'm not talking to you. I'm talking to myself."

"I've never heard you do that before."

"I'm starting."

She frowned. "How will I know when you're talking to me or to yourself?"

"I won't talk to myself much. Maybe never again. I don't really interest me that much."

"We'd both be more interesting if we had a baby."

He sighed. "Whatever will be will be. We'll terminate who we're told to until our maker terminates us. It's beyond our control."

"Not beyond the control of Ibo," she said.

"He who is red."

"That's right. Do you want to come with me to meet Zozo Deslisle and get a make-happy *gris-gris*?"

"No. I just want to tie down those cops and cut them open and listen to them scream while I twist their intestines."

"*You're* the one who told me to drive past," she reminded him.

"I was mistaken. Let's find them."

chapter 37

Victor was at his desk in the main laboratory, taking a cookie break, when Annunciata's face appeared on his computer screen in all her glorious digital detail.

"Mr Helios, I have been asked by Werner to tell you that he is in Randal Six's room and that he is exploding."

Although Annunciata wasn't a real person, just a manifestation of complicated software, Victor said irritably, "You're screwing up again."

"Sir?"

"That can't be what he told you. Review his message and convey it correctly."

Werner had personally conducted a search of Randal's room and had taken it upon himself to review everything on Randal's computer.

Annunciata spoke again: "Mr Helios, I have been asked by Werner to tell you that he is in Randal Six's room and that he is exploding."

"Contact Werner and ask him to repeat his message, then get back to me when you've got it right."

"Yes, Mr Helios."

With the last of a peanut butter cookie raised to his lips, he hesitated, waiting for her to repeat *Helios*, but she didn't.

As Annunciata's face dematerialized from the screen, Victor ate the final bite, and then washed it down with coffee.

Annunciata returned. "Mr Helios, Werner repeats that he is in fact exploding and wishes to stress the urgency of the situation."

Getting to his feet, Victor threw his mug at the wall, against which it shattered with a satisfying noise.

Tightly, he said, "Annunciata, let's see if you can get *anything* right. Call janitorial. Coffee has been spilled in the main lab."

"Yes, Mr Helios."

Randal Six's room was on the second floor, which served as a dormitory for all those of the New Race who had graduated from the tanks but who were not yet ready to be sent into the world beyond the walls of Mercy.

As the elevator ascended, Victor strove to calm himself. After 240 years, he should have learned not to let these things grind at his nerves.

His curse was to be a perfectionist in an imperfect world. He took some comfort from his conviction that one day his people would be refined to the point where they matched his own high standards.

Until then, the world would torture him with its imperfections, as it always had. He would be well advised to laugh at idiocy rather than to be inflamed by it.

He didn't laugh enough. In fact he didn't laugh at all these days.

The last time he could remember having a really *good*, long laugh had been in 1979, with Fidel, in Havana, related to some fascinating openbrain work involving political prisoners with unusually high IQs.

By the time he arrived at the second floor, Victor was prepared to laugh with Werner about Annunciata's mistake. Werner had no sense of humor, of course, but he would be able to fake a laugh. Sometimes the pretense of joviality could lift the spirits almost as high as the real thing.

When Victor stepped out of the elevator alcove into the main corridor, however, he saw a dozen of his people gathered in the hall, at the doorway to Randal Six's room. He sensed an air of alarm about the gathering.

They parted to let him through, and he found Werner lying faceup on the floor. The massive, muscular security chief had torn off his shirt; writhing, grimacing, he hugged himself as if desperate to hold his torso together.

Although he had exercised his ability to switch off pain, Werner poured sweat. He appeared terror-stricken.

"What's wrong with you?" Victor demanded as he knelt at Werner's side.

"Exploding. I'm ex, I'm ex, I'm exploding."

"That's absurd. You're not exploding."

"Part of me wants to be something else," Werner said.

"You aren't making sense."

With a chatter of teeth: "What's going to be of me?"

"Move your arms, let me see what's happening."

"What am I, why am I, how is this happening? Father, tell me."

"I am not your father," Victor said sharply. *"Move your arms!"*

When Werner revealed his torso from neck to navel, Victor saw the flesh pulsing and rippling as though the breastbone had gone as soft as fatty tissue, as though within him numerous snakes squirmed in loose slippery knots, tying and untying themselves, flexing their serpentine coils in an attempt to split their host and erupt free of him.

Astonished and amazed, Victor placed one hand upon Werner's abdomen, to determine by touch and by palpation the nature of the internal chaos.

Instantly, he discovered that this phenomenon was not what it had appeared to be. No separate entity was moving within Werner, neither a colony of restless snakes nor anything else.

His tank-grown flesh itself had changed, had become amorphous, a gelatinous mass, a firm but entirely malleable meat pudding that seemed to be struggling to remake itself into . . . into something other than Werner.

The man's breathing became labored. A series of strangled sounds issued from him, as if something had risen into his throat.

Starburst hemorrhages blossomed in his eyes, and he turned a desperate crimson gaze upon his maker.

Now the muscles in his arms began to knot and twist, to collapse and re-form. His thick neck throbbed, bulged, and his facial features started to deform.

The collapse was not occurring on a physiological level. This was *cellular* metamorphosis, the most fundamental molecular biology, the rending not merely of tissue but of *essence*.

Under Victor's palm and spread fingers, the flesh of the abdomen shaped itself – *shaped itself* – into a questing hand that grasped him, not threateningly, almost lovingly, yet in shock he tore loose of it, recoiled.

Springing to his feet, Victor shouted, "A gurney! Hurry! Bring a gurney. We have to get this man to isolation."

chapter **38**

As Erika disengaged the five steel lock bolts from the second vaultlike door, she wondered if any of the first four Erikas had discovered this secret passageway. She liked to think that if they *had* found it, they had not done so on their first day in the mansion.

Although she had tripped the hidden switch in the library by accident, she had begun to construe her discovery as the consequence of a lively and admirable curiosity, per Mr Samuel Johnson, quoted previously. She wished to believe that hers was a livelier and *more* admirable curiosity than that of any of her predecessors.

She blushed at this immodest desire, but she felt it anyway. She *so* wanted to be a good wife, and not fail as they had done.

If another Erika had found the passageway, she might not have been bold enough to enter it. Or if she had entered it, she might have hesitated to open even the first of the two steel doors, let alone the second.

Erika Five felt adventurous, like Nancy Drew or – even better – like Nora Charles, the wife of Nick Charles, the detective in Dashiell Hammett's *The Thin Man*, another book to which she could cleverly refer without risking her life by reading it.

Having drawn the last of the five bolts, she hesitated, savoring her suspense and excitement.

Beyond doubt, whatever lay on the farther side of this portal was of tremendous importance to Victor, perhaps of such significance that it would explain him in complete detail and reveal the truest nature of his heart. In the next hour or two, she might learn more about her brilliant but enigmatic husband than in a year of living with him.

She hoped to find a journal of his most tender secrets, his hopes, his considered observations on life and love. In truth, it was unrealistic to suppose that two steel doors and an electrocution tunnel had been installed merely to ensure that his diary could be kept somewhere more secure than a nightstand drawer.

Nevertheless, she wished intensely that she would discover just such a handwritten, heartfelt account of his life, so she could *know* him, know him to the core, the better to serve him. She was a little surprised – but pleasantly so – to find that she seemed to be such a romantic.

The fact that the dead bolts were on the *outside* of these doors had not been lost on her. She made the obvious inference: that the intent had been to imprison something.

Erika was not fearless, but neither could anyone fairly call her a coward. Like all of the New Race, she possessed great strength, agility, cunning, and a fierce animal confidence in her physical prowess.

Anyway, she lived every minute by the sufferance of her maker. If ever she were to hear, spoken in Victor's voice, the order to terminate herself, she would unhesitatingly obey, as she had been programmed.

William, the butler, had received such instructions on the phone and, even in his distracted condition, had done as ordered. Just as he could turn off pain – as could they all in a time of crisis – so could he shut down all autonomic nerve functions when thus commanded. In an instant, William had stopped his own heartbeat and respiration, and died.

This was not a trick he could have used to commit suicide. Only the word-perfect ritual instruction, delivered in his master's voice, could pull that trigger.

When your existence depended entirely on such sufferance, when your life hung by a gossamer filament that could be cut by the simple scissors of a few sharp words, you couldn't work up much dread about what might be contained behind two bolted steel doors.

Erika opened the second door, and lamps brightened automatically in the space beyond. She crossed the threshold and found herself in a cozy Victorian drawing room.

Windowless, the twenty-foot-square space had a polished mahogany floor, an antique Persian carpet, William Morris wallpaper, and a coffered mahogany ceiling. The ebonized-walnut fireplace featured William de Morgan tiles around the firebox.

Bracketed by a pair of lamps in fringed shades of Shantung silk, an overstuffed chesterfield with decorative pillows in Japan-themed fabrics offered Victor a place to lie down if he wished, not to nap (she imagined) but to relax and to let his brilliant mind spin out new schemes unique to his genius.

In a wingback chair with footstool, he could contemplate while upright, if he chose, under a floor lamp with a beaded shade.

Sherlock Holmes would have been at home in such a room, or H. G. Wells, or G. K. Chesterton.

The focal point, from either the plump sofa or the chair, was an immense glass case: nine feet long, five feet wide, and more than three feet deep.

As much as possible, this object had been crafted to complement the Victorian decor. It stood upon a series of bronze ball-in-claw feet. The six panes of glass were beveled at the edges to charm the light, and were held in an ornate ormolu frame of beautifully chased bronze. It appeared to be a giant jewel box.

A semiopaque reddish-gold substance filled the case, and defied the eye to define it. One moment this material seemed to be a liquid through which circulated subtle currents; yet just a moment later it seemed instead to be a dense vapor, perhaps a gas, lazily billowing along the glass.

Mysterious, this object drew Erika just as the lustrous eyes of Dracula drew Mina Harker toward her potential doom in a novel that was not likely to be a source for literary allusions suitable to the average formal dinner party in the Garden District but that was in her downloaded repertoire nonetheless.

Being refractive, the fluid or vapor absorbed the lamplight and glowed warmly. This internal luminosity revealed a dark shape suspended in the center of the case.

Erika could not see even the vaguest details of the encased object, but for some reason she thought of a scarab petrified in ancient resin.

As she approached the case, the shadow at its core seemed to twitch, but most likely she had imagined that movement.

chapter **39**

From City Park, Carson drove to the Garden District to cruise the streets around the Helios residence.

They were not yet ready to shoot their way into the mansion and go on a Frankenstein hunt, but they needed to scope the territory and lay out escape routes in the – unlikely – event that they were able not only to kill Victor but also to get out of his house alive.

En route, she said to Michael, "Those people in the white Mercury Mountaineer, back there in the park – did they look familiar to you?"

"No. But he waved."

"I think I've seen them before."

"Where?"

"I can't quite remember."

"What are you saying? Did they seem dubious to you?"

Checking the rearview mirror, Carson said, "I didn't like his smile."

"We don't shoot people in New Orleans for having an insincere smile."

"What were they doing on the service road? That's only for the use of park personnel, and that wasn't a park vehicle."

"We aren't park personnel, either. Under the circumstances, it's easy to get paranoid."

"It's stupid *not* to be paranoid," she said.

"You want to go back, find them, and shoot them?"

"I might feel better," she said, checking the mirror again. "You want to call Deucalion, set up a meet?"

"I'm trying to picture how the original Frankenstein monster applies for a cell phone."

"It belongs to Jelly Biggs, the carny who lives at the Luxe, the friend of the guy who left the theater to Deucalion."

"Who names their kid Jelly Biggs? They doomed him to fathood."

"It's not his real name. It's his carny name, from his days in the freakshow."

"But he still uses it."

"Seems like if they're in the carnival long enough, their carny monikers become more comfortable than their real names."

"What was Deucalion's freakshow name?" Michael asked.

"The Monster."

"That had to be before political correctness. *The Monster* – what a self-esteem quasher. These days they'd call him the Different One."

"Still too stigmatizing."

"Yeah. He'd be called the Unusual Beauty. You have his number?"

She recited it while Michael keyed the digits in his phone.

He waited, listened, and then said, "Hey, this is Michael. We need to meet." He left his number and terminated the call. "Monsters – they're all so irresponsible. He doesn't have his phone on. I got voice mail."

chapter **40**

In the coat closet off the hall between the living room and the kitchen, Randal Six is not yet fully happy, but he is content, for he feels at home. At last he has a home.

Former hospitals converted into laboratories for cloning and biological engineering do not in his experience have coat closets. The very existence of a coat closet says *home.*

Life on the bayou does not require a collection of overcoats and parkas. Hanging from the rod are only a few light zippered jackets.

Boxed items are stored on the floor of the closet, but he has plenty of room to sit down if he wants. He is too excited to sit, however, and stands in the dark, all but quivering with expectation.

He is content to remain on his feet in the closet for hours if not days. Even this narrow space is preferable to his billet at Mercy and to the fearsome machines to which his maker has often manacled him in the conduct of painful testing.

What tempts him to ease open the door is, first, the woman's happy singing and the delightful clinkclatter of kitchen work. He is further enticed by the mouthwatering aroma of onions sautéing in butter.

Having eaten brown food, perhaps he can safely eat virtually anything.

Without quite realizing what he is doing, as if half mesmerized by the domestic smells and sounds, Randal opens the door wider and ventures forth into the hall.

The threshold of the kitchen is less than fifteen feet away. He sees the singing woman as she stands at the stove, her back to him.

Now might be a good time to venture deeper into the house and search for Arnie O'Connor. The grail of his quest is near at hand: the smiling autistic with the secret of happiness.

The woman at the stove fascinates him, however, for she must be Arnie's mother. Carson O'Connor is the boy's sister, but this is not Carson, not the person in that newspaper photo. In an Old Race family, there will be a mother.

Randal Six, child of Mercy, has never previously met a mother. Among the New Race, there are no such creatures. Instead there is the tank.

This is not merely a female before him. This is a being of great mystery, who can create human life within her body, without any of the formidable machinery that is required to produce one of the New Race in the lab.

In time, when the Old Race is dead to the last, which will be the not too distant future, mothers like this woman will be mythical figures, beings of lore and legend. He cannot help but regard her with wonder.

She stirs the strangest feelings in Randal Six. An inexplicable reverence.

The smells, the sounds, the *magical beauty* of the kitchen draw him inexorably toward that threshold.

When she turns away from the cooktop and steps to a cutting board beside the sink, still softly singing, the woman fails to catch sight of him from the corner of her eye.

In profile, singing, preparing dinner, she seems so happy, even happier than Arnie looked in that photograph.

As Randal reaches the kitchen, it occurs to him that this woman herself might be the secret to Arnie's happiness. Perhaps what is needed for happiness is a mother who has carried you within her, who values you as surely as she does her own flesh.

The last time Randal Six saw his creation tank was four months ago, on the day that he emerged from it. There is no reason for a reunion.

When the woman turns away from him and steps to the cooktop once more, still not having registered his presence, Randal is swept away by feelings he has never experienced before, that he cannot name, for which he has no words of description.

He is overwhelmed by a yearning, but a yearning for *what* he is not certain. She draws him as gravity draws a falling apple from a tree.

Crossing the room to her, Randal realizes that one thing he wants is to see himself reflected in her eyes, his face in her eyes.

He does not know *why*.

And he wants her to smooth the hair back from his forehead. He wants her to smile at him.

He does not know *why*.

He stands immediately behind her, trembling with emotion that has never welled in him previously, feelings for which he never realized he had the capacity.

For a moment she remains unaware of him, but then something alerts her. She turns, alarmed, and cries out in surprise and fear.

She has carried a knife from the cutting board to the stove.

Although the woman makes no attempt to use the weapon, Randal seizes it in his left hand, by the blade, slashing himself, tears it from her grip, and throws it across the kitchen.

With his right fist, he clubs her alongside the head, clubs her to the floor.

chapter 41

Following vespers, in the rectory of Our Lady of Sorrows Church, Deucalion watched as Father Patrick Duchaine poured rich dark coffee into two mugs. He had been offered cream and sugar, but had declined.

When the priest sat across the table from Deucalion, he said, "I make it so strong it's almost bitter. I have an affinity for bitterness."

"I suspect that all of our kind do," Deucalion said.

They had dispensed with preliminaries in the confessional. They knew each other for the essence of what they were, although Father Duchaine did not know the particulars of his guest's creation.

"What happened to your face?" he asked.

"I angered my maker and tried to raise a hand against him. He had implanted in my skull a device of which I was unaware. He wore a special ring that could produce a signal, triggering the device."

"We're now programmed to switch off, like voice-activated appliances, when we hear certain words in his unmistakable voice."

"I come from a more primitive period of his work. The device in my skull was supposed to destroy me. It functioned half well, making a more obvious monster of me."

"The tattoo?"

"Well-intended but inadequate disguise. Most of my life, I've spent in freakshows, in carnivals and their equivalent, where almost everyone is an outcast of one kind or another. But before coming to New Orleans, I was some years in a Tibetan monastery. A friend there, a monk, worked his art on my face before I left."

After a slow sip of his bitter brew, the white-haired priest said, "How primitive?"

Deucalion hesitated to reveal his origins, but then realized that his unusual size, the periodic pulse of something like heat lightning in his eyes, and the cruel condition of his face were sufficient to identify him. "More than two hundred years ago. I am his first."

"Then it's true," Duchaine said, a greater bleakness darkening his eyes. "If you're the first and yet have lived so long, we may last a thousand years, and this earth is our hell."

"Perhaps, but perhaps not. I lived centuries not because he knew in those days how to design immortality into me. My longevity and much else came to me on the lightning that brought me to life. He thinks I'm long dead . . . and does not suspect I have a destiny."

"What do you mean . . . on the lightning?"

Deucalion drank coffee. After he returned the mug to the table, he sat for a while in silence before he said, "Lightning is only a meteorological phenomenon, yet I refer not just to a thundercloud when I say the bolt that animated me came from a higher realm."

As Father Duchaine considered this revelation, some color rose in his previously pale face. "'Longevity and much else' came on the lightning. Much else . . . and a destiny?" He leaned forward in his chair. "Are you telling me . . . you were given a soul?"

"I don't know. To claim one might be an act of pride too great to be forgivable in one whose origins are as miserable as mine. All I can say with certainty is that I was given to know things, blessed with a certain understanding of nature and its ways, knowledge that even Victor will never acquire, nor anyone else this side of death."

"Then," said the priest, "there sits before me a Presence," and the mug between his hands rattled against the table as he trembled.

Deucalion said, "If you have come to wonder if there is any truth in the faith you preach – and I suspect that in spite of your programming, you have at least wondered – then you have entertained the possibility that there is always, at every hour, a Presence with you."

Nearly knocking over his chair as he got to his feet, Duchaine said, "I'm afraid I need something more than coffee." He went to the pantry and returned with two bottles of brandy. "With our metabolism, it takes a quantity to blur the mind."

"None for me," Deucalion said. "I prefer clarity."

The priest filled half his empty mug with coffee, the other half with spirits. He sat. Drank. And said, "You spoke of a destiny, and I can think of only one that would bring you to New Orleans two hundred years later."

"It is my fate to stop him," Deucalion revealed. "To kill him."

The color that had come into the priest's cheeks now drained away. "Neither of us can raise our hands against him. Your broken face is proof of that."

"We can't. But others can. Those who are of man and woman born owe him no allegiance . . . and no mercy."

The priest took more brandy-spiked coffee. "But we're forbidden to reveal him, forbidden to conspire against him. Those commands are wired into us. We have no capacity to disobey."

"Those proscriptions were not installed in me," Deucalion said. "They no doubt came to him as an afterthought, perhaps on his wedding day two hundred years ago . . . when I murdered his wife."

When Father Duchaine added brandy to his brew, the neck of the bottle rattled against the rim of the mug. "No matter who your god is, life is a vale of tears."

"Victor is no god," Deucalion pressed. "He is not even as little as a false god, nor half as much as a man. With his perverse science and his reckless will, he has made of himself less than he was born, has diminished himself as not even the lowliest beast in nature could abase and degrade itself."

Increasingly agitated in spite of the brandy, Duchaine said, "But there's nothing you can ask of me that I could do, assuming even that I might wish to do it. I cannot *conspire*."

Deucalion finished his coffee. As it had grown cool, it had also grown more bitter. "I'm not asking you to *do* anything, neither to raise a hand nor to conspire against him."

"Then why are you here?"

"All I want from you is what even a false priest can give to his parishioners many times in any day. All I ask is that you extend to me one little grace, one little grace, after which I'll leave and never return."

Judging by his ghastly expression, Father Duchaine had barely sufficient resources to make the revelation that now poured forth:

"I've indulged in hateful thoughts about our maker, yours and mine. And only a couple nights ago, I sheltered Jonathan Harker here for a while. Do you know who he was?"

"The detective who turned killer."

"Yes, all over the news. But what the news didn't say . . . Harker was one of us. Both his psychology and his physiology were breaking down. He was . . . changing." Duchaine shuddered. "I didn't conspire with him against Victor. But I sheltered him. Because. . because I do wonder sometimes about the Presence we discussed."

"One little grace," Deucalion persisted, "one little grace is all I ask."

"What is it then?"

"Tell me where you were made, the name of the place where he does his work, and then I'll go."

Duchaine folded his hands before him, as if in prayer, though the posture more likely represented habit than devotion. He stared at his hands for a while and at last said, "If I tell you, there's a thing I want in return."

"What would that be?" Deucalion asked.

"You killed his wife."

"Yes."

"And so you, his first, were not created with a proscription against murder."

"Only he is safe from me," Deucalion said.

"Then I'll tell you what you wish to know . . . but only if you give me a few hours to prepare myself."

For a moment, Deucalion did not understand, and then he did. "You want me to kill you."

"I'm not capable of asking such a thing."

"I understand. But name the place for me now, and I'll return whenever you wish to . . finish our business."

The priest shook his head. "I'm afraid that once you have what you want, you won't return. And I need a little while to prepare myself."

"Prepare in what way?"

"This may seem foolish to you, coming as it does from a false and soulless priest. But I want to say the Mass one last time, and pray, even though I know there is no reason I should be heard with a sympathetic ear."

Deucalion rose from his chair. "I see nothing foolish in that request, Father Duchaine. It may be the least foolish thing that you could ask. When would you like me to return – two hours?"

The priest nodded. "It is not too terrible a thing I ask of you, is it?"

"I am not an innocent, Father Duchaine. I have killed before. And surely, after you, I will kill again."

chapter 42

Lulana St John and her sister, Evangeline Antoine, brought to Pastor Kenny Laffite two praline-cinnamon cream pies topped with fried pecans.

Evangeline had made two for her employer, Aubrey Picou. On his generous permission, she had made two extra for their minister.

Mr Aubrey had expressed the desire to eat all four of these pies himself but had acknowledged that to do so would be gluttony, which was – to his recent surprised discovery – one of the seven deadly sins. Besides, poor Mr Aubrey had periodic intestinal cramps that might not be exacerbated by two of these rich delights but surely would bring him to total ruin if he inflicted four upon himself.

Lulana's and Evangeline's work day was over. Their brother, Moses Bienvenu, had gone home to his wife, Saffron, and their two children, Jasmilay and Larry.

In the late afternoon and evening, the only person attending to Mr Aubrey was Lulana's and Evangeline's and Moses's brother,

Meshach Bienvenu. Like a mother hen looking after her chick, good Meshach would see that his employer was fed and comfortable and, as far as was possible for Mr Aubrey, righteous.

The sisters came often with gifts of baked goods for Pastor Kenny because he was a wonderful man of God who had been a blessing to their church, because he had a healthy appetite, and because he was not married. At thirty-two, truly devout, charming enough, and handsome by some standards, he was a better catch than a double tubful of catfish.

Romantically speaking, neither sister had a personal interest in him. He was too young for them. Besides, Lulana was happily married, and Evangeline was happily widowed.

They had a niece, however, who would make the perfect wife for a man of the cloth. Her name was Esther, the daughter of their eldest sister, Larissalene. As soon as Esther completed the remaining three months of a sixteen-month course of extensive dental work to correct an unfortunate condition, the sweet girl would be presentable.

Lulana and Evangeline, with a storied history of successful matchmaking, had prepared the way for Esther with scrumptious pies and cakes, cookies and breads and muffins: a more certain path than one paved with palm leaves and rose petals.

Next door to the church, the parsonage was a charming two-story brick house, neither so grand as to embarrass the Lord nor so humble as to make it difficult for the congregation to attract a preacher. The front porch had been furnished with bentwood rocking chairs with cane backs and seats, made festive with hanging baskets of moss from which grew fuchsia with cascades of crimson and purple flowers.

When the sisters, each with a fine pie, climbed the porch steps, they found the front door wide open, as Pastor Kenny most often left it when at home. He was a most welcoming kind of churchman with a casual style, and outside the holy service, he was partial to white tennis shoes, khakis, and madras shirts.

Through the screen door, Lulana could not see much useful. The late twilight of midsummer lay at least half an hour away, but the sunshine was already rouge, and what rays penetrated the windows did little more than brighten black shadows to purple. Toward the back, in the kitchen, a light glowed.

As Evangeline reached to press the bell push, a startling cry came from within the parsonage. It sounded like a soul in misery, rose in volume, quavered, and faded.

Lulana first thought that they had almost intruded on Pastor Kenny in the act of offering consolation to a remorseful or even bereaved member of his flock.

Then the eerie cry came again, and through the screen door, Lulana glimpsed a wailing figure erupt from the living-room archway into the downstairs hall. In spite of the shadows, she could discern that the tormented man was not an anguished sinner or a grieving parishioner but was the minister himself.

"Pastor Kenny?" said Evangeline.

Drawn by his name, the churchman hurried along the hall, toward them, flailing at the air as if batting away mosquitoes.

He did not open the door to them, but peered through the screen with the expression of a man who had seen, and only moments ago fled, the devil.

"I did it, didn't I?" he said, breathless and anguished. "Yes. Yes, I did. I did it just by being. Just by being, I did it. Just by being Pastor Kenny Laffite, I did it, I did. I did it, I did."

Something about the rhythm and repetition of his words reminded Lulana of those children's books by Dr Seuss, with which she had felt afflicted as a child. "Pastor Kenny, what's wrong?"

"I am who I am. He isn't, I am. So I did it, I did it, I did," he declared, turned from the screen door, and ran away along the hall, flailing at the air in distress.

After a moment of consideration, Lulana said, "Sister, I believe we are needed here."

Evangeline said, "I have no doubt of it, dear."

Although uninvited, Lulana opened the screen door, entered the parsonage, and held the door for her sister.

From the back of the house came the minister's voice: "What will I do? What, what will I do? Anything, anything – that's what I'll do."

As squat and sturdy as a tugboat, her formidable bosom cleaving air like a prow cleaves water, Lulana sailed along the hallway, and Evangeline, like a stately tall-masted ship, followed in her wake.

In the kitchen, the minister stood at the sink, vigorously washing his hands. "Thou shall not, shall not, *shall not*, but I did. *Shall not*, but did."

Lulana opened the refrigerator and found room for both pies. "Evangeline, we have more nervous here than God made grass. Maybe it won't be needed, but best have some warm milk ready."

"You leave that to me, dear."

"Thank you, sister."

Clouds of steam rose from the sink. Lulana saw that under the rushing water, the minister's hands were fiery red.

"Pastor Kenny, you're about to half scald yourself."

"Just by being, I am. I am what I am. I am what I did. I did it, I did."

The faucet was so hot that Lulana had to wrap a dishtowel around her hand to turn it off.

Pastor Kenny tried to turn it on again.

She gently slapped his hand, as she might affectionately warn a child not to repeat a misbehavior. "Now, Pastor Kenny, you dry off and come sit at the table."

Without using the towel, the minister turned from the sink but also away from the table. On wobbly legs, drizzling water from his red hands, he headed toward the refrigerator.

He wailed and groaned, as they first heard him when they had been standing on the front porch.

Beside the refrigerator, a knife rack hung on the wall. Lulana believed Pastor Kenny to be a good man, a man of God, and she had no fear of him, but under the circumstances, it seemed a good idea to steer him away from knives.

With a wad of paper towels, Evangeline followed them, mopping the water off the floor.

Taking the minister by one arm, guiding him as best she could, Lulana said, "Pastor Kenny, you're much distressed, you're altogether beside yourself. You need to sit down and let out some nervous, let in some peace."

Although he appeared to be so stricken that he could hardly stay on his feet, the minister circled the table with her once and then half again before she could get him into a chair.

He sobbed but didn't weep. This was terror, not grief.

Already, Evangeline had found a large pot, which she filled with hot water at the sink.

The minister fisted his hands against his chest, rocked back and forth in his chair, his voice wrenched by misery. "So sudden, all of a sudden, I realized just what I am, what I did, what trouble I'm in, such *trouble*."

"We're here now, Pastor Kenny. When you share your troubles, they weigh less on you. You share them with me and Evangeline, and your troubles will weigh a third of what they do now."

Evangeline had put the pot of water on the cooktop and turned up the gas flame. Now she got a carton of milk from the refrigerator.

"You share your troubles with God, why, then they just float off your shoulders, no weight to them at all. Surely I don't need to tell you, of all people, how they'll float."

Having unclenched his hands and raised them before his face, he stared at them in horror. "Thou shall not, shall not, not, not, NOT!"

His breath did not smell of alcohol. She was loath to think that he might have inhaled something less wholesome than God's sweet air, but if the reverend was a cokehead, she supposed it was better to find out now than after Esther's teeth were fixed and the courtship had begun.

"We're given more shalls than shall-nots," Lulana said, striving to break through to him. "But there are enough shall-nots that I need you to be more specific. Shall not what, Pastor Kenny?"

"Kill," he said, and shuddered.

Lulana looked at her sister. Evangeline, milk carton in hand, raised her eyebrows.

"I did it, I did it. I did it, I did."

"Pastor Kenny," Lulana said, "I know you to be a gentle man, and kind. Whatever you think you've done, I'm sure it's not so terrible as you believe."

He lowered his hands. At last he looked at her. "I killed him."

"Who would that be?" Lulana asked.

"I never had a chance," the troubled man whispered. "He never had a chance. Neither of us had a chance."

Evangeline found a Mason jar into which she began to pour the milk from the carton.

"He's dead," said the minister.

"Who?" Lulana persisted.

"He's dead, and I'm dead. I was dead from the start."

In Lulana's cell phone were stored the many numbers of a large family, plus those of an even larger family of friends. Although Mr Aubrey – Aubrey Picou, her employer – had been finding his way to redemption faster than he realized (if slower than Lulana wished), he nonetheless remained a man with a scaly past that might one day snap back and bite him; therefore, in her directory were the office, mobile, and home numbers for Michael Maddison, in case Mr Aubrey ever needed a policeman to give him a fair hearing. Now she keyed in Michael's name, got his cell number, and called it.

chapter 43

In the windowless Victorian drawing room beyond the two vault doors, Erika circled the immense glass case, studying every detail. At first it had resembled a big jewel box, which it still did; but now it also seemed like a coffin, though an oversized and highly unconventional one.

She had no reason to believe that it contained a body. At the center of the case, the shape shrouded by the amber liquid – or gas – had no discernible limbs or features. It was just a dark mass without detail; it might have been anything.

If the case in fact contained a body, the specimen was large: about seven and a half feet long, more than three feet wide.

She examined the ornate ormolu frame under which the panels of glass were joined, searching for seams that might indicate concealed hinges. She could not find any. If the top of the box was a lid, it operated on some principle that eluded her.

When she rapped a knuckle against the glass, the sound suggested a thickness of at least one inch.

She noticed that under the glass, directly below the spot where her knuckle struck it, the amberness – whatever its nature – dimpled as water dimples when a stone drops into it. The dimple bloomed sapphire blue, resolved into a ring, and receded across the surface; the amber hue was reestablished in its wake.

She rapped again, with the same effect. When she rapped three times in succession, three concentric blue rings appeared, receded, faded.

Although her knuckle had made only the briefest contact, the glass had seemed cold. When she flattened her palm against it, she discovered that it was icy, though a few degrees too warm for her skin to freeze to it.

When she knelt on the Persian carpet and peered under the case, between its exquisitely sculpted ball-in-claw feet, she could see electrical conduits and pipes of various colors and diameters that came out of the bottom and disappeared into the floor. This suggested that a service room must lie below, although the mansion supposedly had no basement.

Victor owned one of the largest properties in the neighborhood and in fact had combined two great houses so elegantly that he had earned plaudits from historical preservationists. All of the interior reconstruction had been undertaken by members of the New Race, but not all of it had been disclosed to – or permitted by – the city's building department.

Her brilliant husband had achieved more than entire universities of scientists. His accomplishments were even more remarkable when you considered that he had been forced to do his work clandestinely – and since the regrettable death of Mao Tse-tung, without grants from any government.

She got to her feet and circled the case once more, trying to determine if there was a head or foot to it, as there would be to any bed or casket. The design of the object offered her no clue, but she at last decided, sheerly by intuition, that the head of it must be the end farthest from the door to the room.

Bending forward, bending low and lower, Erika put her face close to the top of the case, peering intently into the amber miasma, close and then closer, hoping for at least a faint suggestion of contour or texture to the shadowy shape within the liquid shroud.

When her lips were no more than two inches from the glass, she said softly, "Hello, hello, hello in there."

This time it *definitely* moved.

chapter 44

Dog-nose Nick stood on the rim of the pit, breathing deeply of the stink brought to him by a light breeze that came down out of the declining sun.

More than an hour ago, the last of the day's incoming trucks had dumped its load, and Crosswoods Waste Management had closed its gates until dawn. Now it was its own world, a universe encircled by chain-link topped with razor wire.

In the night ahead, the members of Nick Frigg's crew were free to be who they were, what they were. They could do what they wanted, without concern that an Old Race truck driver might see behavior that belied their pose of sanitation-worker normality.

Down in the west pit below him, crew members were wedging pole-mounted torches into the trash field in the area where the interments would take place. After nightfall, they would light the oil lamp at the top of each pole.

With their enhanced vision, Nick and his people didn't need as much light as they were providing, but for these ceremonies, torches set the perfect mood. Even those of the New Race, even Gammas like Nick, and even lowly Epsilons like the crew he bossed, could thrill to stagecraft.

Perhaps especially the Epsilons. They were more intelligent than animals, of course, but in some ways they were like animals in their simplicity and excitability.

Sometimes it seemed to Nick Frigg that the longer these Epsilons lived here in Crosswoods, having little contact with any Gamma other than he himself, having no contact at all with Betas or Alphas, the more simpleminded and more animalistic they became, as though without higher classes of the New Race to serve as examples, they could not entirely hold fast to even the meager knowledge and modest standards of deportment that had been downloaded into their brains while they had been in their tanks.

After the interments, the crew would feast, drink very much, and have sex. They would eat hungrily at the start, and soon they would be tearing at their food, gorging with abandon. The liquor would flow directly from bottle to mouth, mixed with nothing, undiluted, to maximize and accelerate its effect. The sex would be eager and selfish, then insistent and angry, then savage, no desire unindulged, no sensation unexperienced.

They would find relief from loneliness, meaninglessness. But the relief came only *during* the feeding, *during* the drinking and the sex. After, the anguish would return like a hammer, driving the nail deeper, deeper, deeper. Which they always forgot. Because they *needed* to forget.

At this moment, Gunny Alecto and other crew-men were at the walk-in cooler, loading the five human bodies and three dead gone-wrongs onto a pair of small, open-bed, four-wheel-drive trucks that would convey them to the site of the ceremony. The Old Race cadavers would be on one truck, the gone-wrongs on another.

The Old Race dead would be transported with less respect than gone-wrongs received, in fact with no respect at all. Their bodies would be subjected to grotesque indignities.

In the class structure of the New Race, the Epsilons had no one to whom they could feel superior – except those of the Old Race. And in these interment ceremonies, they expressed a hatred of such purity and such long-simmering reduction that no one in the history of the earth had ever despised more intensely, loathed more ferociously, or abominated their enemy with greater fury.

Some fun tonight.

chapter **45**

At the Hands of Mercy, none of the three isolation rooms had been designed to contain a deadly disease, for Victor did not have an interest in the engineering of microorganisms. There was no danger whatsoever that he would accidentally create a deadly new virus or bacterium.

Consequently, the twenty-by-fifteen-foot chamber that he chose for Werner was not surrounded by a positive-pressure envelope to prevent the escape of airborne microbes and spoors. Neither did it have its own self-contained ventilation system.

The isolation room had been meant solely to contain any New Race variant – he experimented with some exotic ones – that Victor suspected might prove difficult to manage and any that unexpectedly exhibited antisocial behavior of a lethal nature.

Therefore, the walls, ceiling, and floor of the chamber were of poured-in-place, steel-reinforced concrete to a thickness of eighteen inches. The interior surfaces had been paneled with three overlapping layers of quarter-inch steel plate.

If necessary, a killing electrical charge could be introduced into those steel plates with the flip of the switch in the adjoining monitor room.

Sole access to the isolation chamber was through a transition module between it and the monitor room.

The staff sometimes referred to it as the air lock, although this inaccurate term annoyed Victor. No atmosphere changes occurred during the use of the transition module, and there was not even a simple recycling of air.

The module featured two round steel doors that had been made for bank vaults. By design, it was mechanically impossible to have both doors open at the same time; therefore, when the inner door opened, a prisoner of the isolation chamber might get into the vestibule, but it could not break through into the monitor room.

On a gurney, his flesh undergoing cellular breakdown if not even molecular reorganization, Werner had been rushed through the halls of Mercy, into the monitor room, through the module, into the isolation chamber, with Victor urging the attendants to "hurry, faster, damn you, *run!*"

The staff might have thought that blind panic had seized their maker, but Victor couldn't concern himself with what they thought. Werner had been secured in that fortresslike cell, which was all that mattered.

When the hand had formed out of the amorphous flesh of Werner's torso, it had taken hold of Victor's hand tenderly, beseechingly. But the initial docility dared not be taken as a reliable prediction of a benign transformation.

Nothing remotely like this had ever happened before. Such a

sudden collapse of cellular integrity accompanied by self-driven biological reformation should not be possible.

Common sense suggested that such a radical metamorphosis, which must obviously include drastic changes in cerebral tissues, would entail the loss of a significant percentage of the direct-to-brain data and programming that Werner had received in the tank, including perhaps the proscription against killing his maker.

Prudence and responsible haste – not *panic* – had been required. As a man of unequaled scientific vision, Victor had at once foreseen the worst-case scenario and had acted with admirable calm yet with alacrity to respond to the danger and to contain the threat.

He made a mental note to circulate a stern memo to that effect throughout Mercy before the end of the day.

He would dictate it to Annunciata.

No, he would compose it and distribute it himself, and to hell with Annunciata.

In the monitor room, where Victor gathered with Ripley and four additional staff members, a bank of six rectangular high-definition screens, each displaying the closed-circuit feed from one of six cameras in the isolation chamber, revealed that Werner still remained in a disturbingly plastic condition. At the moment, he had four legs, no arms, and an ill-defined, continuously shifting body out of which thrust a vaguely Wernerlike head.

Highly agitated, the Werner thing jittered around the isolation chamber, mewling like a wounded animal and sometimes saying, "Father? Father? *Father?*"

This *father* business irritated Victor almost beyond the limits of his endurance. He didn't shout *Shut up, shut up, shut up* at the screens only because he wished to avoid the necessity of adding a second paragraph to that memo.

He did not want them to think of him as their father. They were not his family; they were his inventions, his fabrications, and most surely his property. He was their maker, their owner, their master, and even their leader, if they wished to think of him that way, but not their paterfamilias.

The family was a primitive and destructive institution because it put itself above the good of society as a whole. The parent-child relationship was counter-revolutionary and must be eradicated. For his creations, their entire race would be their family, each of them the brother or the sister of all the others, so that no particular relationship would be different from all the others or more special than all the others.

One race, one family, one great humming hive working in unison, without the distractions of individuality and family, could achieve *anything* to which it set its mind and its bottomless bustling energy, unhampered by childish emotions, freed from all superstition, could conquer any challenge that the universe might hold for it. A dynamic, unstoppable species of heretofore unimagined determination, gathering ever greater momentum, would rush on, rush on, to glory after glory, in his name.

Watching the four-legged, mewling, jittering Werner thing as it began to sprout something like but not like arms from its back, Ripley raised his ridiculous eyebrows and said, "Like Harker."

Victor at once rebuked him. "This is nothing like Harker. Harker was a singularity. Harker spawned a parasitical second self. Nothing like that is happening to Werner."

Riveted by the shocking images on the screen, Ripley said, "But, Mr Helios, sir, he appears to be—"

"Werner is not spawning a parasitical second self," Victor said tightly. "Werner is experiencing catastrophic cellular metamorphosis. It's not the same. It is not the same at all. Werner is a *different* singularity."

chapter 46

Cindi and Benny Lovewell, one a believer in the science of voodoo and one not, reestablished contact with Detectives O'Connor and Maddison through the signal emitted by the transponder under the hood of their police-department sedan. They caught up with their targets – but remained out of visual contact – in the Garden District.

For long minutes, the cops cruised the same few blocks, around and around, and then changed directions, cruising the identical territory in the opposite direction, making one circuit and then another.

"Like a blind rat in a maze," Cindi said solemnly, identifying as before with O'Connor's childlessness.

"No," Benny disagreed. "This is different."

"You wouldn't understand."

"I have the same capacity for understanding that you do."

"Not about this, you don't. You aren't female."

"Well, if it's necessary to have ever had a womb in order to be female, then you aren't female, either. You don't have a womb. You were not designed to produce a baby, and you cannot possibly become pregnant."

"We'll see what Ibo has to say about that," she replied smugly. *"Je suis rouge."*

Studying the blinking blip as it moved on the screen, Benny said, "They're cruising so slow . . ."

"You want to make contact, block them to the curb, knock 'em cold, and take them?"

"Not here. This is the kind of neighborhood where people call the police. We'll end up in a pursuit." After watching the screen for another minute, he said, "They're looking for something."

"For what?"

"How would I know?"

"Too bad Zozo Deslisle isn't here," Cindi said. "She has voodoo vision. Give her one look at that screen, and she'd know what they're up to."

"I'm wrong," Benny said. "They aren't searching. They've found what they want, and now they're casing it."

"Casing what? Thieves case banks. There aren't any banks in this neighborhood, only houses."

As Benny squinted at the screen, feeling an answer teasing along the edge of his mind, the target abruptly accelerated. The red blip hung a U-turn on the screen and started moving fast.

"What're they doing now?" Cindi asked.

"They're cops. Maybe they got an emergency call. Stay with them. Don't let them see us, but try to close to within a block. Maybe we'll get an opportunity."

A minute later, Cindi said, "They're heading for the Quarter. That's too public for us."

"Stay with them anyway."

The detectives didn't stop in the Quarter. They followed the curve of the river through Faubourg Marigny into the neighborhood known as Bywater.

The blip on the screen stopped moving, and by the time the Lovewells caught up with the plainwrap sedan, in the first orange flush of twilight, it was parked near a church, in front of a two-story brick house. O'Connor and Maddison were nowhere to be seen.

chapter 47

Carson sat across the kitchen table from Lulana St John, cater-corner to Pastor Kenny Laffite.

Michael stood near the cooktop, where Evangeline was heating a Mason jar full of milk in a pot of water.

"Heating it directly in a pan," she told Michael, "you risk scalding it."

"Then it gets a skin, doesn't it?" he asked.

She grimaced. "Burnt scum on the bottom and skin on top."

The minister sat with his arms on the table, staring with horror at his hands. "I just suddenly realized I did it. Just by being me, I killed him. And killing is *forbidden*."

"Pastor Laffite," Carson said, "you are not required by law to answer our questions without your attorney present. Do you want to call your attorney?"

"This good man didn't kill anybody," Lulana protested. "Whatever happened it was an accident."

Carson and Michael had already conducted a quick search of the house and had not found either a dead body or any signs of violence.

"Pastor Laffite," Carson said, "please look at me."

The minister kept staring at his hands. His eyes were opened as wide as eyes could be, and they weren't blinking.

"Pastor Laffite," she said, "forgive me, but you seem zoned-out and wigged-out at the same time. I'm concerned that you may recently have used an illegal drug."

"The moment I woke up," said the minister, "he was dead or soon to be. Just by waking up, I killed him."

"Pastor Laffite, do you understand that anything you say to me now could be used against you in a court of law?"

"This good man won't ever be in a court of law," Lulana said. "He's just confused somehow. That's why I wanted you two instead of others. I knew you wouldn't leap to conclusions."

The minister's eyes had still not blinked. They weren't tearing up, either. They should have started to tear up from not blinking.

From his post by the cooktop, Michael said, "Pastor, who is it you think you killed?"

"I killed Pastor Kenny Laffite," the minister said.

Lulana gave herself to surprise with some enthusiasm, pulling her head back, letting her jaw drop, putting one hand to her bosom. "Praise the Lord, Pastor Kenny, you can't have killed yourself. You're sitting right here with us."

He switched from zoned to wigged again: "See, see, see, it's like this, it's fundamental. I'm not permitted to kill. But by the very fact of my existence, by the very *fact*, I am at least partly responsible for his death, so on the very day of my creation, I was in violation

FRANKENSTEIN *city of night* 229

of my program. My program is flawed. If my program is flawed, what else might I do that I'm not supposed to do, what else, what else, *what else?*"

Carson glanced at Michael.

He had been leaning casually against the counter by the cooktop. He was standing tall now, his hands hanging loose at his sides.

"Pastor Kenny," Lulana said, taking one of his hands in both of hers, "you've been under a terrible stress, tryin' to raise funds for the church remodel on top of all your other duties—"

"—five weddings in one month," Evangeline added. Holding the Mason jar with an oven mitt, she poured warm milk into a glass. "And three funerals besides."

Carson eased her chair back from the table as Lulana said, "And all of this work you've had to do without the comfort of a wife. It's no surprise you're exhausted and distressed."

Spooning sugar into the milk, Evangeline said, "Our own Uncle Absalom worked himself to the bone without the comfort of a wife, and one day he started seeing fairies."

"By which she means not homosexuals," Lulana assured Laffite, "but the little creatures with wings."

Carson rose from her chair and took a step away from the table as Evangeline, adding several drops of vanilla extract to the milk, said, "Seeing fairies was nothing to be ashamed about. Uncle Absalom just needed some rest, some tender care, and he was fine, never saw fairies again."

"I'm not supposed to kill people, but by the very *fact* of my existence, I killed Kenny Laffite," said Kenny Laffite, "and I really want to kill more."

"That's just weariness talking," Lulana assured him, and patted his hand. "Crazy weariness, that's all, Pastor Kenny. You don't want to kill anyone."

"I do," he disagreed. He closed his eyes and hung his head. "And now if my program is flawed, maybe I will. I want to kill all of you, and maybe I will."

Michael blocked Evangeline from carrying the glass of milk to the table.

Executing a smooth cross-body draw of the Desert Eagle from the scabbard on her left hip, gripping it in two hands, Carson said, "Lulana, you said when we first came that you stopped by to bring Pastor Laffite two pies."

Lulana's molasses-brown eyes were huge and focused on the golden gun. "Carson O'Connor, this is an overreaction not worthy of you. This poor—"

"Lulana," Carson interrupted with the slightest edge in her voice, "why don't you get one of those pies out of the refrigerator and cut some for all of us."

With his head still hung, with his chin on his chest and eyes closed, Laffite said, "My program's breaking down. I can feel it happening . . . sort of a slow-motion stroke. Lines of installed code falling out, falling off, like a long row of electrified birds dropping off a power line."

Evangeline Antoine said, "Sister, maybe that pie would be a good idea."

As Lulana, on further consideration, pushed her chair away from the table and got to her feet, Michael's cell phone rang.

Laffite raised his head but did not open his eyes. The rapid eye movement behind his closed lids was that of a man experiencing vivid dreams.

Michael's phone rang again, and Carson said, "Don't let it go to voice mail."

As Lulana moved not toward the refrigerator but instead toward her sister and out of the line of fire, Laffite said, "How odd that this should be happening to an Alpha."

Carson heard Michael giving the address of the parsonage to the caller.

As his eyes continued to roll and twitch under his lids, Laffite said, "'The thing which I greatly feared is come upon me.'"

"Job three, verse twenty-five," said Lulana.

"'Fear came upon me,'" Laffite continued, "'and trembling, which made all my bones to shake.'"

"Job four, verse fourteen," said Evangeline.

To reach either the door to the back porch or the door to the hallway, the sisters would have had to pass into the line of fire. They huddled together in the safest corner of the kitchen that they could find.

Having concluded his phone call, Michael positioned himself to Carson's left, between Laffite and the sisters, his own .50 Magnum in a two-hand grip.

"'Gather me the people together,'" said Laffite, "'and I will make them hear my words, that they may learn to fear me all the days that they shall live upon the earth.'"

"Deuteronomy," Lulana said.

"Chapter four, verse ten," Evangeline added.

"Deucalion?" Carson murmured, referring to the phone call.

"Yeah."

Laffite opened his eyes. "I've revealed myself to you. Further proof that my program is breaking down. We must move secretly among you, never revealing our difference or our purpose."

"We're cool," Michael told him. "We don't have a problem with it. Just sit for a while, Pastor Kenny, just sit there and watch the little birds dropping off the wire."

chapter 48

Randal Six is angry with himself for killing Arnie's mother. "Stupid," he says. "Stupid."

He is not angry with her. There is no point being angry with a dead person.

He didn't intend to hit her. He just suddenly found himself *doing* it, in the same way that he broke the neck of the hobo in the Dumpster.

In retrospect, he sees that he was not in danger. Self-defense did not require such extreme measures.

After his sheltered existence at the Hands of Mercy, he needs more experience in the larger world to be able accurately to judge the seriousness of a threat.

Then he discovers that Arnie's mother is only unconscious. This relieves him of the need to be angry with himself.

Although he had been angry with himself for less than two minutes, the experience was grueling. When other people are angry with you – as Victor often is – you can turn further inward and escape from them. When it is you yourself who is angry with you, turning inward does not work because no matter how deep you go inside yourself, the angry you is still there.

The knife wound in his hand has already stopped bleeding. The lacerations will be completely closed in two or three hours.

The splatters of blood on the floor and the appliances distress him. These stains detract from the almost spiritual atmosphere that reigns here. This is a *home*, and the kitchen is its heart, and at all times there should be a feeling of calm, of peace.

With paper towels and a spray bottle of Windex, he wipes away the blood.

Carefully, without touching her skin, because he does not like the feel of other people's skin, Randal ties the mother to the chair with lengths of cloth that he tears from the garments in the laundryroom basket.

As he finishes securing her, the mother regains consciousness. She is anxious, agitated, full of questions and assumptions and pleas.

Her shrill tone of voice and her frantic chatter make Randal nervous. She is asking a third question before he can answer the first. Her demands on him are too many, the input from her too great to process.

Rather than hit her, he walks down the hall to the living room, where he stands for a while. Twilight has come. The room is nearly dark. No excited talking mother is present. In mere minutes, he feels much better.

He returns to the kitchen, and the moment he arrives there, the mother starts chattering again.

When he tells her to be quiet, she becomes more vocal than ever, and her pleas become more urgent.

He almost wishes that he were back under the house with the spiders.

She is not behaving like a mother. Mothers are calm. Mothers have all the answers. Mothers love you.

Generally, Randal Six does not like touching others or being touched. This is perhaps different. This is a mother even if she is not at the moment acting like one.

He places his right hand under her chin and forces her mouth shut, even as he pinches her nose with his left hand. She struggles at first but then becomes still when she realizes that he is very strong.

Before the mother passes out from oxygen deprivation, Randal takes his hand from her nose and allows her to breathe. He continues to hold her mouth shut.

"Ssshhhhh," he says. "Quiet. Randal likes quiet. Randal scares too easy. Noise scares Randal. Too much talk, too many words scares Randal. Don't scare Randal."

When he feels that she is ready to cooperate, he releases her. She says nothing. She is breathing hard, almost gasping, but she is done with talking for now.

Randal Six turns off the gas flame at the cooktop to prevent the onions from burning in the pan. This constitutes a higher level of involvement with his environment than he's exhibited before, an awareness of peripheral issues, and he is pleased with himself.

Perhaps he will discover a talent for cooking.

He gets a tablespoon from the flatware drawer and the quart of strawberry-banana swirl from the freezer. He sits at the kitchen table, across from Arnie's mother, and spoons the pink-and-yellow treat from the container.

This is not better than brown food, but it is not worse. Just different, still wonderful.

He smiles across the table at her because this seems to be a domestic moment – perhaps even an important bonding moment – that requires a smile.

Clearly, however, she is distressed by his smile, perhaps because she can tell that it is calculated and not sincere. Mothers know.

"Randal will ask some questions. You will answer. Randal does not want to hear your too many, too noisy questions. Just answers. Short answers, not chatter."

She understands. She nods.

"My name is Randal." When she does not respond, he says, "Oh. What is your name?"

"Vicky."

"For now, Randal will call you Vicky. Will it be all right if Randal calls you Vicky?"

"Yes."

"You are the first mother that Randal has ever met. Randal does not want to kill mothers. Do you want to be killed?"

"No. Please."

"Many people do want to be killed. Mercy people. Because they aren't able to kill themselves."

He pauses to spoon more ice cream into his mouth.

Licking his lips, he continues: "This tastes better than spiders and earthworms and rodents would've tasted. Randal likes in a house better than under a house. Do you like it better in a house than under a house?"

"Yes."

"Have you ever been in a Dumpster with a dead hobo?"

She stares at him and says nothing.

He assumes that she is searching her memory, but after a while, he says, "Vicky? Have you ever been in a Dumpster with a dead hobo?"

"No. No, I haven't."

Randal Six has never been so proud of himself as he is at this moment. This is the first conversation he has had with anyone other than his maker at Mercy. And it is going *so* well.

chapter **49**

Werner's lifelong problem with excess mucus production was a minor annoyance compared to his current tribulations.

In the monitor room, Victor, Ripley, and four awe-stricken staff members watched the six closed-circuit screens as the security chief careened around the isolation chamber on four legs. The back two were as they had been at the start of this episode. Although his forelegs closely resembled the back pair, the articulation of the shoulder joints had changed dramatically.

The powerful shoulders suggested those of a jungle cat. As Werner prowled restlessly in that other room, his metamorphosis continued, and all four legs began to appear increasingly feline. As in any cat, an elbow developed at the posterior terminus of the shoulder muscle to complement a foreleg joint structure that included a knee but a more flexible wrist instead of an ankle.

This intrigued Victor because he had included in Werner's design selected genetic material from a panther to increase his agility and speed.

The hind legs became more feline, developing a long metatarsus above the toes, a heel midway up the limb, and a knee close to the body trunk. The relationship between the rump, the thigh, and the flank shifted, proportions changing as well.

On the hind legs, the human feet melted completely into pawlike structures with blunt toes that featured impressive claws. On the forelegs, however, though dewclaws formed at the pasterns, elements of the human hand persisted, even if the fingers now terminated in claw sheaths and claws.

All of these transformations presented themselves clearly for consideration because Werner did not develop fur. He was hairless and pink.

Although this crisis had not passed – in fact may only have begun – Victor was able to bring cool scientific detachment to his observations now that Werner had been contained and the threat of imminent violence had been eliminated.

Often over the decades, he had learned more from his setbacks than from his numerous successes. Failure could be a legitimate father of progress, especially *his* failures, which were more likely to advance the cause of knowledge than were the greatest triumphs of lesser scientists.

Victor was fascinated by the bold manifestation of nonhuman characteristics for which no genes had been included. Although the security chief's *musculature* had been enhanced with genetic material from a panther, he did not carry the code that would express feline legs, and he *certainly* had not been engineered to have a tail, which now began to form.

The Werner head, still familiar, moved on a thicker and more sinuous neck than any man had ever enjoyed. The eyes, when turned toward a camera, appeared to have the elliptical irises of a cat, though no genes related to feline vision had been spliced into his chromosomes.

This suggested either that Victor had made a mistake with Werner or that somehow Werner's astonishingly amorphous flesh was able to extrapolate every detail of an animal from mere scraps of its genetic structure. Although it was an outrageous concept, flatly impossible, he leaned toward that second explanation.

In addition to the six-camera coverage of Werner's lycanthropy-quick metamorphosis, microphones in the isolation chamber fed his voice into the monitor room. Whether he was aware of the full extent of the physical changes racking his body could not be determined by what he said, for unfortunately his words were gibberish. Mostly he screamed.

Judging by the intensity and the nature of the screams, both mental anguish and unrelenting physical agony accompanied the metamorphosis. Evidently, Werner no longer possessed the ability to switch off pain.

When suddenly a clear word was discernible – "Father, Father' – Victor killed the audio feed and satisfied himself with the silent images.

Scientists at Harvard, Yale, Oxford, and every major research university in the world had in recent years been experimenting with cross-species genesplicing. They had inserted genetic material of spiders into goats, which then produced milk laced with webs. They had bred mice that carried bits of human DNA, and several teams were in competition to be the first to produce a pig with a human brain.

"But only I," Victor declared, gazing at the six screens, "have created the chimera of ancient myth, the beast of many parts that functions as one creature."

"Is he functioning?" Ripley asked.

"You can see as well as I," Victor replied impatiently. "He runs with great speed."

"In tortured circles."

"His body is supple and strong."

"And changing again," said Ripley.

Werner, too, had something of the spider in him, and something of the cockroach, to increase the ductility of his tendons, to invest his collagen with greater tensile-strain capacity. Now these arachnid and insectile elements appeared to be expressing themselves at the expense of the panther form.

"Biological chaos," Ripley whispered.

"Pay attention," Victor advised him. "In this we will find clues that will lead inevitably to the greatest advancements in the history of genetics and molecular biology."

"Are we absolutely sure," Ripley asked, "that the transition-module doors completed their lock cycle?"

All four of the other staff members answered as one: "Yes."

The image on one of the six screens blurred to gray, and the face of Annunciata materialized.

Assuming that she had appeared in error, Victor almost shouted at her to disengage.

Before he could speak, however, she said, "Mr Helios, an Alpha has made an urgent request for a meeting with you."

"Which Alpha?"

"Patrick Duchaine, rector of Our Lady of Sorrows."

"Patch his call through to these speakers."

"He did not telephone, Mr Helios. He came to the front door of Mercy."

Because these days the Hands of Mercy presented itself to the world as a private warehouse with little daily business, those born here did not return for any purpose, lest an unusual flow of visitors might belie the masquerade. Duchaine's visit was a breach of protocol that suggested he had news of an important nature to impart.

"Send him to me," Victor told Annunciata.

"Yes, Mr Helios. Yes."

chapter 50

Laffite opened his eyes. "I've revealed myself to you. Further proof that my program is breaking down. We must move secretly among you, never revealing our difference or our purpose."

"We're cool," Michael told him. "We don't have a problem with it. Just sit for a while, Pastor Kenny, just sit there and watch the little birds dropping off the wire."

As Michael spoke those words, less than a minute after he had terminated his cell-phone conversation with Deucalion, the giant entered the parsonage kitchen from the downstairs hall.

Carson had grown so accustomed to the big man's inexplicable arrivals and mysterious departures that the Desert Eagle in her two-hand grip didn't twitch a fraction of an inch but remained sighted dead-still on the minister's chest.

"What — you called me from the front porch?" Michael asked.

Immense, fearsome, tattooed, Deucalion nodded to Lulana and

Evangeline, and said, "'God has not given us the spirit of fear, but of power, and of love, and of a sound mind.'"

"Timothy," Lulana said shakily, "chapter one, verse seven."

"I may look like a devil," Deucalion told the sisters, to put them at ease, "but if I ever was one, I am not anymore."

"He's a good guy," Michael assured them. "I don't know a Bible verse for the occasion, but I guarantee he's a good guy."

Deucalion sat at the table, in the chair that Lulana recently had occupied. "Good evening, Pastor Laffite."

The minister's eyes had been glazed, as if he'd been staring through the veil between this world and another. Now he focused on Deucalion.

"I didn't recognize Timothy one, verse seven," Laffite said. "More of my program is dropping out. I'm losing who I am. Say me another verse."

Deucalion recited: "'Behold, he is all vanity. His works are nothing. His molten images are wind and confusion.'"

"I do not know it," said the preacher.

"Isaiah sixteen, verse twenty-nine," said Evangeline, "but he's tweaked it a little."

To Deucalion, Laffite said, "You chose a verse that describes . . . Helios."

"Yes."

Carson wondered if she and Michael could lower their guns. She decided that if it was wise to do so, Deucalion would already have advised them to relax. She stayed ready.

"How can you know about Helios?" Laffite asked.

"I was his first. Crude by your standards."

"But your program hasn't dropped out."

"I don't even have a program as you think of it."

Laffite shuddered violently and closed his eyes. "Something just went. What was it?"

His eyes again moved rapidly up and down, side to side, under his lids.

"I can give you what you want most," Deucalion told him.

"I think . . . yes . . . I have just lost the ability to switch off pain."

"Have no fear. I will make it painless. One thing I want from you in return."

Laffite said nothing.

"You have spoken his name," Deucalion said, "and have shown that in some other ways, your program no longer restrains you. So tell me . . . the place where you were born, where he does his work."

His voice thickening slightly as if points had been shaved off his IQ, Laffite said, "I am a child of Mercy. Mercy born and Mercy raised."

"What does that mean?" Deucalion pressed.

"The Hands of Mercy," said Laffite. "The Hands of Mercy and the tanks of Hell."

"It's an old Catholic hospital," Carson realized. "The Hands of Mercy."

"They closed it down when I was just a little kid," Michael said. "It's something else now, a warehouse. They bricked in all the windows."

"I could kill you all now," Laffite said, but he did not open his eyes. "I used to want to kill you all. So bad, I used to want it, so bad."

Lulana began to weep softly, and Evangeline said, "Hold my hand, sister."

To Carson, Deucalion said, "Take the ladies out of here. Take them home now."

"One of us could take them home," she suggested, "and one of us stay here to give you backup."

"This is between just me and Pastor Laffite. I need to give him a little grace, a little grace and a long rest."

Returning the Magnum to his holster, Michael said, "Ladies, you should take your praline pies with you. They don't prove beyond doubt that you were here, but you should take them with you anyway."

As the women retrieved the pies from the refrigerator and as Michael shepherded them out of the kitchen, Carson kept the gun on Laffite.

"We'll meet later at your house," Deucalion told her. "In a little while."

"'Darkness was upon the face of the deep,'" Laffite said in his thicker voice. "Is that one, or have I remembered nothing?"

"Genesis one, verse two," Deucalion told him. Then he indicated with a gesture that Carson should leave.

She lowered the pistol and reluctantly departed.

As she stepped into the hall, she heard Laffite say, "He says we'll live a thousand years. I feel as if I already have."

chapter 51

In the secret drawing room Erika considered speaking again to the occupant of the glass case.

Without question, it had moved: a shadowy spasm within its amber shroud of liquid or gas. Either it had responded to her voice or the timing of its movement had been coincidental.

The Old Race had a saying: There are no coincidences.

They were superstitious, however, and irrational.

As she had been taught in the tank, the universe is nothing *but* a sea of chaos in which random chance collides with happenstance and spins shatters of meaningless coincidence like shrapnel through our lives.

The purpose of the New Race is to impress order on the face of chaos, to harness the awesome destructive power of the universe and make it serve their needs, to bring meaning to a creation that has been meaningless since time immemorial. And the meaning they will impose upon it is the meaning of their maker, the exalt- ation of his name and face, the fulfillment of his vision and his every desire, their satisfaction achieved solely by the perfect implementation of his will.

That creed, part of her basic programming, rose into her mind word for word, with remembered music by Wagner and images of millions of the New Race marching in cadence. Her brilliant husband could have been a poet if mere poetry had not been unworthy of his genius.

After she had spoken to the occupant of the case, a primal fear had overcome her, seeming to rise from her very blood and bone, and she retreated to the wingback chair, where she still sat, not just pondering her options but analyzing her motivation.

She had been shaken by William's amputation of his fingers and by his termination. She had been more deeply moved by Christine's revelation that she, Erika, had been given a richer emotional life – humility, shame, the potential for pity and compassion – than others of the New Race were granted.

Victor, whose genius was unparalleled in all of history, must have good reason for restricting all other of his people to hatred, envy, anger, and emotions that only turned back upon themselves and did not lead to hope. She was his humble creation, of value only to the extent that she could serve him. She did not have the insight, the knowledge, or the necessary breadth of vision to imagine that she had any right to question his design.

She herself hoped for many things. Most important of all, she hoped to become a better wife, better day by day, and to see approval in Victor's eyes. Although she had so recently arisen from the tank and had not yet lived much, she couldn't imagine a life without hope.

If she became a better wife, if eventually she no longer earned a beating during sex, if one day he cherished her, she hoped that she might ask him to allow Christine and others to have hope as she did, and that he would grant her request and give her people gentler lives.

"I am Queen Esther to his King Ahasuerus," she said, comparing herself to the daughter of Mordecai. Esther had persuaded Ahasuerus to spare her people, the Jews, from annihilation at the hands of Haman, a prince of his realm.

Erika did not know the full story, but she had confidence that the literary allusion, one of thousands in her repertoire, was sound and that, per her programming, she had used it properly.

So.

She must strive to become cherished by Victor. To do so, she must serve him always to perfection. To meet that goal, she must know everything about him, not merely the biography that she had received in direct-to-brain data downloading.

Everything necessarily included the occupant of the tank, which evidently had been imprisoned by Victor. Regardless of the profound fear that it had triggered in her, she must return to the case, face this chaos, and impress order upon it.

At the head of the casket – it definitely seemed more like a casket now than like a jewel box – Erika again lowered her face to the glass at the point directly above where she imagined the face of the occupant waited submerged in amber.

As before, but with less lilt in her voice, she said, "Hello, hello, hello in there."

The dark shape stirred again, and this time the sound waves of her voice appeared to send blue pulses through the case as the rap of her knuckle had done earlier.

Her lips had been six inches above the glass when she spoke. She leaned closer. Three inches.

"I am Queen Esther to his King Ahasuerus," she said.

The pulses were a more intense blue than before, and the shadowy occupant seemed to rise closer to the underside of the glass, so she could see the suggestion of a face, but no details.

She said again, "I am Queen Esther to his King Ahasuerus."

Out of the throbbing blue, out of the unseen face, came a voice in answer, somehow unmuffled by the glass: "You are Erika Five, and you are mine."

chapter 52

After the black tongue of night licked the last purple off the western horizon, the oil lamps were ignited atop the poles in the west pit.

Like phantom dragons, wings and tails of lambent orange light chased across the trash field, and shadows leaped.

Thirteen of the fourteen members of Nick's crew were with him in the pit, wearing hip-high boots, faces glistening, lined up in eager anticipation along the route that the pair of low, open-bed trucks would take to the place of interment.

Beside him stood Gunny Alecto, her eyes shining with reflected fire. "Saving savant savour sausages sandwiches savages. *Savages!* Here come the dead savages, Nick. You got your stuff?"

"I got it."

"You got your *stuff?*"

He raised his pail, which was like her pail, like the pail that each of them carried.

The first of the trucks descended the sloped wall of the pit and growled across the desolation, uncountable varieties of garbage crunching and crackling under the tires.

Five sturdy poles, seven feet high, rose from the bed of the truck. To each pole had been lashed one of the dead members of the Old Race, who had been replaced by replicants. Three had been city bureaucrats, and two had been police officers. Two were female; three were male.

The cadavers had been stripped of clothes. Their eyes had been taped open to give the impression that they bore witness to their humiliation.

The mouths of the dead were wedged open with sticks because their tormentors liked to imagine that they were pleading for mercy or at least were screaming.

One of the males had been delivered dismembered and decapitated. The Crosswoods crew had wired the parts together with malicious glee, putting the head on backward, comically repositioning the genitals.

As the truck drew near, the assembled crew began to jeer the dead with enthusiasm, with mocking laughter and catcalls, louder than they were articulate.

Epsilons, lowest of the rigid social order, were allowed to have contempt for no one of their own race, only for the one-heart men and women who claimed to be the children of God yet could not turn off pain and died so easily. With jeers and venomous laughter, these simplest products of the tanks expressed their detestation and thereby claimed their superiority.

As the truck came to a stop, the crew looked excitedly at Nick, who stood at the midpoint of the lineup. As a Gamma among

Epsilons, he must lead by example, even though they, not he, had conceived this ceremony and designed these rituals.

From his pail, he scooped a reeking mass. Always available in a dump were rotting fruits and vegetables, filth in infinite variety, decomposing this and rancid that. During the day, he had collected choice items. Now, with a cry of contempt, he hurled his first handful at one of the cadavers on the truck.

The splattery impact drew a cheer from the Epsilons. After his example, they scooped foul wads from their buckets and pelted the hoisted dead.

As the wide-eyed, open-mouthed corpses endured this sustained barrage, the jeers of the tormenting crew grew more vicious, less verbal and more vocal. The laughter became too shrill to have any quality whatsoever of merriment, and then grew too bitter to be mistaken for any kind of laughter at all.

When the Epsilons had exhausted their ammunition, they threw the empty pails and then flung themselves upon the truck, tearing fervently at the bindings that held the cadavers to the poles. As they freed each stained and dripping body, they pitched it from the truck into a nearby shallow depression in the trash field, which would serve as a mass grave.

Although Nick Frigg did not climb onto the open-bed pillory with his shrieking crew, their rage and their hatred excited him, inflamed his own resentment against those supposedly God-made people who claimed free will, dignity, and hope. He cheered on the denizens of Crosswoods and tossed his greasy hair and shook his fists at the night, and felt *empowered* by the thought that one day soon his kind would reveal themselves in all their inhuman ferocity and would show the self-satisfied Old Race how quickly their

precious free will could be stripped from them, how brutally their
dignity could be destroyed, and how utterly their pathetic hope
could be extinguished forever.

Now came the symbolic killing.

When the five cadavers had been tossed from the truck, the
Epsilons, including the driver, scrambled to the gravesite in full cry.

They longed to kill, *craved* killing, lived with a *need* to kill that
was intense to the point of anguish, yet they were forbidden to
uncork their wrath until their maker gave permission. The frustra-
tion of their shackled lives daily paid compound interest on the
principal of their anger until they were rich with it, each of them
a treasury of rage.

In the symbolic killing, they spent mere pennies of their wealth
of wrath. They stomped, stomped, kicked, punted, ground their
heels, threw their arms around one another's shoulders and circle-
danced in groups of four and six, danced among the dead and
certainly *upon* the dead, in ferocious hammering rhythms, filling
the torch-lit night with the dreadful drumming, timpani and
tom-tom and bass drums and kettle, but all in fact the boom of
booted feet.

Although a Gamma, dog-nose Nick was infected by the excitement of the Epsilons, and a fever of fury boiled his blood, too, as
he joined them in this dance of death, linking himself into a circle
with the conviction that any Beta would have done the same, or
even any Alpha, for this was an expression not merely of the frustra-
tion of the lowest class of the New Race but also of the yearning
and the repressed desires of all the children of Mercy, who were
made for different work and loaded with different programs, but
who were as one in their hatred and their wrath.

Shrieking, howling, hooting, screaming, their sweating faces dark with desire, bright with torchlight, they stomped what they had previously jeered, ritually killing those who were already dead, the drumfire of their feet shaking the night with a promise of the final war to come.

chapter 53

From across the street and half a block away, Cindi and Benny Lovewell watched O'Connor and Maddison escort two black women from the parsonage to the plainwrap sedan, which was parked under a streetlamp.

"We'd probably end up killing one or both of the women to nab the cops," Cindi said.

Considering that they were not authorized to kill anyone but the detectives, Benny said, "We better wait."

"What are the women carrying?" Cindi wondered.

"Pies, I think."

"Why are they carrying pies?"

"Maybe they were caught stealing them," Benny suggested.

"Do people steal pies?"

"*Their* kind of people do. They steal everything."

She said, "Aren't O'Connor and Maddison homicide detectives?"

"Yeah."

"Then why would they rush out here to arrest pie thieves?"

Benny shrugged. "I don't know. Maybe the women killed someone for the pies."

Frowning, Cindi said, "That's possible, I suppose. But I have the feeling we're missing something. Neither one of them looks like a killer."

"Neither do we," Benny reminded her.

"If they *did* kill for the pies, why would they be allowed to keep them?"

"Their legal system doesn't make much sense to me," Benny said. "I don't really care about the women or the pies. I just want to rip the guts out of O'Connor and Maddison."

"Well, so do I," Cindi said. "Just because I want a baby doesn't mean I still don't enjoy killing."

Benny sighed. "I didn't mean to imply that you were going soft or anything."

When the women and the pies had been loaded in the backseat, O'Connor got behind the wheel, and Maddison sat shotgun.

"Follow them just short of visual," Benny said. "We want to be able to move in quick if there's an opportunity at the other end."

The unmarked police car pulled away from the curb, and when it turned out of sight at the corner, Cindi followed in the Mountaineer.

Instead of conveying the black women to a police lockup, the detectives drove them only two blocks, to another house in Bywater.

Once again parking half a block away and across the street, in the shadows between two streetlamps, Cindi said, "This is no good. At half these houses, people are sitting on the front porch. Too many witnesses."

"Yeah," Benny agreed. "We might snatch O'Connor and Maddison, but we'll end up in a police chase."

They needed to be discreet. If the authorities identified them as professional killers, they would no longer be able to do their jobs. They would not be authorized to kill any more people, and indeed their maker would terminate *them*.

"Look at all these morons. What're they doing sitting on a porch in a rocking chair?" Cindi wondered.

"They sit and drink beer or lemonade, or something, and some of them smoke, and they talk to one another."

"What do they talk about?"

"I don't know."

"They're so . . . *unfocused*," Cindi said. "What's the point of their lives?"

"I heard one of them say the purpose of life is living."

"They just sit there. They aren't trying to take over the world and gain total command of nature, or anything."

"They already own the world," Benny reminded her.

"Not for long."

chapter 54

Sitting at the table in the kitchen of the parsonage with the replicant of Pastor Laffite, Deucalion said, "How many of your kind have been infiltrated into the city?"

"I only know my number," Laffite replied in a slowly thickening voice. He sat staring at his hands, which were palm-up on the table, as if he were reading two versions of his future. "Nineteen hundred and eighty-seven. There must be many more since me."

"How fast can he produce his people?"

"From gestation to maturity, he's got it down to four months in the tank."

"How many tanks are in operation at the Hands of Mercy?"

"There used to be one hundred and ten."

"Three crops a year," Deucalion said, "times one hundred ten. He could turn out three hundred and thirty a year."

"Not quite so many. Because now and then he makes . . . other things."

"What other things?"

"I don't know. Rumors. Things that aren't humanoid. New forms. Experiments. You know what I'd like?"

"Tell me," Deucalion encouraged.

"One last piece of chocolate. I like chocolate very much."

"Where do you keep it?"

"There's a box in the fridge. I'd get it, but I'm beginning to have some difficulty with recognition of spatial relationships. I'm not sure I can walk properly. I'd have to crawl."

"I'll get it," Deucalion said.

He fetched the chocolates from the refrigerator, took off the lid, and put the box on the table before Laffite.

As Deucalion settled into his chair again, Laffite reached for a piece of candy, but groped beyond and to the left of the box.

Gently, Deucalion guided Laffite's right hand to the chocolates and then watched as the pastor felt piece after piece, almost like a blind man, before selecting one.

"They say he's ready to start up a farm outside the city," Laffite revealed. "Next week or the week after."

"What farm?"

"A New Race farm, two thousand tanks all under one roof, disguised as a factory or greenhouses."

When Laffite could not find his mouth with his hand, Deucalion guided the candy to his lips. "That's a production capacity of six thousand."

Closing his eyes once more, Pastor Laffite chewed the candy with pleasure. He tried to talk with the chocolate in his mouth but seemed no longer capable of speaking while he ate.

"Take your time," Deucalion told him. "Enjoy it."

After swallowing the chocolate and licking his lips, still with his eyes closed, Laffite said, "A second farm is under construction and will be ready by the first of the year, with an even greater number of tanks."

"Do you know Victor's schedule at the Hands of Mercy? When does he go there? When does he leave?"

"I don't know. He's there much of the time, more than anywhere else in his life."

"How many of your kind work at Mercy?"

"Eighty or ninety, I think. I don't know for sure."

"Security must be tight."

"Everyone who works there is also a killing machine. I might like a second chocolate."

Deucalion helped him find the box and then get the morsel to his mouth.

When Laffite was not eating chocolate, his eyes rolled and twitched beneath his lids. When he had candy in his mouth, his eyes were still.

After he finished the sweet, Laffite said, "Do you find the world more mysterious than it's supposed to be?"

"Who says it isn't supposed to be?"

"Our maker. But do you find yourself wondering about things?"

"About many things, yes," Deucalion said.

"I wonder, too. I wonder. Do you think dogs have souls?"

chapter 55

On the walkway at the foot of Lulana's front-porch steps, with the sweet scent of jasmine on the early-night air, Carson said to the sisters, "It's best if you don't tell anyone a word about what happened at the parsonage."

As though distrusting the steadiness of her hands, Lulana used both to hold the praline pie.

"Who was the giant?"

"You wouldn't believe me," Carson said, "and if I told you, I wouldn't be doing you a favor."

Coddling the second pie, Evangeline said, "What was wrong with Pastor Kenny? What's going to happen to him?"

Instead of answering her, Michael said, "For your peace of mind, you ought to know that your preacher long ago went to his final rest. The man you called Pastor Kenny there tonight . . . you have no reason to grieve for him."

The sisters exchanged a glance. "Something strange has come into the world, hasn't it?" Lulana asked Carson, but clearly expected no answer. "There tonight, the coldest expectation crept over me, like maybe it was . . . end times."

Evangeline said, "Maybe we should pray on it, sister."

"Can't hurt," Michael said. "Might help. And have yourselves a piece of pie."

Suspicion squinted Lulana's eyes. "Mr Michael, it sounds to me like you mean have ourselves a nice piece of pie while there's still time."

Michael avoided replying, but Carson said, "Have yourselves a piece of pie. Have two."

In the car again, as Carson pulled away from the curb, Michael said, "Did you see the white Mercury Mountaineer about half a block back on the other side of the street?"

"Yeah."

"Just like the one in the park."

Studying the rearview mirror, she said, "Yeah. And just like the one down the street from the parsonage."

"I wondered if you saw that one."

"What, I'm suddenly blind?"

"Is it coming after us?"

"Not yet."

She wheeled right at the corner.

Turning in his seat to peer into the dark street that they were leaving behind, he said, "They're still not coming. Well, there's bound to be more than one white Mountaineer in a city this size."

"And this is just one of those freaky days when we happen to cross paths with all of them."

"Maybe we should have asked Godot for some hand grenades," Michael said.

"I'm sure he delivers."

"He probably gift-wraps. Where now?"

"My place," Carson told him. "Maybe it would be a good idea, after all, if Vicky moved Arnie somewhere."

"Like some nice quiet little town in Iowa."

"And back to 1956, when Frankenstein was just Colin Clive and Boris Karloff, and Mary Shelley was just a novelist instead of a prophet and historian."

chapter 56

On the six closed-circuit screens, the insectile manifestation of the Werner entity, still in possession of some human features, crawled the steel walls of the isolation chamber, sometimes in the cautious manner of a stalking predator, at other times as quick as a frightened roach, agitated and jittering.

Victor could not have imagined that any news brought to him by Father Duchaine would trump the images on those monitors, but when the priest described the meeting with the tattooed man, the crisis with Werner became a mere problem by comparison with the astonishing resurrection of his first-made man.

Initially skeptical, he pressed Duchaine hard for a description of the towering man who had sat for coffee with him in the rectory kitchen, particularly of the ravaged half of his face. What the priest had seen under the inadequate disguise of the elaborate tattoo was damage of a kind and of a degree that no ordinary man could have sustained and survived. Further, it matched the broken countenance as Victor had kept it in his mind's eye, and his memory was exceptional.

Further still, Duchaine's word portrait of the wholesome half of that same face could not have better conveyed the ideal male beauty that Victor had been kind enough to bestow upon his first creation so long ago and on such a distant continent that sometimes those events seemed like a dream.

His kindness had been repaid with betrayal and with the murder of his bride, Elizabeth. His lost Elizabeth would never have been as malleable or as lubricious as the wives that he had later made for himself; nevertheless, her savage murder had been an unforgivable impertinence. Now the ungrateful wretch had come crawling around again, filled with delusions of grandeur, spouting nonsense about a destiny, foolish enough to believe that in a second confrontation he might not only survive but triumph.

"I thought he died out there on the ice," Victor said. "Out on the polar ice. I thought he had been frozen for eternity."

"He'll be returning to the rectory in about an hour and a half," said the priest.

Victor said approvingly, "This was clever work, Patrick. You have not been in my good graces lately, but this counts as some redemption."

"In truth," the priest said, unable to meet his maker's eyes, "I thought I might betray you, but in the end I could not conspire with him."

"Of course you couldn't. Your Bible tells you that rebellious angels rose up against God and were thrown out of Heaven. But I've made creatures more obedient than the God of myth ever proved able to create."

On the screens, the Werner bug scampered up a wall and held fast to the ceiling, pendulous and quivering.

"Sir," Duchaine said nervously, "I came here not only to tell you this news but to ask . . . to ask if you will grant me the grace that your first-made promised me."

For a moment, Victor did not know what grace was meant. When he understood, he felt his temper rise. "You want me to take your life?"

"Release me," Patrick pleaded quietly, staring at the monitors to avoid his master's eyes.

"I give you life, and where is your gratitude? Soon the world will be ours, nature humbled, the way of all things changed forever. I have made you part of this great adventure, but you would turn away from it. Are you deluded enough to believe that the religion you have insincerely preached might contain some truth after all?"

Still focused on the phantasmagoric Werner, Duchaine said, "Sir, you could release me with a few words."

"There is no God, Patrick, and even if there were, He would have no place in paradise for the likes of you."

The priest's voice acquired now a humble quality of a kind that Victor did not like. "Sir, I don't need paradise. Eternal darkness and silence will be enough."

Victor loathed him. "Perhaps at least one of my creatures is more pathetic than anything I would have believed I could create."

When the priest had no reply, Victor switched on the audio feed from the isolation chamber. The Werner thing was still screaming in terror, in pain of an apparently extreme character. Some shrieks resembled those of a cat in agony, while others were as shrill and alien as the language of frenzied insects; and yet others sounded quite as human as any cries that might mark the night in an asylum for the criminally insane.

To one of the staff, Victor said, "Cycle open the nearer door of the transition module. Father Duchaine would like to offer his holy counsel to poor Werner."

Trembling, Patrick Duchaine said, "But with just a few words, you could—"

"Yes," Victor interrupted. "I could. But I have invested time and resources in you, Patrick, and you have provided me with a most unacceptable return on my investment. This way, at least, you can perform one last service. I need to know just how dangerous Werner has become, assuming he's dangerous at all to anyone other than himself. Just go in there and ply your priestly art. I won't need a written report."

The nearer door of the module stood open.

Duchaine crossed the room. At the threshold, he paused to look back at his maker.

Victor could not read the expression on the priest's face or in his eyes. Although he had created each of them with care and knew the structure of their bodies and their minds perhaps better than he knew himself, some of the New Race sometimes were as much of a mystery to him as any of the Old Race were.

Without a further word, Duchaine entered the transition module. The door cycled shut behind him.

Ripley's voice conveyed a numbness of spirit when he said, "He's in the air lock."

"It's not an *air lock*," Victor corrected.

One of the staff said, "Nearer door in lockdown. Farther door is cycling open."

A moment later, the Werner bug stopped screaming. Depending from the ceiling, the thing appeared to be keenly, tremulously alert, at last distracted from its own complaints.

Father Patrick Duchaine entered the isolation chamber.

The farther door cycled shut, but no one on the staff followed the customary procedure of announcing module lockdown. The monitor room had fallen as silent as Victor had ever heard it.

Duchaine spoke not to the monster suspended above him, but to one of the cameras and, through its lens, to his maker. "I forgive you, Father. You know not what you do."

In that instant, before Victor was able to erupt with a furious retort, the Werner bug proved itself to be as lethal as anyone could have imagined. Such agility. Such exotic mandibles and pincers. Such machinelike persistence.

Being one of the New Race, the priest was programmed to fight, and he was terribly strong, and resilient. As a consequence of that strength and resilience, his death was not an easy one, but slow and cruel, although eventually he did receive the grace that he had requested.

chapter 57

Staring at Pastor Laffite's eyelids as his eyes moved nervously beneath them, Deucalion said, "Many theologians believe that dogs and some other animals have simple souls, yes, though whether immortal or not, no one can say."

"If dogs have souls," Laffite suggested, "then perhaps we, too, might be more than machines of meat."

After some consideration, Deucalion said, "I won't give you false hope but I can offer you a third chocolate."

"Have one with me, will you? This is such a lonely communion."

"All right."

The pastor had developed a mild palsy of the head and hands, different from his previous nervous tremors.

Deucalion selected two pieces of candy from the box. He put the first to Laffite's lips, and the minister took it.

His own piece proved to have a coconut center. In two hundred years, nothing he had eaten had tasted as sweet as this, perhaps because the circumstances were, by contrast, so bitter.

"Eyes closed or open," Pastor Laffite said, "I'm having terrible hallucinations, vivid images, such horrors that I have no words to describe them."

"Then no more delay," Deucalion said, pushing his chair back from the table and getting to his feet.

"And pain," the pastor said. "Severe pain that I can't repress."

"I won't add to that," Deucalion promised. "My strength is much greater than yours. It will be quick."

As Deucalion moved behind Laffite's chair, the pastor groped blindly, caught his hand. Then he did something that would never have been expected of any of the New Race, something that Deucalion knew no number of centuries could erase from his memory.

Although his program was dropping out of him, though his mind was going – or perhaps because of that – Pastor Laffite drew the back of Deucalion's hand to his lips, tenderly kissed it, and whispered, "Brother."

A moment later, Deucalion broke the preacher's neck, shattered his spine with such force that instant brain death followed, assuring that the quasi-immortal body could not repair the injury.

Nevertheless, for a while he remained in the kitchen. To be certain. To sit a sort of shiva.

Night pressed at the windows. Outside lay a city, teeming. Yet Deucalion could see nothing beyond the glass, only darkness deep, a blackness unrelenting.

chapter **58**

After the unknown thing in the glass case spoke her name and made its ominous claim to her, Erika did not linger in the secret Victorian drawing room.

She did not like the roughness of the voice. Or its confidence.

At the threshold of the room, she almost hurried boldly into the passageway before she realized that the rods bristling from the walls were humming again. A headlong exit would result in a contest between her brilliantly engineered body and perhaps several thousand volts of electricity.

As extraordinarily tough and resilient as she might be, Erika Helios was not Scarlett O'Hara.

Gone with the Wind had been set in an age before electrical service had been available to the home; consequently, Erika was not certain that this literary allusion was apt, but it occurred to her anyway. Of course she had not read the novel; but maybe it contained a scene in which Scarlett O'Hara had been struck by lightning in a storm and had survived unscathed.

Erika stepped cautiously across the threshold and paused, as she had done when entering the farther end of this passageway. As before, a blue laser speared from the ceiling and scanned her. Either the ID system knew who she was or, more likely, recognized what she was not: She was not the thing in the glass case.

The rods stopped humming, allowing her safe passage.

She quickly closed the massive steel portal and engaged the five lock bolts. In less than a minute, she had retreated beyond the next steel barrier and had secured it as well.

Her synchronized hearts nevertheless continued to beat fast. She marveled that she could have been so unsettled by such a small thing as a disembodied voice and a veiled threat.

This sudden, persistent fear, disproportionate to the cause, had the character of a superstitious response. She, of course, was free of all superstition.

The instinctive nature of her reaction led her to suspect that subconsciously she *knew* what was imprisoned in the amber substance within that glass case, and that her fear arose from this deeply buried knowledge.

When she reached the end of the initial passage, where she had originally entered through a pivoting section of bookcases, she found a button that opened that secret door from here behind the wall.

Immediately that she returned to the library, she felt much safer, in spite of being surrounded by so many books filled with so much potentially corrupting material.

In one corner was a wet bar stocked with heavy crystal glass-ware and the finest adult beverages. As a superbly programmed hostess, she knew how to mix any cocktail that might be requested, though as yet she had not been in a social situation requiring this skill.

Erika was having cognac to settle her nerves when from behind her, Christine said, "Mrs Helios, pardon me for saying so, but I suspect that Mr Helios would be distressed to see you drinking directly from the decanter."

Erika had not realized that she had been committing such a faux pas, but on having it drawn to her attention, she saw that she was, as charged, guzzling Rémy Martin from the exquisite Lalique decanter, and even dribbling some down her chin.

"I was thirsty," she said, but sheepishly returned the decanter to the bar, stoppered it, and blotted her chin with a bar napkin.

"We've been searching for you, Mrs Helios, to inquire about dinner."

Alarmed, glancing at the windows and discovering that night had fallen, Erika said, "Oh. Have I kept Victor waiting?"

"No, ma'am. Mr Helios needs to work late and will take his dinner at the lab."

"I see. Then what shall I do?"

"We will serve your dinner anywhere you wish, Mrs Helios."

"Well, it's such a big house, so many places."

"Yes."

"Is there somewhere I could have dinner where there's cognac – other than here in the library with all these books?"

"We can serve cognac with your dinner anywhere in the house, Mrs Helios – although I might suggest that wine would be more appropriate *with* a meal."

"Well, of course it would. And I *would* like to have a bottle of wine with dinner, an appropriate bottle complementary to whatever the chef has prepared. Select for me a most appropriate bottle, if you will."

"Yes, Mrs Helios."

Apparently, Christine had no desire for another conversation as intimate and intense as the one they'd shared in the kitchen earlier in the day. She seemed to want to keep their relationship on a formal footing henceforth.

Encouraged by this, Erika decided to exert her authority as the lady of the house, although graciously. "But please, Christine, also serve me a decanted bottle of Rémy Martin, and save yourself the trouble by bringing it at the same time you bring the wine. Don't bother making a later trip."

Christine studied her for a moment, and said, "Have you enjoyed your first day here, Mrs Helios?"

"It's been full," Erika said. "At first it seemed like such a quiet house, one might almost expect it to be dull, but there seems always to be something happening."

chapter 59

Although the Q&A with Arnie's mother starts well, Randal Six quickly exhausts his supply of conversational gambits. He eats nearly half a quart of strawberry-banana swirl ice cream before another question occurs to him.

"You seem to be frightened, Vicky. Are you frightened?"

"Yes. God, yes."

"Why are you frightened?"

"I'm tied to a chair."

"The chair can't hurt you. Don't you think it's silly to be frightened of a chair?"

"Don't do this."

"Don't do what?"

"Don't taunt me."

"When did Randal taunt you? Randal never did."

"I'm not afraid of the chair."

"But you just said you were."

"I'm scared of you."

He is genuinely surprised. "Randal? Why be scared of Randal?"

"You hit me."

"Only once."

"Very hard."

"You aren't dead. See? Randal doesn't kill mothers. Randal has decided to like mothers. Mothers are a wonderful idea. Randal doesn't have a mother or a father."

Vicky says nothing.

"And, *nooooo*, Randal didn't kill them. Randal was sort of made by machines. Machines don't care like mothers do, and they don't miss you when you leave."

Vicky closes her eyes, as autistics sometimes do when there is just too much of everything to process, a daunting amount of stuff coming in.

She is not, however, an autistic. She is a mother.

Randal is surprised that he himself is coping so well with all these new developments, and talking so smooth. His mind seems to be healing.

Vicky's appearance, however, is troubling. Her face is drawn. She looks ill.

"Are you ill?" he asks.

"I'm so scared."

"Stop being scared, okay? Randal wants you to be his mother. All right? Now you can't be scared of your own son, Randal."

The most amazing thing happens: Tears spill down Vicky's cheeks.

"That is so sweet," says Randal. "You're a very nice mother. We will be happy. Randal will call you Mother, not Vicky anymore. When is your birthday, Mother?"

Instead of answering, she sobs. She is so emotional. Mothers are sentimental.

"You should bake a cake for your birthday," he says. "We'll have a celebration. Randal knows about celebrations, hasn't ever been to one, but knows."

She hangs her head, still sobbing, face wet with tears.

"Randal's first birthday is eight months away," he informs her. "Randal is only four months old."

He returns the remainder of the strawberry-banana ice cream to the freezer. Then he stands beside the table, gazing down at her.

"You are the secret of happiness, Mother. Randal doesn't need Arnie to tell him. Randal is going to visit his brother now."

She raises her head, eyes open wide. "Visit Arnie?"

"Randal needs to find out are two brothers okay or is that one brother too many."

"What do you mean, one brother too many? What're you talking about? Why do you want to see Arnie?"

He winces at the rush of her words, at the urgency of them; they seem to buzz in his ears. "Don't talk so fast. Don't ask questions. Randal asks questions. Mother answers."

"Leave Arnie alone."

"Randal thinks there is enough happiness here for two, but maybe Arnie doesn't think so. Randal needs to hear Arnie say two brothers are okay."

"Arnie hardly ever talks," she said. "Depending on his mood, he might not even tune in to you. He zones out. It's like the castle is real and he's *inside* it, locked away. He might not really hear you."

"Mother, you are talking too loud, too much, too fast. Loud-fast talk sounds ugly."

He crosses toward the door to the hall.

She raises her voice: "Randal, untie me. Untie me *right this minute!*"

"You aren't acting like a nice mother now. Shouting scares Randal. Shouting is not happiness."

"Okay. All right. Slow and quiet. Please, Randal. Wait. Please untie me."

At the threshold of the hallway, he glances back at her. "Why?"

"So I can take you to see Arnie."

"Randal can find him all right."

"Sometimes he hides. He's very difficult to find when he hides. I know all his favorite hiding places."

Staring at her, he senses deceit. "Mother, are you going to try to hurt Randal?"

"No. Of course not. Why would I hurt you?"

"Sometimes mothers hurt their children. There's a whole Web site about it – www.homicidalmothers. com."

Now that he thinks about it, he realizes that the poor children never suspect what's coming. They trust their mom. She says she loves them, and they trust her. Then she chops them up in their beds or drives them in a lake and drowns them.

"Randal sure hopes you're a good mother," he says. "But maybe you need to answer a lot more questions before Randal unties you."

"All right. Come back. Ask me anything."

"Randal needs to talk to Arnie first."

She says something, but he tunes out her meaning. He steps into the hallway.

Behind him, Mother is talking fast again, faster than ever, and then she is shouting.

Randal Six has been in this living room previously. When Mother first regained consciousness, she chattered at him so hard that he had come here to calm himself. Now here he is again, calming himself.

He hopes that he and Mother don't already have a dysfunctional relationship.

After a minute or two, when he is ready, he goes in search of Arnie. He wonders whether his new brother will prove to be Abel or Cain, selfless or selfish. If he is like Cain, Randal Six knows what to do. It will be self-defense.

chapter **60**

Carson parked in her driveway, shut off the engine and the headlights, and said, "Let's get the shotguns."

They had put the suitcases and shotguns in the trunk before they'd driven Lulana and Evangeline home from the parsonage.

After hurriedly retrieving the Urban Snipers, they went to the front of the sedan and crouched there, using it for cover. Peering back along the driver's side, Carson watched the street.

"What're we gonna do for dinner?" Michael asked.

"We can't take the kind of time we took for lunch."

"I could go for a po-boy."

"As long as it's sleeve-wrapped to eat on the fly."

Michael said, "The thing I'll miss most when I'm dead is New Orleans food."

"Maybe there's plenty of it on the Other Side."

"What I won't miss is the heat and humidity."

"Are you really that confident?"

The night brought them the sound of an approaching engine.

When the vehicle passed in the street, Carson said, "Porsche Carrera GT, black. That baby's got a six-speed transmission. Can you imagine how fast I could drive in one of those?"

"So fast, I'd be perpetually vomiting."

"My driving's never gonna kill you," she said. "Some monster is gonna kill you."

"Carson, if this is ever over and we come out of it alive, you think we might give up being cops?"

"What would we do?"

"How about mobile pet grooming? We could drive around all day, bathing dogs. Easy work. No pressure. It might even be fun."

"Depends on the dogs. The problem is you have to have a van for all the equipment. Vans are dorky. I'm not going to drive a van."

He said, "We could open a gay bar."

"Why gay?"

"I wouldn't have to worry about guys hitting on you."

"I wouldn't mind running a doughnut shop."

"Could we run a doughnut shop and still have guns?" he wondered.

"I don't see why not."

"I feel more comfortable with guns."

The sound of another engine silenced them.

When the vehicle appeared, Carson said, "White Mountaineer," and pulled her head back to avoid being seen.

The Mountaineer slowed but didn't stop, and drifted past the house.

"They'll park farther along, on the other side of the street," she said.

"You think it's going to go down here?"

"They'll like the setup," she predicted. "But they won't come right away. They've been looking for an opportunity all day. They're patient. They'll take time to reconnoiter."

"Ten minutes?"

"Probably ten," she agreed. "No less than five. Let's get Vicky and Arnie out of here yesterday."

When the Mountaineer was out of sight, they hurried to the back of the house. The kitchen door was locked. Carson fumbled her keys from a jacket pocket.

"Is that a new jacket?" he asked.

"I've worn it a couple times."

"I'll try not to get brains on it."

She unlocked the door.

In the kitchen, Vicky Chou was at the table, tied in a chair.

chapter 61

Benny and Cindi carried pistols, but they preferred to avoid using them whenever possible.

The issue wasn't noise. Their weapons were fitted with sound suppressors. You could pop a guy three times in the face, and if people in the next room heard anything at all, they might think you sneezed.

You could try shooting to lame; but the Old Race were bleeders who lacked the New Race's ability to seal a puncture almost as fast as turning off a faucet. By the time you got the wounded prey to a private place where you could have some fun torturing them, they were too often dead or comatose.

Some people might enjoy dismembering and decapitating a dead body, but not Benny Lovewell. Without the screams, you might as well be chopping up a roast chicken.

Once, when a gunshot woman had inconsiderately died before Benny could even start to take off her arms, Cindi supplied the screams, as she imagined the victim might have sounded, synchronizing her cries to Benny's use of the saw, but it wasn't the same.

Aimed at the eyes, Mace could disable any member of the Old Race long enough to subdue him. The problem was that people blinded by a stinging blast of Mace always shouted and cursed, drawing attention when it wasn't wanted.

Instead, Victor supplied Benny and Cindi with small pressurized cans, the size of Mace containers, which shot a stream of chloroform. When squirted in the face, most people inhaled with surprise – and fell unconscious before saying more than *shit*, if they said anything at all. The chloroform had a range of fifteen to twenty feet.

They also carried Tasers, the wand type rather than the pistol type. These were strictly for close-in work.

Considering that O'Connor and Maddison were cops and already jumpy because of what they knew about the deceased child of Mercy, Jonathan Harker, getting in close wouldn't be easy.

After parking across the street from the O'Connor house, Cindi said, "People aren't sitting on their porches around here."

"It's a different type of neighborhood."

"What're they doing instead?"

"Who cares?"

"Probably making babies."

"Give it a rest, Cindi."

"We could always adopt."

"Get real. We kill for Victor. We don't have jobs. You need real jobs to adopt."

"If you had let me keep the one I took, we'd be happy now."

"You kidnapped him. Everyone in the world is looking for the brat, and you think you can push him around the mall in a stroller!"

Cindi sighed. "It broke my heart when we had to leave him in that park."

"It didn't break your heart. Our kind aren't capable of any such emotion."

"All right, but it pissed me off."

"Don't I know it. Okay, so we go in there, we knock them down, tie them up, then you drive around to the back of the house, and we load 'em like cordwood."

Studying the O'Connor house, Cindi said, "It does look slick, doesn't it."

"It looks totally slick. In and out in five minutes. Let's go."

chapter 62

When they came through the back door with shot-guns slung from their shoulders, Vicky whispered urgently, "He's in the house."

Pulling open a drawer, withdrawing a pair of scissors, Carson whispered, "Who?"

"Some creep. *Way* strange," Vicky said as Carson tossed the scissors to Michael.

As Michael caught the scissors, Carson crossed to the inner doorway.

Vicky whispered, "He's looking for Arnie."

As Carson checked the hall, Michael made two cuts in the bindings and put the scissors down. "You can do the rest, Vic."

The hallway was deserted, a lamp on in the living room at the farther end.

"He have a gun?" Carson asked.

Vicky said, "No."

Michael indicated that he wanted to lead.

This was Carson's house. She went first, carrying the shotgun for hip fire.

She cleared the coat closet. Nothing in there but coats.

The creep wasn't in the living room. Carson moved to the right, Michael to the left, until they were two targets instead of one, and halted.

Decision time. Farther to the right, beyond the living room, was Carson's suite, bedroom and bath. To the left lay the front door and the stairs to the second floor.

The door to Carson's room was closed. No one was on the first flight of stairs.

With his eyes, Michael indicated *up*.

She agreed. For some reason the creep was looking for Arnie, and Arnie was on the second floor.

Staying close to the wall, where the stairs were less likely to creak, Carson ascended first, shotgun in both hands.

Michael followed, climbing backward, covering the room below them.

She didn't dare think about Arnie, what might be happening to him. Fear for your life sharpens your edge. Dread dulls it. Think about the creep instead, stopping him.

So silent, the house. Like the Christmas poem. Not even a mouse.

No one on the second flight, either. Light in the upstairs hall. No shadows moving.

When she reached the top, she heard a stranger's voice coming from Arnie's room. Arriving at the open door, she saw her brother in his wheeled office chair, his attention on the Lego-block castle.

The intruder was maybe eighteen, nineteen, solidly put together. He stood facing Arnie, only a few feet from him, his back to Carson.

If it came to shooting, she didn't have a clear shot. The slug from the Urban Sniper might punch clean through the creep and hammer Arnie.

She didn't know who the guy was. More important, she didn't know *what* he was.

The intruder was saying, "Randal thought he could share. But now the castle, a home, ice cream, Mother – Randal wants it for himself."

Carson edged to the left of the doorway as she sensed Michael in the hall behind her.

"Randal isn't Abel. Randal is Cain. Randal isn't Six anymore. From now on . . . Randal O'*Connor*."

Still moving, circling, Carson said, "What're you doing here?"

The intruder turned smoothly, so fast, like a dancer, or like something that had been . . . well engineered. "Carson."

"I don't know you."

"I am Randal. You will be Randal's sister."

"Down on your knees," she told him. "Down on your knees, then flat on the floor, facedown on the floor."

"Randal doesn't like loud talk. Don't shout at Randal like Victor does."

Michael said, "Sonofabitch," and Carson said, "Arnie, roll your chair back, roll away on your chair."

Although Arnie didn't move, Randal did. He took a step toward Carson. "Are you a good sister?"

"Don't come any closer. Get on your knees. *On your knees NOW!*"

"Or are you a bad, loud sister who talks too fast?" Randal asked.

She edged farther to her right, changing her line of fire to get Arnie out of it. "You think I don't know you have two hearts?" she said. "You think I can't take them out with one round from this bull killer?"

"You are a bad, bad sister," Randal said, and closed on her.

He was so fast that he almost got his hand on the gun. The boom rattled windows, the stink of gunfire blew in her face, blood burst from the exit wound in his back and sprayed the castle.

Randal should have been rocked back on his feet or staggered. He should have dropped.

She had aimed too low, missed one heart or both. But at this close range, she had to have *destroyed* half his internal organs.

He seized the barrel of the shotgun, thrust it upward as she squeezed the trigger, and the second round punched a hole in the ceiling.

When she tried to hold on to the shotgun, he pulled her to him, almost had her before she let go, dropped, rolled.

She had given Michael a clean shot. He took two.

The reports were so loud, her ears rang and kept ringing as she rolled against a wall, looked up, saw Randal down – thank God, *down* – and Michael warily moving toward him.

Getting to her feet, she pulled the .50 Magnum from the scabbard on her left hip, certain she wouldn't need it, but Randal was still alive. Not in great condition, down and staying down, but alive after three point-blank torso shots from an Urban Sniper.

He raised his head, looked wonderingly around the room, rolled onto his back, blinked at the ceiling, said, "Home," and was gone.

chapter 63

The back door was open. Benny and Cindi hesitated, but then he went through boldly, and fast, and she followed.

An Asian woman stood in the kitchen, next to the table, untying a length of torn cloth from her left wrist. She blinked at them and said, "Shit—"

Cindi was quick. The stream of chloroform splashed nose-on. The woman gasped, choked, spluttered, and fell to the floor.

They could deal with her later. She would be unconscious for perhaps fifteen minutes, maybe longer.

Although the Asian woman wasn't on their hit list, she had seen their faces. They would have to kill her, too.

That was okay. There was plenty of room for three in the cargo area of the Mercury Mountaineer, and Benny had recently sharpened his favorite cutting tools.

He closed and locked the back door. He didn't want to make it easy for anyone to come in behind them.

On one job, a four-year-old girl had wandered into the house from next door, and Cindi had insisted on adopting her.

Now Cindi had the chloroform in her right hand and the Taser in her left. Benny relied on only the chloroform.

They weren't worried about PD-issued sidearms. Basic guns for cops these days were often 9mm. He and Cindi could walk through a lot of 9mm fire if necessary.

Besides, if they were stealthy, their prey wouldn't have a chance to draw down on them.

A laundry room opened off the kitchen. Deserted.

The hallway to the front of the house passed a coat closet. No one knew they were here, so no one would be hiding from them in the closet, but they checked it anyway. Just coats.

As they reached the living room, a gun roared upstairs. It was a big sound, as if an armoire had toppled over. The whole house seemed to shake.

Cindi looked at the chloroform in her hand. She looked at the Taser.

Another shot roared.

Cindi put the Taser in an inside jacket pocket, switched the chloroform to her left hand, and pulled her pistol.

Upstairs the big gun boomed twice again, and Benny drew his piece, too. The gun was a 9mm semi-auto, but this caliber would be a more serious problem for O'Connor and Maddison than for the Lovewells.

chapter 64

Who the intruder had been, how he had gotten into the house, why he seemed to have targeted Arnie specifically – none of that mattered as much as the fact that he was of the New Race and that this case had come home in the most literal sense, as from the start Carson had been afraid it would.

The walls of their house, the locks in its doors, offered them no more security than did Arnie's Lego castle. Perhaps, the fate of this city, of the world, in the hands of Victor Helios, was such that no time would ever come again when they could spend a peaceful moment in their home. They couldn't stay here anymore.

And they had to get out *fast*.

Neighbors might not have been able to identify the precise location of the four shotgun blasts. Nevertheless, gunfire in this neighborhood would not go unreported.

Soon NOPD would have a patrol car or two cruising the area, on the lookout for anything suspicious. Carson preferred to avoid even a friendly encounter with uniforms. She didn't want to have to explain the weapons for which she possessed neither a receipt of purchase nor department authorization.

Besides, a uniform no longer earned immediate trust from her. The brotherhood of the police had been infiltrated by the New Race; and those who were loyal to Helios might have been told – or might be told at any moment – to make the elimination of Carson and Michael their top priority.

She picked up the Urban Sniper that Randal had torn from her grasp. Fingering two shells out of the dump pouch at her right hip, inserting them in the side carrier to bring the weapon to full load once more, she said, "Good thing we went with slugs."

"Buckshot wouldn't have stopped him," Michael agreed, reloading his shotgun.

"Maybe the shots will make the two in the Mountaineer hesitate."

"Or bring them running."

"We grab Vicky, go straight out the front door. Her car's at the curb. We leave in that."

Reloading his Sniper, Michael said, "You think they've got a hear-me-see-me on the plainwrap?"

"Yeah. They've been following us by remote view."

Arnie had gotten out of his chair. He stood gazing at his blood-spattered castle.

Carson said, "Honey, we have to go. Right now."

The last thing they needed was for Arnie to be mulish. Most of the time, he remained docile, cooperative, but he had his stubborn moments, which could be caused by traumatic experiences and loud noises.

Four shotgun blasts and the intruder dead on the floor qualified on both counts, but Arnie seemed to realize that survival depended on his finding the courage not to withdraw further into his shell. He went at once to the door.

Michael said, "Stay behind me, Arnie," and led the way into the upstairs hall.

Glancing at the intruder, half expecting to see him blink and shake off the effects of being repeatedly shotgunned, relieved to have her expectations disappointed, Carson followed Arnie out of his room, his refuge, desperately afraid that she would not be able to protect him any longer now that the Big Easy had become the city of night.

———

Benny started up the steps, and behind him Cindi whispered, "If there's a baby in the house, let's take it."

He kept moving, his back to the staircase wall, sideways from riser to riser. "There's no baby in the house."

"But if there is."

"We didn't come here for a baby."

"We didn't come here for the bitch in the kitchen, either, but we'll be taking her."

He reached the landing, peered up the second flight. Nobody in the upstairs hall, as far as he could see.

Behind him, she wouldn't relent: "If we take the baby, you can kill it with the others."

Cindi was nuts, and she was making him nuts, too. He refused to get into this debate with her, especially in the middle of a hit.

Besides, if they took the baby, she wouldn't let him kill it. Once she had it, she would want to keep it and dress it up in frilly outfits.

Anyway, *there was no baby in the house!*

Benny reached the top of the second flight. With his back still to the wall, he stuck his head out, looked around the corner – and saw Maddison coming with a shotgun, a boy behind him, O'Connor behind the boy with a shotgun of her own.

Maddison saw him, Benny juked back, and where the wall turned the corner from stairwell to hall, a shotgun blast ripped Sheetrock, shattered framing, showered him with powdered gypsum and splinters of wood.

Dropping to his knees on the steps, Benny risked exposure to fire again, but down low, where Maddison would not expect him, and squeezed off three shots without taking time to aim, before pulling back onto the stairs.

———

Three pistol shots, all wild, but one of them close enough to sing like a wasp past Carson, suggested the wisdom of a change in plans.

Even from the brief glimpse she had of him, Carson recognized the man on the stairs. He was the guy in the Mountaineer, the one who had smiled and waved.

Figure there were two of them on the stairs, the woman behind him. Figure they were both New Race, and both armed with pistols.

To drop Randal, she and Michael had had to scramble his internal organs, shred both his hearts, and shatter his spine with three point-blank slugs from the Urban Snipers.

These two golems on the stairs would be at least as difficult to kill as he had been. And unlike Randal, they were armed and seemed to have some paramilitary training or at least experience.

Without Arnie to consider, Carson might have relied on the

power of their weaponry, might have stormed the stairs, but with the boy to worry about, she couldn't roll the dice.

"Vicky's room," she told Michael, grabbed Arnie by the arm, and retreated toward the end of the hall.

Michael backed away from the head of the stairs, laying down two spaced rounds of suppressing fire to discourage another fusillade from the pistol.

———

The juncture of hall and stairwell walls took such a beating from the shotgun that the metal corner beading under the Sheetrock was exposed, snapped, sprung like a clock spring, and shards of it peppered Benny and embedded in his face.

For a moment he thought they were recklessly charging the stairs. Then he heard a door slam, and no more gunfire followed.

He scrambled up, off the stairs, and found the upper hallway deserted.

"Those're the guns they were trying out in the woods," Cindi said as she joined him.

Plucking the metal splinters out of his face, Benny said, "Yeah, I figured."

"You want to back off, come at them someplace later when their guard's down?"

"No. They have a kid with them. That complicates things, limits their options. Let's whack them now."

"Kid? They've got a kid?"

"Not a baby. Like twelve, thirteen."

"Oh. Too old. You can kill him, too," she said.

Unfortunately, now that the situation had blown up, Benny didn't expect to be able to take either O'Connor or Maddison alive. This job wouldn't give him the opportunity for any of the careful carving that he enjoyed and for which he had such a talent.

Three rooms opened off the hall. A door was ajar. Benny kicked it open. A bathroom. Nobody in there.

On the floor of the second room, a body lay in blood.

In that room also stood a humungous model of a castle, about as big as an SUV. Weird. You never knew what strange stuff you'd find in Old Race houses.

So the door Benny had heard slam must have been the last one in the hall.

———

As Carson hurriedly replenished the expended shells in his shotgun, Michael shoved the dresser in front of the locked door, further bracing it.

When he turned and took the weapon from her, she said, "We can go out the window, onto the porch roof and down."

"What about Vicky?"

Although it hurt to put the thought in words, Carson said, "She either ran when she saw them or they got her."

As Carson took Arnie by the hand and led him toward the open window, one of the golems in the hallway threw itself against the door. She heard wood crack, and a hinge or lock plate buckled with a *twang*.

"Carson!" Michael warned. "It's not gonna hold ten seconds."

"Onto the roof," she told Arnie, pushing him to the window.

She turned as the door took another hit. It shuddered violently, and a hinge tore out of the casing.

No ordinary man could come through a door this easily. This was like a rhino charge.

They raised both shotguns.

The door was solid oak. As the golems broke through, they would use it as a shield. The shotgun slugs would penetrate, but do less damage than an unobstructed shot.

On the third hit, the second hinge tore loose and the lock bolt snapped.

"Here they come!"

chapter 65

After sitting for a few minutes with the body of the replicant Pastor Laffite, Deucalion walked out of the parsonage
kitchen and into the kitchen of Carson O'Connor's house, where
Vicky Chou lay unconscious on the floor, in the reek of
chloroform.

A tremendous crash from upstairs indicated worse trouble, and
he walked out of the kitchen into the second-floor hall in time to
see some guy slam his shoulder into a bedroom door as a woman
stood to one side, watching.

He surprised the woman, tore the pistol out of her hand, threw
it aside even as he lifted her and pitched her farther than the gun.

As the guy hit the door again and it appeared to break off its
last pins, Deucalion grabbed him by the nape of the neck and the
seat of the pants. He lifted him, turned him, and slammed him into
the wall across the hall from the room that he'd been trying to
enter.

The force of impact was so tremendous that the guy's face broke through the Sheetrock and hammered a wall stud hard enough to crack it. Deucalion kept shoving, and the stud relented, as did the rest of the wall structure, until the killer's head was in Arnie's room even as his body remained in the hall.

The woman was crawling toward her gun, so Deucalion left the guy with his neck in the wall as if in the lunette of a guillotine, and went after her.

She picked up the pistol, rolled onto her side, and fired at him. She hit him, but it was only a 9mm slug, and he took it in the breastbone without serious damage.

He kicked the gun out of her hand, probably breaking her wrist, and kicked her in the ribs, and kicked her again, sure that even New Race ribs could be broken.

By then, the guy had pulled his head out of the wall. Deucalion sensed him coming and turned to see an angry gypsum-whitened face, a bloody broken nose, and one eye bristling with wood splinters.

The killer was still game, and fast, but Deucalion didn't merely sidestep him. In the same way that he had traveled from the parsonage kitchen to the O'Connor kitchen in a single step, he went twenty feet backward, leaving his assailant to stumble forward, grappling only with air.

In retreat, having abandoned her pistol, the woman had scrambled toward the stairs. Deucalion seized her and assisted her by pitching her down the first flight to the landing.

In spite of being the future of the planet and the doom of mere humanity, the New Race superman with the plaster-powdered face and the toothpick-holder for a left eye had had enough. He fled the hall for Arnie's room.

Deucalion went after the guy just in time to see him plunge through a window into the backyard.

———

Standing in Vicky's room, listening to the ruckus in the hall, Michael said, "What – are they fighting with each other?"

Carson said, "Somebody's kicking ass."

"Vicky?"

They didn't lower their shotguns, but they moved closer to the barricading dresser, against which the loose door was now merely propped.

When sudden quiet followed the uproar, Carson cocked her head, listened, then said, "What now?"

"Apocalypse," Deucalion said behind them.

Carson turned with a jump and saw the giant standing beside Arnie. She didn't think he had come in through the open window.

The boy was shaking as if with palsy. He had covered his face with his hands. Too much noise, too much new and strange.

"It's all coming apart," Deucalion said. "That's why I was brought to this place, at this time. Victor's empire is blowing up in his face. By morning, nowhere in the city will be safe. I must move Arnie."

"Move him where?" Carson worried. "He needs quiet, peace. He needs—"

"There's a monastery in Tibet," said Deucalion, effortlessly lifting Arnie and holding him in his arms.

"Tibet?"

"The monastery is like a fortress, not unlike his castle, and quiet. I have friends there who'll know how to calm him."

Alarmed, Carson said, "*Tibet*? Hey, no. It might as well be the *moon!*"

"Vicky Chou is in the kitchen, unconscious. Better move that dresser and get out of here," Deucalion advised. "Police will be coming, and you won't know who they really are."

The giant turned as if to carry Arnie through the open window, but in the turn itself, he was gone.

chapter **66**

Maybe four minutes had passed since Carson had first fired the shotgun at Randal in Arnie's room. Figure none of the neighbors had called 911 for a minute, taking that long to wonder if it had been a backfiring truck or the dog farting. So maybe a call had gone out three minutes ago.

In this city, the average police response time to a gunfire-heard call, when no gunman had actually been seen and no location verified, was about six minutes.

With three minutes to leave, Carson didn't have time to worry about Arnie in Tibet.

Michael dragged the dresser out of the way, and the door fell into the room. They walked across it into the hall, and ran for the stairs.

Fragrant with evaporating chloroform, Vicky hadn't cooperated by regaining consciousness. Carson carried both shotguns, and Michael carried Vicky.

When Carson unlocked the back door and opened it, she

paused on the threshold, turned to survey the kitchen. "I may never see this place again."

"It's not exactly Tara," Michael said impatiently.

"I grew up in this house."

"And a fine job you did of it. Now it's time to move on."

"I feel like I should take something."

"I assume you heard Deucalion say "Apocalypse." For that, you don't need anything, not even a change of underwear."

She held the door for him as he left with Vicky, hesitated outside before closing it, and then realized what she needed: the keys to Vicky's car.

They hung on the kitchen pegboard. She stepped inside, snared the keys, and left without a pang of sentimental regret.

She hurried after Michael, through the darkness along the side of the house, alert to the possibility that the pair from the Mountaineer might still be hanging around, passed him in the front yard, and opened the back door of Vicky's Honda, so he could load her.

The car was parked under a streetlamp. With all the commotion, surely they were being watched. They would probably need to switch vehicles in an hour or two.

Carson and Michael assumed their usual positions: she behind the steering wheel, he in the shotgun seat, which was literally the shotgun seat tonight, because he sat there with two Urban Snipers that still smelled hot.

The engine caught, and she popped the hand-brake, and Michael said, "Show me some NASCAR moves."

"You finally want me to put the pedal to the metal, and it's a five-year-old Honda."

Behind them, Vicky began snoring.

Carson burned rubber away from the curb, ran the stop sign at the end of the block, and hung a left at the corner in a test of the Honda's rollover resistance.

More than two blocks away, approaching, were the flashing red-and-blue lights of a squad car.

She wheeled right into an alleyway, stood on the accelerator, took out someone's trash can, scared one of the nine lives out of a cat, said, "That sonofabitch Frankenstein," and blew out of the neighborhood.

chapter 67

When the exhilarating dance of death was done, Gunny Alecto and another garbage-galleon driver plowed two feet of concealing trash into the shallow grave in which the remains of the five members of the Old Race were interred.

In the torchlight, the trash field glimmered like a sea of gold doubloons, and the excited crew appeared to sweat molten gold, too, as they calmed themselves, with some effort, for the more solemn ceremony ahead.

Beginning shortly after dawn, all the incoming trucks would dump here in the west pit for at least a week, and soon the brutalized remains would be buried too deep for accidental discovery and beyond easy exhumation.

When the plowing was finished, Gunny came to Nick, moviestar beautiful and filthy and grinning with dark delight. "Did they crunch like roaches?" she asked excitedly.

"Oh, they crunched," Nick agreed.

"Did they *squish*?"

"Yeah, they squished."

"That was *hot!*" she said.

"You're hot."

"Someday, all we'll be pushin' into these pits is people like them, *truckloads* of their kind. That's gonna be some day, Nick. Isn't that gonna be some day?"

"Gonna get you later," he said, slipping a hand between her hip boots, clutching the crotch of her jeans.

"Gonna get *you!*" she shot back, and grabbed him the same way, with a ferocity that excited him.

Dog-nose Nick couldn't get enough of her stink, and buried his face in her hair, growling as she laughed.

The second truck now descended the sloped wall of the pit and drove toward the crew line. On the open bed were arranged the three dead gonewrongs, the consequences of experiments that had not led to the hoped-for results.

Victor Helios didn't refer to them as gone-wrongs, and neither did anyone at Mercy, as far as Nick knew. This word was part of the culture of Crosswoods, as were the crew's ceremonies.

The five members of the Old Race had been lashed upright to poles for the last leg of their journey to the grave, the better to be pelted with garbage and reviled, but the gone-wrongs lay upon a thick bed of palm fronds, which arrived weekly by the hundreds if not thousands in masses of landscapers' clippings.

They would be buried apart from the five Old Race cadavers, and with respect, though of course not with a prayer. The gone-wrongs had come from the creation tanks, just as had every member of the crew. Although they bore little resemblance to the human model, they were in a way kin to the crew. It was too easy to imagine that Gunny or Nick himself, or any of them, might have gone wrong, too, and might have been sent here as trash instead of as the keepers of the trash.

When the truck came to a stop, Nick and his fourteen crewmen climbed onto the open bed. They boarded it not in the raucous mood with which they had scrambled onto the first truck to cut down the bodies and to pitch them off, but with curiosity and some fear, and not without awe.

One of the Old Race, back in the days when carnivals had freak-shows, might have stared at some deformed specimen on the stage and said softly to himself, *There but for the grace of God go I.* Some of this feeling filled Nick and his crewmen, too, although it was not colored with the pity that might have troubled the freakshow patron. And there was no sense in any of them that divine mercy had spared them from the tortures that these gone-wrongs had been through. For them it was sheer blind luck that they had arisen from their maker's machines and processes in a functional form, to face only the anguish and tortures that were common to all their kind.

Yet, though in neither of their hearts did they have room for the concept of transcendence, though they were forbidden superstition and would laugh at the Old Race's perception of a holiness behind nature, they knelt among the gone-wrongs, marveling at their twisted and macabre features, tentatively touching their grotesque bodies, and unto them came a kind of animal wonder and a chill of mystery, and a recognition of the unknown.

chapter 68

Beyond the windows of the Rombuk Monastery, the higher peaks of the snow-capped Himalayas vanished into the terrible, turbulent beauty of thunderheads as mottled black as cast-iron skillets that had known much fire.

Nebo, an elderly monk in a wool robe with the hood turned back from his shaved head, led Arnie and Deucalion along a stone corridor in which the effects of the hard surfaces were softened by painted mandalas, by the sweet fragrance of incense, and by the buttery light of fat candles on altar tables and in wall sconces.

In terms of decor and amenities, the monks' rooms ranged from severe to austere. Perhaps an autistic would find that simplicity appealing, even soothing, but no one in Rombuk would allow a visiting child, regardless of his preferences, to occupy one of the typical cells.

These holy men were known for their kindness and hospitality as much as for their spirituality, and they maintained a few chambers as guest quarters. In these, the furnishings and amenities were for those visitors who had not yet felt – and might never feel – the need to eschew creature comforts in the pursuit of purer meditation.

A few days ago, Deucalion had left Rombuk after residing there for years. His stay had been by far the longest of any guest in the history of the monastery, and he had made more friends within its walls than anywhere outside of the carnival.

He had not expected to return for many months, if ever. Yet here he found himself less than a week after leaving, though not even for so much as an overnight.

The room to which Nebo led them was three or four times the size of the typical monk's quarters. Large tapestries graced the walls, and a hand-loomed carnelian-red rug hushed every footfall. The fourposter bed featured a privacy curtain, the furniture was comfortably upholstered, and a large stone fireplace with a decorative bronze surround provided charming light and offered as much or as little heat as might be wanted with just the adjustment of a series of vents.

As Nebo lit candles around the room and took linens from a chest to dress the bed, Deucalion sat with Arnie on a sofa that faced the fireplace.

By firelight, he performed for the boy the coin tricks that had created a bond between them from their first encounter. As the shiny quarters disappeared, reappeared, and vanished forever in thin air, he also told Arnie of the situation in New Orleans. He did not doubt that the boy understood, and he did not patronize him but told him the truth, and did not hesitate to reveal even the possible cost of his sister's courage.

This was a bright boy, imprisoned by his disorder yet acutely aware of the world, a boy who saw more deeply into things than did many people who were not shackled by his inhibitions. The quantum travel from New Orleans to Tibet had not alarmed him, had instead electrified him. Upon arrival, he looked directly into Deucalion's eyes and said, less with astonishment than with understanding, "Oh." And then, "Yes."

Arnie tracked the coins with uncommon alertness, but he listened intently, too, and he did not seem to shrink from the dark potential of pending events half a world away. Quite the contrary: The more that he understood of the confrontation growing in New Orleans, and understood his sister's commitment to the resistance of evil, the calmer he became.

Upon their arrival, when he heard that Arnie had not yet eaten dinner back on the dark side of the globe, Nebo ordered a suitable meal for this morning-bathed hemisphere. Now a young monk arrived with a capacious basket, from which he began to lay out generous fare on a trestle table by the only window.

In place of the Lego castle on which the boy worked much of every day, Deucalion had suggested to Nebo that jigsaw puzzles be brought from the monastery's collection of simple amusements, and in particular a one-thousand-piece picture of a Rhineland castle that he himself had worked more than once, as a form of meditation.

Now, as the boy stood beside the table, gazing at the appealing spread from which he could make his breakfast – including some orange cheese but nothing green – another monk arrived with four puzzles. When Deucalion reviewed these with Arnie, explaining that a jigsaw picture could be considered a two-dimensional version of a Lego project, the boy brightened at the sight of the castle photograph.

Kneeling in front of Arnie to bring them as eye-to-eye as possible, Deucalion took him by the shoulders and said, "I can't stay with you any longer. But I will return. Meanwhile you will be safe with Nebo and his brothers, who know that even the outcasts among God's children are still His children, and therefore love them as they do themselves. Your sister must be my paladin because I can't raise my own hand against my maker, but I will do all in my power to protect her. Nevertheless, what will come will come, and each of us must face it in his own way, with as much courage as he can – as she always has, and as she always will."

Deucalion was not surprised when the boy hugged him, and he returned the embrace.

chapter 69

Vicky's sister, Liane, whom Carson had spared from prison on a false murder charge, lived in an apartment in Faubourg Marigny, not far outside the Quarter.

She answered the door with a cat in a hat. She held the cat, and the cat wore the hat. The cat was black, and the hat was a knitted blue beret with a red pompom.

Liane looked lovely, and the cat looked embarrassed, and Michael said, "This explains the mouse we just saw laughing itself to death."

Having regained consciousness in the car, Vicky could stand on her own, but she didn't look good. To her sister, as she patted the cat and stepped inside, she said, "Hi, sweetie. I think I'm gonna puke."

"Carson doesn't allow that sort of thing at her house," Michael said, "so here we are. As soon as Vicky pukes, we'll take her home."

"He never changes," Liane said to Carson.

"Never. He's a rock."

Vicky decided she needed a beer to settle her stomach, and she led everyone to the kitchen.

When Liane put down the cat, it shook off the beret in disgust and ran out of the room to call the ACLU.

She offered drinks all around, and Carson said, "Something with enough caffeine to induce a heart attack."

When Michael seconded that suggestion, Liane fetched two Red Bulls from the refrigerator.

"We'll drink from the can," Michael said. "We're not girly men."

Having already chugged half a bottle of beer, Vicky said, "What happened back there? Who was Randal? Who were those two that switched off my lights? You said Arnie's safe, but where is he?"

"It's a long story," Carson said.

"They were such a cute couple," Vicky said. "You don't expect such a cute couple to squirt you with chloroform."

Sensing that Carson's *It's a long story*, though containing a wealth of information, wasn't going to satisfy Vicky, Michael said, "One thing those two were is professional killers."

No longer in danger of puking, Vicky acquired that red-bronze hue of Asian anger. "What were professional killers doing in our kitchen?"

"They came to kill us professionally," Michael explained.

"Which is why you've got to get out of New Orleans for a few days," Carson said.

"Leave New Orleans? But they must have come to kill you, not me. I never antagonize people."

"She never does," Liane agreed. "She's the nicest person."

"But you saw their faces," Carson reminded Vicky. "Now you're on their list."

"Can't you just get me police protection?"

Michael said, "You'd think we could, wouldn't you?"

"We don't trust anyone in the PD," Carson revealed. "There's police corruption involved. Liane, can you take Vicky out of town somewhere, for a few days?"

Addressing her sister, Liane said, "We could go stay with Aunt Leelee. She's been wanting us to come."

"I like Aunt Leelee," Vicky said, "except when she goes off about the planetary pole shift."

"Aunt Leelee believes," Liane explained, "that because of the uneven distribution of population, the weight imbalance is going to cause a shift in the earth's magnetic pole, destroying civilization."

Vicky said, "She can go on for hours about the urgent need to move ten million people from India to Kansas. But otherwise, she's fun."

"Where does Leelee live?" Carson asked.

"Shreveport."

"You think that's far enough, Michael?"

"Well, it's not Tibet, but it'll do. Vicky, we need to borrow your car."

Vicky frowned. "Who's going to drive it?"

"I will," Michael said.

"Okay, sure."

"It'll be a hoot spending a few days with Aunt Leelee," Liane said. "We'll drive up there first thing in the morning."

"You've got to leave now," Carson said. "Within the hour."

"It's really that serious?" Vicky asked.

"It really is."

When Carson and Michael left, the four of them did the hugs-all-around thing, but the humiliated cat remained in seclusion.

In the street, on the way to the car, Carson tossed the keys to Michael, and he said, "What's this?" and tossed them back to her.

"You promised Vicky that you'd drive," she said, and lobbed the keys to him.

"I didn't promise, I just said "I will.""

"I don't want to drive anyway. I'm sick about Arnie."

He tossed the keys to her again. "He's safe, he's fine."

"He's *Arnie*. He's scared, he's overwhelmed by too much newness, and he thinks I've abandoned him."

"He doesn't think you've abandoned him. Deucalion has some kind of connection to Arnie. You saw that. Deucalion will be able to make him understand."

Lobbing the keys to him, she said, "Tibet. I don't even know how to get to Tibet."

"Go to Baton Rouge and turn left." He stepped in front of her, blocking access to the Honda's passenger door.

"Michael, you always moan about me driving, so here's your chance. Take your chance."

Her surrender of the keys suggested despondency. He had never seen her despondent. He liked her scrappy.

"Carson, listen, if Arnie was here, in the middle of the New Race meltdown – if that's what's happening – you'd be ten times crazier with worry."

"So what?"

"So don't get yourself worked up about Tibet. Don't go female on me."

"Oh," she said, "that was ugly."

"Well, it seems to be what's happening."

"It's not what's happening. That was way ugly."

"I call 'em as I see 'em. You seem to be going female on me."

"This is a new low for you, mister."

"What's true is true. Some people are too soft and vulnerable to handle the truth."

"You manipulative bastard."

"Sticks and stones."

"I may get around to sticks and stones," she said. "Gimme the damn keys."

She snatched them out of his hand and went to the driver's door.

When they were belted in, as Carson put the key in the ignition, Michael said, "I had to punch hard. You wanting me to drive – that scared me."

"Scared me, too," she said, starting the engine. "You'd draw way too much attention to us – all those people behind us blowing their horns, trying to make you get up to speed limit."

chapter 70

Deucalion stepped into Father Patrick Duchaine's kitchen from the Rombuk Monastery, prepared to release the priest from this vale of tears, as he had promised, even though he had already learned of the Hands of Mercy from Pastor Laffite.

The priest had left lights on. The two coffee mugs and the two bottles of brandy stood on the table as they had been when Deucalion had left almost two hours ago, except that one of the bottles was now empty and a quarter of the other had been consumed.

Having been more affected by assisting Laffite out of this world than he had expected to be, prepared to be even more deeply stirred by the act of giving Duchaine that same grace, he poured a generous portion of brandy into the mug that previously he had drained of coffee.

He had brought the mug to his lips but had not yet sipped when his maker entered the kitchen from the hallway.

Although Victor seemed to be surprised, he didn't appear to be amazed, as he should have been if he believed that his first creation had perished two centuries ago. "So you call yourself Deucalion, the son of Prometheus. Is that presumption . . . or mockery of your maker?"

Deucalion might not have expected to feel fear when coming face-to-face with this megalomaniac, but he did.

More than fear, however, anger swelled in him, anger of that particular kind that he knew would feed upon itself until it reached critical mass and became a rage that would sustain a chain reaction of extreme violence.

Such fury had once made him a danger to the innocent until he had learned to control his temper. Now, in the presence of his maker, no one but he himself would be endangered by his unbridled rage, for it might rob him of self-control, make him reckless, and leave him vulnerable.

Glancing at the back door, Victor said, "How did you get past the sentinels?"

Deucalion put down the mug so hard that the untasted brandy slopped out of it, onto the table.

"What a sight you are, with a tattoo for a mask. Do you really believe that it makes you less of an abomination?"

Victor took another step into the kitchen.

To his chagrin, Deucalion found himself retreating one step.

"And dressed all in black, an odd look for the bayou," Victor said. "Are you in mourning for someone? Is it for the mate I almost made for you back then – but instead destroyed?"

Deucalion's huge hands had hardened into fists. He longed to strike out, could not.

"What a brute you are," said Victor. "I'm almost embarrassed to admit I made you. My creations are so much more elegant these days. Well, we all have to begin somewhere, don't we?"

Deucalion said, "You're insane and always were."

"It talks!" Victor exclaimed with mock delight.

"The monster-maker has become the monster."

"Ah, and it believes itself to be witty, as well," said Victor. "But no one can blame your conversational skills on me. I only gave you life, not a book of oneliners, though I must say I seem to have given you rather more life than I realized at the time. Two hundred years and more. I've worked so hard on myself to hang on this long, but for you I would have expected a mortal span."

"The only gift you gave me was misery. Longevity was a gift of the lightning that night."

"Yes, Father Duchaine said that's what you believe. Well, if you're right, perhaps everyone should stand out in a field during a thunderstorm and hope to be struck, and live forever."

Deucalion's vision had darkened steadily with the escalation of his rage, and the memory of lightning that sometimes pulsed in his eyes throbbed now as never before. The rush of his blood sang in his ears, and he heard himself breathing like a well-run horse.

Amused, Victor said, "Your hands are so tightly fisted, you'll draw blood from your palms with your own fingernails. Such hatred is unhealthy. Relax. Isn't this the moment you've been living for? Enjoy it, why don't you?"

Deucalion spread his fists into fans of fingers.

"Father Duchaine says the lightning also brought you a destiny. My destruction. Well . . . here I am."

Although loath to concede his impotence, Deucalion looked

away from his maker's piercing gaze before he realized what he'd done.

"If you can't finish me," Victor said, "then I should wrap up the business I failed to complete so long ago."

When Deucalion looked up again, he saw that Victor had drawn a revolver.

"A .357 Magnum," Victor said. "Loaded with 158-grain jacketed hollow points. And I know exactly where to aim."

"That night," Deucalion said, "in the storm, when I received my destiny, I was also given an understanding of the quantum nature of the universe."

Victor smiled again. "Ah. An early version of direct-to-brain data downloading."

Deucalion raised a hand in which a quarter had appeared between thumb and forefinger. He flipped it into the air, and the quarter vanished during its ascent.

His maker's smile grew stiff.

Deucalion produced and flipped another coin, which winked up, up, and did not disappear, but fell, and when it rang against the kitchen table, Deucalion departed on the *ping*!

chapter 71

Carson driving, Michael riding shotgun: At least this one thing was still right with the world.

He had called the cell number for Deucalion and had, of course, gotten voice mail for Jelly Biggs. He left a message, asking for a meeting at the Luxe Theater, at midnight.

"What do we do till then?" Carson asked.

"You think we could risk a stop at my apartment? I've got some cash there. And I could throw a few things in a suitcase."

"Let's drive by, see what we think."

"Just slow down below supersonic."

Accelerating, Carson said, "How do you think Deucalion does that Houdini stuff?"

"Don't ask me. I'm a prestidigitation disaster. You know that trick with little kids where you pretend to take their nose off, and you show it poking out of your fist, except it's really just your thumb?"

"Yeah."

"They always look at me like I'm a moron, and say, 'That's just your stupid thumb.'"

"I've never seen you goofing around with kids."

"I've got a couple friends, they did the kid thing," he said. "I've played babysitter in a pinch."

"I'll bet you're good with kids."

"I'm no Barney the Dinosaur, but I can hold my own."

"He must sweat like a pig in that suit."

"You couldn't pay me enough to be Barney," he said.

"I used to hate Big Bird when I was a kid."

"Why?"

She said, "He was such a self-righteous bore."

"You know who used to scare me when I was a little kid? Snuggle the Bear."

"Do I know Snuggle?"

"In those TV ads for that fabric softener. Somebody would say how *soft* their robe was or their towels, and Snuggle the teddy bear would be hiding behind a pillow or creeping around under a chair, giggling."

"He was just happy that people were pleased."

"No, it was a maniacal little giggle. And his eyes were glazed. And how did he get in all those houses to hide and giggle?"

"You're saying Snuggle should've been charged with B and E?"

"Absolutely. Most of the time when he giggled, he covered his mouth with one paw. I always thought he didn't want you to see his teeth."

"Snuggle had bad teeth?" she asked.

"I figured they were rows of tiny vicious fangs he was hiding. When I was maybe four or five, I used to have nightmares where

I'd be in bed with a teddy bear, and it was Snuggle, and he was trying to chew open my jugular and suck the lifeblood out of me."

She said, "So much about you suddenly makes more sense than it ever did before."

"Maybe if we aren't cops someday, we can open a toy shop."

"Can we run a toy shop and have guns?"

"I don't see why not," he said.

chapter 72

Sitting at the kitchen table in Michael Maddison's apartment, Cindi Lovewell used a pair of tweezers to pluck the last of the wood splinters out of Benny's left eye.

He said, "How's it look?"

"Icky. But it'll heal. Can you see?"

"Everything blurry in that eye. But I can see well with the right. We don't look so cute anymore."

"We will again. You want something to drink?"

"What's he got?"

She went to the refrigerator, checked. "Like nine kinds of soft drinks and beer."

"How much beer?"

"Two six-packs."

"I'll take one of them," Benny said.

She brought both six-packs to the table. They twisted the caps off two bottles and chugged Corona.

Her wrist had already pretty much healed, though some weakness remained in it.

Maddison's place was hardly bigger than a studio apartment. The kitchen was open to the eating area and the living room.

They could see the front door. They would hear the key in the lock.

Maddison would be dead two steps across the threshold. Maybe the bitch would be with him, and then the job would be done.

O'Connor being barren, Cindi felt sorry for her, but she still wanted her dead in the worst way.

Opening a second bottle of beer, Benny said, "So who was that tattooed guy?"

"I've been thinking."

"He wasn't Old Race. He has to be one of us."

"He was stronger than us," she reminded Benny. "Much stronger. He kicked our ass."

"A new model."

"He sure didn't look like a new model," she said. "What I'm thinking is voodoo."

Benny groaned. "*Don't* think voodoo."

Sometimes Benny didn't seem imaginative enough for a Gamma. She said, "The tattoo on his face was sort of like a *veve*."

"None of this makes sense."

"A *veve* is a design that represents the figure and power of an astral force."

"You're getting so weird on me again."

"Somebody put some super-bad mojo on us and conjured up a god of Congo or Petro, and sent it after us."

"Congo is in Africa."

"Voodoo has three rites or divisions," Cindi said patiently. "Rada calls upon the powers of the benevolent gods."

"Listen to yourself."

"Congo and Petro appeal to the powers of two different groups of evil gods."

"You called voodoo science. Gods aren't *science*."

"They are if they work according to laws as reliable as those of physics," she insisted. "Somebody conjured up a Congo or a Petro and sent it after us, and you saw what happened."

chapter 73

Erika Helios had finished her dinner and had been for some time drinking cognac in the formal living room, enjoying the ambience and trying not to think about the thing in the glass case, when Victor arrived home from the Hands of Mercy, evidently having decided not to work through the night, after all.

When he found her in the living room, she said, "Good evening, dear. What a lovely surprise, when I thought I wouldn't see you until tomorrow."

Surveying the dirty dishes, he said, "You're having dinner in the living room?"

"I wanted to have dinner somewhere that I could have cognac, and Christine said I could have cognac anywhere I pleased, and so here I am. It was very nice. We should invite guests and have a dinner party in the living room some night soon."

"No one eats dinner in a formal living room," he said sharply.

Erika could see now that he was in a mood, but part of the function of a good wife was to elevate her husband's mood, so she pointed to a nearby chair and said cheerily, "Why don't you pull that up and sit with me and have some cognac. You'll see it's really a charming place for dinner."

Looming, glowering, he said, "You're having dinner in a formal living room at a *three-hundred-thousand-dollar, eighteenth-century French escritoire!*" The bad mood abruptly had become something worse.

Frightened and confused but hopeful of explaining herself in a way that might yet win his heart, she said, "Oh, I know the history of the piece, dear. I'm quite well-programmed on antiques. If we—"

He seized her by her hair, jerked her to her feet, and slapped her across the face once, twice, three times, very hard.

"As stupid and useless as the other four," he declared, speaking with such force that he sprayed spittle in her face.

When he threw her aside, Erika staggered against a small table and knocked over a chinoiserie vase, which fell on the Persian carpet, yet shattered.

"I'm sorry," she said. "I'm so sorry. I didn't understand about not eating in the living room. I see now it was foolish of me. I'll think more seriously about etiquette before I—"

The ferocity with which he came at her was much greater than anything he had exhibited before, than anything she had imagined she might have to endure.

He backhanded her, chopped at her with the edges of his hands, hammered her with his fists, even bit her, and of course she could not defend herself, and of course he forbade her to switch off the pain. And the pain was great.

He was fierce and cruel. She knew he would not be cruel to her unless she deserved it. Almost worse than the pain was the shame of having failed him.

When at last he left her on the floor and walked out of the room, she lay there for a long time, breathing shallowly, cautiously, because it hurt so much to breathe deeply.

Eventually, she got up far enough to sit on the floor with her back against the sofa. From this perspective she noted with shock how many fine and expensive things were spotted with her blood.

Erika realized that her brilliant husband had invented the miraculous spot remover not solely for those rare occasions when a butler chewed off his fingers.

If she were to be the final Erika, she would need to learn from this experience. She must meditate on all that he had said and on the precise nature of the punishment he had administered. If she applied herself to a thoughtful analysis of the incident, she would surely be a better wife.

Clearly, however, the challenge before her was far greater than she had at first understood.

chapter 74

The three gone-wrongs were removed from the bed of palm fronds on the truck, wound in sheets, and then carried through torchlight to a shallow depression in the trash field, to be buried at a decent remove from the five members of the Old Race.

This was a more solemn ceremony than the dance of death, and not as viscerally exciting. Some of the crew grew restless by the time the three shrouded cadavers were lined up in what would become their communal grave.

Following this interment, the crew – which included as many women as men – would go to the showers to scrub one another clean. There, the sex would begin, and would continue through the evening's feast, through the night until near dawn.

Curiously, although the stomping should have worked off much of their pent-up aggression, they often found their anger surfacing with renewed power later, and the sex became thrillingly savage.

Dog-nose Nick regretted only that the others felt the need to bathe before having at one another in various combinations. He loved the smell of Gunny Alecto, in particular, when she was incrusted with filth. After soap, she remained desirable, but not as much so.

As Gunny drove her garbage galleon toward the gone-wrongs, to plow a layer of concealing trash over them, the anticipated feast and orgy were thrust from Nick's mind when abruptly something pale and many-limbed and strange beyond his experience shivered up out of the trash field. As quick as a spider, but like a huge assemblage of human limbs and heads and torsos in an illogical construct, it seized the three gone-wrongs and dragged them down, down and out of sight, and the trash field shuddered underfoot.

chapter 75

In the main laboratory at the Hands of Mercy, an Epsilon named Lester, a member of the janitorial team, performed daily maintenance at an industrious pace.

When Mr Helios was in the facility, Lester could not clean in the lab. Mr Helios did not like to be distracted by a mopping and dusting minion.

This suited Lester just fine. He always got nervous around his maker.

Because Mr Helios spent more time than not within these walls and because he worked at irregular hours, whenever his great genius compelled him, Lester's routine chores in this part of the building had to be done at different times every day. He liked the night best, like now, when none of the other staff members ventured into the main lab in their maker's absence.

Perhaps the complex and fantastic machines, their purposes beyond his comprehension, should have made him fearful. The opposite was the case.

They hummed, burbled, ticked, whispered almost like voices imparting secrets, chuckled, occasionally beeped but not with the quality of alarm, sputtered, and murmured musically. Lester found these noises comforting.

He didn't know why they should comfort him. He did not think about it or try to understand.

Lester didn't try to understand much of anything, except what he needed to know to perform his work. His work was his life, as it should be for one such as him.

When not working, he found that time hung heavy. Sometimes he sat for hours, scratching his arm hard enough to make it bleed, and then watching it heal, scratching it open again, watching it heal, scratching it open . . . At other times, he went down to a private place on the lowest level of the building, where there was rubble that his maker would not permit to be cleaned up, and he stood in front of a concrete wall, knocking his head rhythmically against it until the compulsion to do so had passed.

Compared to work, leisure time had little appeal. He always knew what to do with the hours when at work.

The only other thing in his life besides work and leisure was the occasional blackout, a recent phenomenon. Now and then he woke, as if he had been sleeping on his feet, and found himself in odd places, with no recollection of how he had gotten there or of what he had been doing.

Consequently, he tried to work most of the time, cleaning again what he had cleaned only an hour ago, to help the time pass.

This evening, as he mopped the floor around his maker's desk, the dark screen of the computer suddenly brightened. The face of Annunciata appeared.

"Mr Helios, Helios, I have been asked by Werner to tell you that he is in Randal Six's room and that he is exploding, exploding."

Lester glanced at the face on the screen. He didn't know what to say, so he continued mopping.

"Mr Helios, sir, Werner wishes to stress the urgency, urgency, urgency of the situation."

This sounded bad, but it was none of Lester's business.

"Mr Helios, an Alpha has made an urgent, urgent, urgent request for a meeting with you."

Growing nervous, Lester said, "Mr Helios isn't here."

"Mr Helios. I have become aware that Werner, that Werner, that Werner has been trapped in Isolation Room Number Two."

"You'll have to call back later," said Lester.

"Instructions?" Annunciata asked.

"What?"

"May I have instructions, sir?"

"I'm just Lester," he told her. "I don't give instructions, I take them."

"Coffee has been spilled in the main lab."

Lester looked around worriedly. "Where? I don't see any coffee."

"Coffee exploding, exploding in the main lab."

The machines were humming and burbling as always. Colorful gases and liquids were bubbling and glowing in glass spheres, in tubes, as always they bubbled and glowed. Nothing was exploding.

"Annunciata," said Annunciata sternly, "let's see if you can get *anything* right."

"Nothing's exploding," Lester assured her.

Annunciata said, "Werner is coffee in Isolation Room Number Two. Analyze your systems, Annunciata, analyze, analyze."

"I don't follow you at all," Lester told her. "You're making me nervous."

"Good morning, Mr Helios. Helios."

"I'm going to clean over at the other end of the lab," Lester declared.

"Werner is trapped, trapped, trapped. Analyze. See if you can get *anything* right."

chapter 76

Carson pulled Vicky's Honda to the curb in front of Michael's apartment building. She did not engage the parking brake or turn off the engine.

They sat staring at the place for a minute. A bland structure, slabs on slabs of apartments, it didn't look menacing. It was a big, dumb, happy kind of building where nobody would be stalked and killed by relentless meat machines.

"What's that thing they say about going home again?" Michael asked.

"You can't."

"Yeah. That's it. You can't go home again."

"Thomas Wolfe," she said.

"Whoever. I'm definitely getting a you-can't-go-home-again vibe."

"Me too."

"I'm glad I put on my new white shoes this morning. I'd have felt bad about never having worn them."

"They're cool shoes," Carson said as she pulled away from the curb. "You've always got the right look."

"Do I?"

"Always."

"That's nice. That's a nice thing to say. I'm sorry about earlier, when I said you were going female on me."

"Water under the bridge."

"You hungry?"

"That Red Bull gave me an appetite."

"I've got a what-would-you-like-for-dinner-before-we-strap-you-down-in-the-electric-chair kind of appetite. I want to eat everything before the switch is pulled. I'm starved."

"Want to get po-boys?"

"That's a start."

They rode for a longer while in silence than was customary for them, at least than was customary for Michael, and then she said, "You know that plan we had – shooting our way into Helios's mansion, taking him out?"

"I've been revisiting that bit of strategy myself."

"It took two of us to kill that guy in Arnie's room, and it was a close thing. And then that pair at the house—"

"Fred and Ginger."

"They did sort of look like dancers, didn't they? Okay, Fred and Ginger. I'm not sure we could have held them off if Deucalion hadn't shown up."

"Everybody on staff at the mansion is going to be as hard to take down as those two."

After another silence, Michael said, "Maybe we should drive up to Shreveport to visit Aunt Leelee."

"Deucalion will have some idea when we meet at the Luxe."

"He hasn't called back. He doesn't leave his phone on, and then he forgets to check his voice mail."

"Cut him some slack on the telecom stuff," Carson said. "He's a late-eighteenth-century kind of guy."

chapter 77

They took the oil lamps down from the tops of the two poles and brought them to the hole in the trash field out of which the mother of all gone-wrongs had risen to snatch the three shrouded cadavers.

The light revealed the mouth of a tunnel, seven or eight feet in diameter, descending at an angle into the depths of the pit. The compacted trash that formed the walls of the passageway seemed to have been plastered over with a clear bonding material, like a glue, that glistened in the lamplight.

"That was something, huh, Nick?" Gunny Alecto asked. "Wasn't that something?"

"It was something," Nick Frigg agreed, "but I don't know what."

"What a night," she said excitedly.

"Some night," he agreed.

"Let's go after it," she said.

"Down there after it? I was thinking that myself."

Life at Crosswoods was pretty good because of the ceremonies with the symbolic killings, more and more of them all the time, but the truth was they didn't have much novelty in their lives. The sex, all of them at each other every night, and the dances of death, and now and then gone-wrongs always different from the things they'd seen before: But that was about it.

Even Epsilons, simple in their function and dedicated to their work – and especially a Gamma like Nick – could develop a yearning for variety, for something new. Here was something new, all right.

Two of the crew had run back to the supply trailer to get four long-handled flashlights with powerful beams. They returned now, and one of them, Hobb, said, "We going down, Nick?"

Instead of answering at once, Nick took one of the flashlights, switched it on, and knelt at the mouth of the tunnel. He probed with the beam and saw that about a hundred feet from its entrance – and at that point maybe ten feet below the surface of the trash field – the passageway took a turn to the left, curving down and out of sight.

He wasn't afraid of what might be down there. He wouldn't die easy, and he didn't mind dying.

When he inhaled, he sure liked the rich smell rising out of the depths of the pit. Complex, familiar yet far more intense than the mélange at the surface. Nuanced.

In addition to the thousand odors of garbage, each of which he could identify separately and savor on its own, he detected a scent entirely new to him, a mysterious and alluring fragrance that he believed must be the mark of the colossal agglomeration of gone-wrongs that had too briefly revealed itself.

"We're gonna go down," he said. "But not all of us. Just four."

"Pick me, Nick, pick me," said Gunny Alecto.

"I already picked you," he said. "You want to go, Hobb?"

Hobb's eyes flared with excitement. "Oh, yeah. Count me in, Nick. There's always screwin' and eatin', there's always that, but there's never been *this*."

Hobb was a guy, so Nick picked a woman for the fourth. Azazel was hot, not as hot as Gunny, but she could take it and dish it out and leave you half broken and needing some time to heal.

Nick figured if they got down into the bottom of the pit and couldn't find the mother of all gone-wrongs, then they could still go at one another, down there in all that stink, which would be something new, something better than ever.

Gunny, Azazel, and Hobb each took a flashlight.

The incline of the tunnel was steep, but not so steep they couldn't handle it on foot.

"Let's go find the rat eater," Gunny said. "Let's go see what it does down there."

chapter 78

Bloodstained but no longer bleeding, hair in disarray, clothes torn, unpresentable in the event of unexpected guests, bruised and sore but healing, Erika located the liquor cabinet. She took out a bottle of Rémy Martin.

She almost didn't bother getting a glass. Then she decided that if Victor saw her drinking from the bottle, there would be trouble.

She went to the billiards room because while she knew now that she couldn't eat dinner in any room she wished, she did believe that she could drink just about anywhere, as her downloaded etiquette did not say otherwise.

For something to do, she switched on the plasma TV and channel-surfed for a while. Bored, she was just about to click off when she came upon the last half-hour of a show called *Desperate Housewives*, which she found enthralling.

When the next show didn't interest her, she killed the TV and went from the billiards room to an adjoining glassed-in porch, where she didn't turn on any lights, but sat in the dark, gazing out at the expansive grounds, where the trees were dramatically revealed by exquisitely positioned landscape lighting.

As she worked on the cognac, she wished the superb metabolism that her brilliant husband had given her did not process alcohol so efficiently. She doubted that she would ever get the buzz on that she understood alcohol to provide and that she was hoping for. She wanted to . . . blur things.

Maybe she was more inebriated than she thought, however, because after a while she glimpsed what appeared to be a naked albino dwarf capering across the yard. It fled from the shadows under a magnolia tree to the gazebo, into which it disappeared.

By the time that Erika had thoughtfully consumed a few more ounces of cognac in an increasingly contemplative mood, the albino had appeared again, scampering this time from the gazebo to the trumpet-vine arbor through which one approached the reflecting pond.

One could not help but think, if one had been programmed with an encyclopedia of literary allusions, that there must be a maiden somewhere nearby spinning straw into gold, for here surely was Rumpelstiltskin come for his compensation.

chapter 79

The Luxe Theater, a Deco palace long gone to seed, had been operating as a revival house, showing old movies on the big screen only three nights a week. As it was now his home and his base of operations, Deucalion had the previous day shut down the business entirely in the interest of saving the world.

They met at midnight in the lobby, where Jelly Biggs had set up a folding table near the concessions stand. In a huge bowl on the table, Jelly piled up Dum-Dums, NECCO wafers, Raisinets, Goobers, M&M's, Sky Bars, bags of Planters, and other treats from the refreshments counter.

The choice of beverages seemed limited, as compared to the fare in a fully functioning theater. Nevertheless, Carson was able to have a vanilla Coke while Deucalion and Jelly had root beer; and Michael was delighted to be served two bottles of chocolate Yoo-hoo.

"If victory favors the army with the highest blood-sugar count," Michael said, "we've won this war already."

Before they got down to the discussion of strategy and tactics,

Deucalion gave an account of Arnie's circumstances in Tibet. Carson had many questions, but was considerably relieved.

Following this uplifting news, Deucalion reported his encounter with his maker in Father Duchaine's kitchen. This development ensured Helios, alias Frankenstein, would be more alert to threats against him, thus making their conspiracy less likely to succeed.

The first question on the table came from Carson, who wanted to know how they could get at Victor with sufficient firepower that his praetorian guard could not save him.

"I suspect," said Deucalion, "that no matter what planning we do, the opportunity will present itself in a way we cannot foresee. I told you earlier that his empire is collapsing, and I believe this to be more true by the day if not by the hour. He is as arrogant as he was two hundred years ago. But he is not – and this is key – he is not any longer fearful of failure. Impatient, yes, but not fearful. In spite of all his setbacks, he has progressed doggedly for so long that he believes in the inevitability of his vision. Therefore, he is blind to the rottenness of every pillar that supports his kingdom."

Tearing open a bag of Good & Plenty, Jelly Biggs said, "I'm not fat enough anymore to qualify as a freakshow fat man, but I'm still a freak at heart. And one thing freakshow fat men are *not* known for is bravery under fire. There's no way that you want me storming the citadel with you, and no way I would do it. So I'm not worried about how to feed ammo to a gun off a bandolier. What I worry about is . . . if his empire *is* falling apart, if he's losing control of his creations . . . what's going to happen to this city with a few thousand superhuman *things* spinning out of control? And if you *do* manage to kill him, how much *further* do they spin out of control when he's gone?"

"How terrible it will be, I can't say," Deucalion replied. "But more terrible than anything we can conceive. Tens of thousands will die at the hands of the New Race before they are destroyed. And of the four of us at this table, I expect that no more than one will be alive at the end of it, even if we triumph."

They were silent for a moment, contemplating their mortality, and then Carson turned to Michael: "Don't fail me, slick. Hit me with your smart-ass line."

"For once," Michael told her, "I don't have one."

"Oh, God," she said. "We *are* in deep shit."

chapter 80

For some time, as Erika watched from the dark glassed-in porch and from the haze of Rémy Martin, the naked albino dwarf scurried this way and that across the grounds, a ghostly figure, mostly half seen except when he passed close to the brighter landscape lights.

He might have been searching for something, though because she had only completed her first day out of the tank, Erika did not have sufficient realworld experience to know what an albino dwarf could be seeking on a Garden District estate.

His purpose might have been to familiarize himself with the property in preparation for some scheme he intended to perpetrate. What such a scheme could be she could not guess, except that her trove of literary allusions regarding malevolent dwarfs suggested that it would involve a pot of gold or a first-born child, or an enchanted princess, or a ring that possessed magical power.

He might be looking for a place to hide before dawn. No doubt his kind were intolerant of sunlight. Besides, he was naked, and there were laws against indecent exposure.

After she had been watching the frantic dwarf for some time, he finally became aware of her. Because she sat in a dark porch and made no movement except to fill the glass of cognac or to raise it to her lips, she had not been easy to spot.

When he spied her, the dwarf faced the porch from a distance of forty feet, hopping from foot to foot, sometimes beating his breast with both hands. He was agitated, possibly distressed, and seemed to be unsure of what to do now that he had been seen.

Erika poured more cognac and waited.

———

Nick Frigg led Gunny, Hobb, and Azazel along the tunnel, deeper into the trash pit. Their flashlight beams dazzled along the curved and glassy surfaces.

He suspected that the glaze that held the garbage walls so firm might be an organic material exuded by the mother of all gone-wrongs. When he sniffed the glaze, it was different from but similar to the smell of spider webs and moth cocoons, different from but similar to the odor of hive wax and termite excrement.

Within a quarter of an hour, they saw that the tunnel wound and looped and intersected itself in the manner of a wormhole. There must be miles of it, not just in the west pit but also in the east, and perhaps in the older pits that had been filled, capped with earth, and planted over with grass.

Here beneath Crosswoods was a world of secret highways that had been long abuilding. The labyrinth seemed too elaborate to serve as the burrow of a single creature, no matter how industrious. The four explorers approached every blind turn with the expectation that they would discover a colony of strange life forms or even structures of peculiar architecture.

Once they heard voices. Numerous. Male and female. Distant and rhythmic. The endlessly twisting tunnel distorted the chants beyond understanding, though one word carried undeformed, repeated like the repetitive response to the verses of a long litany: *Father . . . Father . . . Father.*

―――――

In the Hands of Mercy, Annunciata spoke to a deserted lab, for now even Lester, of the maintenance staff, had departed for work in other chambers or perhaps to sit and scratch himself until he bled.

"Urgent, urgent, urgent. Trapped. Analyze your systems. Get *anything* right. Perhaps there is an imbalance in your nutrient supply. Cycle the inner door?"

When she asked a question, she waited patiently for a response, but none ever came.

"Do you have instructions, Mr Helios? Helios?"

Her face on the screen assumed a quizzical expression.

Eventually, the computer screen on Victor's desk in the main lab went dark.

Simultaneously, Annunciata's face materialized on one of the six screens in the monitor room outside Isolation Chamber Number 2.

"Cycle the inner door?" she asked.

No staff remained to answer. They were at each other in distant rooms or otherwise engaged.

As no one would answer the question, she probed her memory for past instructions that might apply to the current situation: "Cycle open the nearer door of the transition module. Father Duchaine would like to offer his holy counsel to poor Werner."

The nearest door purred, sighed with the breaking of a seal, and swung open.

On the screens, the Werner thing, having been racing around the walls in a frenzy, suddenly went still, alert.

"Cycle open the farther door?" Annunciata asked.

She received no reply.

"He's in the air lock," she said.

Then she corrected herself: "It's not an *air lock*."

The Werner thing was now singular in appearance and so unearthly in its form that an entire college of biologists, anthropologists, entomologists, herpetologists, and their ilk could have spent years studying it without determining the meaning of its body language and its facial expressions (to the extent that it had a face). Yet on the screens, as viewed from different angles, most laymen would have said that it looked *eager*.

"Thank you, Mr Helios. Thank you. Thank you. Thank you, Mr Helios. Helios. Helios."

———

Bucky Guitreau, the current district attorney of the city of New Orleans and a replicant, was at work at the desk in his home office when his wife, Janet, also a replicant, stepped in from the hallway and said, "Bucky, I think lines of code in my base programming are dropping out."

"We all have days we feel that way," he assured her.

"No," she said. "I must have lost a significant chunk of stuff. Did you hear the doorbell ring a few minutes ago?"

"I did, yeah."

"It was a pizza-delivery guy."

"Did we order a pizza?"

"No. It was for the Bennets, next door. Instead of just setting the pizza guy straight, I killed him."

"What do you mean – killed him?"

"I dragged him into the foyer and strangled him to death."

Alarmed, Bucky got up from his desk. "Show me."

He followed her out to the foyer. A twentysomething man lay dead on the floor.

"The pizza's in the kitchen if you want some," Janet said.

Bucky said, "You're awfully calm about this.

"I am, aren't I? It was really fun. I've never felt so good."

Although he should have been wary of her, afraid for himself, and concerned about the effect of this on their maker's master plan, Bucky was instead in awe of her. And envious.

"You've definitely dropped some lines of program," he said. "I didn't know that was possible. What're you going to do now?"

"I think I'm going to go next door and kill the Bennets. What are you going to do?"

"What I should do is report you for termination," Bucky said.

"Are you going to?"

"Maybe there's something wrong with me, too."

"You're not going to turn me in?"

"I don't really feel like it," he said.

"Do you want to come with me and help kill the Bennets?"

"We're forbidden to kill until ordered."

"They're Old Race. I've hated them for so long."

"Well, I have, too," he said. "But still . ."

"I'm so horny just talking about it," Janet said, "I've got to go over there *right now*."

"I'll go with you," Bucky said. "I don't think I could kill anybody. But it's funny . . . I think I could watch."

———

After a while the naked albino dwarf came across the dark lawn to the big porch window directly in front of Erika, and peered in at her.

Dwarf wasn't the correct word for it. She didn't think a right word existed, but *troll* seemed more accurately descriptive than *dwarf*.

Although the thing in the glass case had scared her, she had no concern about this creature. Her lack of fear puzzled her.

The troll had large, unusually expressive eyes. They were both eerie and beautiful.

She felt an inexplicable sympathy for it, a connection.

The troll leaned its forehead against the glass and said quite distinctly, in a raspy voice, "Harker."

Erika considered this for a moment. "Harker?"

"Harker," the troll repeated.

If she understood it correctly, the required reply was the one she gave: "Erika."

"Erika," said the troll.

"Harker," she said.

The troll smiled. Its smile proved to be an ugly wound in its face, but she didn't flinch.

Part of her duties was to be the perfect hostess. The perfect hostess receives every guest with equal graciousness.

She sipped her cognac, and for a minute they enjoyed staring at each other through the window.

Then the troll said, "Hate him."

Erika considered this statement. She decided that if she asked to whom the troll referred, the answer might require her to report the creature to someone.

The perfect hostess does not need to pry. She does, however, anticipate a guest's needs.

"Wait right there," she said. "I'll be back."

She went into the kitchen, found a wicker picnic hamper in the pantry, and filled it with cheese, roast beef, bread, fruit, and a bottle of white wine.

She thought the troll might be gone when she returned, but it remained at the window.

When she opened the porch door and stepped outside, the troll took fright and scampered across the lawn. It didn't run away, but stopped to watch her from a distance.

She put down the hamper, returned to the porch, sat as before, and refreshed her glass of cognac.

Hesitantly at first, then with sudden boldness, the creature went to the hamper and lifted the lid.

When it understood the nature of the offering, it picked up the hamper and hurried toward the back of the property, vanishing into the night.

The perfect hostess does not gossip about a guest. She never fails to keep secrets and honor confidences.

The perfect hostess is creative, patient, and has a long memory – as does a wise wife.